The Dedalus Book of Surrealism 2

(The Myth of the World)

edited by Michael Richardson

Dedalus

Dedalus would like to express its gratitude to The French Ministry of Foreign Affairs and The Eastern Arts Board for their assistance in producing this book.

Published in the UK by Dedalus Ltd, Langford Lodge, St Judith's Lane, Sawtry, Cambs, PE17 5XE

ISBN 1 873982 36 4

Distributed in Canada by Marginal Distribution,
Unit 103, 277 George Street North, Peterborough, Ontario, KJ9 3G9
Distributed in Australia & New Zealand by Peribo Pty Ltd, 26 Tepko Road, Terrey Hills, N.S.W. 2084

Typeset by Datix International Ltd, Bungay, Suffolk
Printed in Finland by Wsoy

A C.I.P. listing for this title is available on request from the British Library.

List of Contents

NOTE ABOUT THE EDITOR

Michael Richardson also edited *The Dedalus Book of Surrealism* (*The Identity of Things*).

The Myth of the World comprises, along with *The Identity of Things*, two volumes published by Dedalus exploring surrealist storytelling. This project would not have been possible without considerable help from many people. It is not possible to credit all help, but the editor would like to give special thanks to all the help given by the translators, many of whom have done far more than simply translate the stories included. Particular thanks for this volume also to Heribert Becker, Guy Flandre, Raúl Henao, Stuart Inman, Alain Joubert, François Leperlier, Rik Lina, Věra Linhartová, Conroy Maddox, Anne Marbrun, Floriano Martins, Bernard Roger, Zuca Sardan, Gerald Stack, Nanos Valaoritis and Laurens Vancrevel.

The Myth of the World is dedicated to the memories of Marcel Mariën and of my father, both of whom, in different ways, showed the path to be followed.

addenda to *The Identity of Things:*

The biographical note for Raul Fiker should read: **RAUL FIKER** (Sao Paolo, 1947). Participated in the Brazilian Surrealist Group from 1964 to 1969. His poetical and theoretical works have been published in Brazil and Portugal, his most important work being *O Equivocrata* (1976). He is currently a lecturer at Universidade Estadual Paulista and is researching Francis Bacon at Cambridge University.

The dates of Gilbert Lely should be (Paris, 1904 – Paris, 1984)

It should be pointed out that the text by Paul Nougé is a 'correction' of a text by Baudelaire originally published by Nougé as part of a series entitled 'Le mot est à Baudelaire'.

ANDRÉ BRETON

Once Upon A Time

Imagination is not a gift but an object of conquest par excellence. "Where," Huysmans wondered, "in what age, under what latitudes, in what localities, could this immense palace actually be located with its cupolas rising up into the sky, its phallic columns and its pillars emerging from a hard glittering block of stone?"[1] To gradually efface everything one thinks and that should be calls for an at once totally lyrical and totally pessimistic means. This palace was *raised up*, this *palace*. . . This imperfect, this useless splendour tending to repudiate in quasi-legendary gratuity the need one feels – these *phallic columns* – to behave (be it only from the sexual point of view) differently from how one usually behaves, bearing witness to a guilty lassitude and an inadmissible doubt concerning the real forces of the mind. The lamentable expression: "But it was only a dream", the increasing use of which – among others in the domain of the cinema – has contributed not a little to encourage such hypocrisy, has for a long while ceased to merit discussion. Why not come right out and say it? Huysmans knew perfectly well that such visions as he had – as we can have them: outside time – were no less fated to drag the world 'forward' as 'backward'. What is the point, unless one retires unhappily into safety, what is the point in conforming with what, once again, must be, the fearful faculty of having existed and no longer existing! I know the objection: "But this spirit stumbles at each step against the vestiges of time and place. Its representations are slaves of the greater or lesser emotions these vestiges more or less

[1] *En Rade.*

give it. Fetishist *in extremis*! What is generally called the past undeniably takes it on its weakest side. Nights of Anthony, Mexico before the arrival of the Spaniards, a photograph of an unknown woman from the last century: you, here, over there, if you move try not to make too much noise."

But where are the snows of tomorrow? I say that the imagination, from whatever it borrows and – as far as I am concerned this remains to be demonstrated – if it actually does *borrow*, does not need to humiliate itself in the face of life. There will always be, notably, between those so-called 'accepted' ideas and the idea. . . who knows, to be accepted – a difference liable to restore the imagination to being mistress of the domain of the Mind. Everything connected with the problem of transformation of energy is once more proposed. To mistrust as one does, excessively, the practical virtue of the imagination, is to desire to deny oneself, at all costs, the aid of electricity, in the hope of leading hydro-electric power to its absurd consciousness of being a waterfall.

The imaginary is what tends to become real.

It is for this reason that I would like to rent (I do not even say buy) a property on the outskirts of Paris.[2] Nothing grand. Just around thirty rooms with, as far as possible, long corridors that would be very dark or that I would myself make dark. There would be ten or twelve acres of wooded land all around. It would not be unwelcome to see a few streams or, preferably, a couple of ponds. Naturally I would make the decisions about the security of the place (and when I speak about security, thieves will do me the honour of believing that I don't have them in mind). Let it be possible for anyone – *all sorts* of people with whom I'd have made appointments – to enter or to leave, day or night, without causing any scenes. All these pre-conditions are, on the whole, easy to put into practice.

[2] only money prevents me.

An underground passage, to be excavated or not, would also present few problems.

Its outward appearance, in order also not to appear completely out of place, would be that of a stopover point rather than a hotel or an inn. But inside, as you will see, it is a stopover point in which those who, according to me, are entitled to it, could always come to partake of exhausting ideas in exchange for ideas that are exhausted.

It will be offered with board and lodging prepared *on time*. . . Let's say three girls will be invited for a stay there and these young girls being the last to be marked out in some haunted house scandal or another. The first thing to do is to put them at ease by convincing them they're really 'at home'. If there is a manifest inadequacy on their part, replacements would be provided as soon as possible. In an urgent case, supplementary help can be brought in. (An appeal can even be made for a young man unwittingly specialised in these sorts of questions – but never more than one at a time). Some other young girls and some young women (incidentally capable of presenting attractive medianimique phenomena or distinguished by their strangeness of mind or their beauty) will be given as occasional companions to these young people.

For each bedroom, a large clock made of black glass will be set to chime especially *well* at midnight.

It will be strictly forbidden, under penalty of immediate and definitive expulsion, for anyone at all, notwithstanding all the provocations to which they would be exposed, to fulfil the act of love within the boundaries marked by the wall surrounding the grounds.

There will be hardly be anything but small study lamps with green lampshades that will be dimmed very low. The blinds will remain lowered day and night.

Only the white-washed reception hall will be lit with an invisible ceiling light and it will contain no other furniture, besides two authentic Merovingian chairs, and a stool on which will sit the perfume bottle tied up with a pale ribbon, inside which a discoloured rose will be immersed with its stems and leaves equally lifeless, such as one can see today, the 9th June, in the south window of the chemist's on the corner of rue Lafayette and rue du faubourg Montmartre.

And that will bring the arbitrary to an end.

But the butterflies released by nature will later be seized by men and *commented upon*. We shall finally see whether the bedsheets are made to serve as an envelope for the bodies of men and women (how must it be addressed?) or whether they are constructed – given their incomprehensible height when they rise up – to render a body, imaginary or not, imaginary in order to prove that the human mind, no matter what they say, has never *escaped from it with nothing more than a fright* (I was recently told this charming ghost story: two men, dressed as you might expect, played at frightening the ignorant world by doing the rounds of a cemetery on several consecutive nights. Finally, one night an 'unbeliever' discretely joined them at a turning and followed on their heels, having been careful to dress up in the same grotesque way. Having become aware of such a presence behind them the two men made off. I prefer these first two men to the latter.)

There will be a 'wishing well', a pure and simple replica of the one at Luna-Park, although at first sight less *free*, but more diverse, more emphatic, and so much prettier.

Five rooms with boarded-up doors and windows, access to which is rendered almost impossible without prejudicing sworn oaths not to try to see into them. I conjecture that in the first, and largest, would be grouped the most important examples of mannequins and wax figures, neither piled on top of one another nor with each playing a role but arranged the way they would have appeared before being walled up, to arouse the greatest possible spirit of surrender. In the second adjoining room eccentric luggage, large sunflowers and other carnival gifts of the mind will be strewn about pell-mell; it will be decorated completely with love letters. In the third, in which an attempt will have been made to make it the most luxurious nursery possible, with only a slashed cradle embellished in the proper place with a dagger, will tilt, like a ship in distress, over a floor of too-blue waves. It is necessary that I alone know what takes place in the fourth room so one reliable man may know the purpose of the fifth without possessing, any more than I or anyone else would, the ideological key to everything.[3] The worst thing is that not a single external detail will distinguish the first room from the second or the fifth. Decorating will be done in such a way as to make any indiscretion impossible.

Since I wish today to stick to a simple outline I won't dwell futilely on the furnishing of the occupiable rooms. Of course, this could only be thoroughly austere – the extreme disparateness of the whole responding more to necessity than impulse. Moreover our taste is to be relied upon.

The most exacting conditions of physical hygiene will be meticulously observed.

Certainly I don't yet know whether two white greyhounds or two white pedigree bull dogs will be entrusted to domestic service or whether it will be possible to dispense with such animals.

. . . .

What I want to defend here above all else is simply the principle of an association having the advantage of placing the mind in the position which seems to be as poetically receptive as possible. For the moment it would not be a question of penetrating any further into the secrets of such a community. As I write these lines, I repeat that I am momentarily making an abstraction of any point of view other than the poetic, which is not in the least to say that I accept taking the debate into the domain of utopia. I'm content to indicate a source of unusual, and to a great extent unforeseeable, *movements*, a source which, if one

[3] somewhat puerile? so much the better.

once agrees to follow its course (and my wager is that it will be accepted) would be the promise of a magnificent torrent after confronting masses and masses of difficulties. It is hard not to think and see into the future, faced with today's blind architecture – a thousand times more stupid and more revolting than that of other ages. How bored we shall be inside! Ah, we may be quite sure that nothing will happen there. But suppose, straightaway, that someone heard, even in such a domain, that something had happened! If he dared venture, alone or almost so, into lands struck with chance? Suppose, with his mind unencumbered with those stories which, as children, gave us such delight while at the same time starting to deepen the disappointment in our hearts, that person took the risk of tearing its mysterious prey from the past? Suppose this poet wanted himself to enter into the Lair? If he was genuinely determined to open his mouth simply to say, "Once upon a time. . ."?

★★★★★

originally published in *Le Surréalisme au service de la Révolution* issue no 1 (1930) and reprinted as a preface to André Breton, *Le Révolver à cheveux blancs* (1932). Included in his *Oeuvres complètes* Vol 2 Paris: Gallimard (1992)

★★★★★

ANDRÉ BRETON (see volume one p 18)

ROBERT DESNOS

I Looked At Myself In The Fountain

I looked at myself in the fountain, I don't know how, and I was startled to see a bird, tired out by the wind, and high grasses that had collapsed under the rain, on my face. I wanted to put out my tongue to read the course of my health in its colour, but what was my amazement to see a blue helicopter coming out of the mouth of my image which parted from my lips like a smoke-ring. As I contemplated this phenomenon, I returned slowly to my house and my eyes fixed on the gleaming snail tracks were no more than dead granite under my eyelids, when suddenly – was it the storm in the skiffs of sulphur or the Greek fire over the sea? – I was less conscious than an orange peel and there was a man in front of me.

He must have been about thirty. He looked the very image of those Messmers in which liquid steel is covered with an incandescent scoria. His green tie protected him from flies. Nonchalantly leaning on a boxwood cane, he waved his free hand. "Kind sir," he addressed me. "Give me your hand." I was unable to hide my fear and felt my hair turn into columns of water, while a heavy sweat flowed over my face. The stranger was still smiling: he transformed himself into a rose-bush and entwined me.

My Christian education meant that ever since childhood I've had a horror of vice and it was not without a quite understandable terror that I discerned the pleasure I felt in the embrace of this vigorous bush whose branches gradually mingled with my limbs, my hair and my looks. When one of its flowers came apart in my mouth, I could feel myself grasping the sorcerer in my arms in my turn. He was transformed into a torrent and I was a barge, into the desert and I was smoke, into a car and I was a road, into a man and I was a woman. "What we are doing is very wrong," he said and was off.

How did a house with six floors come to be in the forest with an advertisement for Parlo on the back, a small wicker balcony on the fourth floor and my mother, who is a saint, on the balcony with a small yellow dog at her feet? In her left hand my mother had a finger biscuit and in her right hand an opera glass, that's what I can't explain. She had still not lost a mouthful of the performance nor of her biscuit which was pink inside, just like certain kisses. "Jacques," she called out, pretending she had to tie herself to the convolvulus which crept up the wall, "do you want to make me die?" At the same time the ball of pink wool I thought was a biscuit fell through the bars and unwound as it fell. The dog said, woof, woof, and I realised that my mother's house was forever closed to me.

I had the idea of finding something out about my loathsome seducer so I could complain and ask him for some money. But he had left France and some days later I found myself alone with an elderly woman who cooked up mysterious plans. I'll leave you to envisage how I escaped from that scrape.

Passing in front of a mirror, I praised the Lord for overwhelming me with his gifts and took a room in a sort of squirrel's cage whose landlady was exactly a fifty cent stamp for overseas postage. While looking out of the window, as I had been taught to, the setting sun set and I was fascinated by the comings and goings of a middle-aged individual crossing the road in all directions, two steps to the right, four to the left, three back, and so on as he pleased. He had properly placed his bowler beneath a tree on one of those grills I am assured serve as water outlets. On his head he had a binauricular telephone head-set which would have allowed an observer from above to notice his incipient baldness. The head-set was linked by a thread to a wooden frame the man held in his left hand.

His right hand seemed to be used as a counterbalance to stabilise his progress and beat in the air like a wing. You might have said that this odd character was dancing on a tightrope. The passers-by did not seem to notice his performance. I went down and asked the strange stroller for a light. He nimbly twisted round, took off his head-set and politely asked me to hold it for a moment. As he prepared to kindle a match a gust of wind blew his bowler away. He ran after it. I was unable to resist the desire to put on the telephone head-set and no sooner had I done so than everything under my feet became transparent and I saw a land completely different from the home of King Dagobert and Tambour d'Arcole.

It was a difficult kind of town to describe. The surprising thing one first realised was that the stone houses were naturally formed, while the trees, rivers and so on were the work of man's hand. The inhabitants walked around naked, with gloves on their hands and veils on their faces, so that for a civilised young man like me, whose mother had kept him in ignorance of the marvels of nature, it was almost impossible to work out the sex of the charming marionettes with fresh skin who evolved around under me.

In a romantic courtyard where some tall agricultural machines and garden hoses had rather haphazardly been left to grow, one group chatted at the foot of a large dandelion which served as a statue. The conversation floated up and I could even smell the odour of each of the speakers. "Oh," said a very white body as it threw a wrist watch to the ground which broke without attracting anyone's attention, "Oh, how can anyone not love poetry, natural machines, large white houses, the brilliance of steel, crimes and wild passions? Must there be people today so complicated as to prefer these stupid ornaments that the municipal authorities entrust to artists unworthy of the name to the delightful oscillations of pressure-gauges." And the woman (I think it was a woman) pointed to the dandelion. Another spoke in turn ardently: "How can anyone go into ecstasies faced with the foolishness of nature with its phonographs and roller skates? Especially when we make such pretty little fur animals which, if you'll pardon the expression, I am unable to refrain from placing to my lips." At this last word the whole group went into a concert of protest: "How dreadful! Don't use such words, my good chap. Where do you think you are?" "I am amazed," he went on, "that you still use the word poetry to talk about something other than the wind, the oaks and the blue sky. How much longer are you going to cry after reading the idiotic story of the gyroscope lost at the bottom of a naphtha well. Is it still necessary to teach such inanities in government schools?" The woman who had spoken first declaimed:

> Secret decor on wheels
> my paper money body
> plays bingo in the fireplace
> like a crank

"No, but you don't know anything more ridiculous? I'll suffer you not to speak ill of Pierre Serin, who was a great poet." "Then it is in the name of poetry. . ." "And what do you know about poetry with your flowers and all this Saint-Frippery?" "I see," a third voice interposed, "that you agree only about your love of poetry." "Who wouldn't love it," said a fourth "it's like the yeast for beer and the salt for celery." "Me," said a fifth. It was a fine how do you do. Ernest, of course, always Ernest, the paradoxical Ernest. "One can," said Ernest "remain unmoved before a cloud as before an automatic ticket machine. I don't like poetry, I don't like flowers, I don't like machines, I don't like sugar, I don't like pepper, I don't like what you like." This was addressed to whoever attacked Ernest. A woman (to judge from the voice) cried out: "Pervert, Pervert! I will say everything, everything, everything. What can one expect from a man who has shown his eyes to men, my dear?" I think she said, "His eyes, yes, his eyes, the word is shameful, to men, to my lover." I couldn't hear any more: the cries went up around

Ernest like swords, and I moved away, passing over strange parades, where the odd veiled and gloved people walked with bodies that I began to watch carefully without dreaming of doing them ill. I went from one discovery to another, but one question obsessed me: why the devil do these men have breasts? I've always been told that divine providence does nothing without reason. The only response I could find seemed to me to be whispered by hell and I didn't give it a second thought, any more than these forests, these avenues, these ports, these mountains, which unravel in the world below. Suddenly there was a fault in the apparatus, the earth became opaque again and I had to throw the frame and head-set to the side of the pavement. I found myself in a part of Paris I didn't know.

A woman came to meet me. She was young and healthy on her right side, old and wrinkled on the left. Her left side had abundant silver hair, while on her right side her hair was not so thick but was of a fine blackness. She wore a dress of grassland velvet gathered at the waist. There were no less than eight darns in brown cotton on the front of the dress. The woman held a sugar bowl in her right hand while with her left she pretended to lift up her skirt. On the side of her hat perched a robin which held in its beak a bunch of cherries. The lady's stockings were of a thousand colours. The following story was printed on it, illustrated by a member of the Institute:

My young friend Jean Dubonnet
Was eating his breakfast.
He heard in the clearing
A gunshot and then nothing more
He then gave free rein
To his imagination.
It is a horse or a lady
A priest or a king of diamonds
It is a crackling oriflamme
A wolf, a zouave, a brazier
Tired of dipping bread fingers

in an under-cooked egg
he put on a spangled robe
and went out. His dog Fanfan followed
In the meantime
A cloud in the form of love
Above the ballroom
Came to kneel down in its turn
Oh my Lord give me I pray
Everyday my café au lait

The woman bowed and asked if my name was René. When she discovered my name: "Jacques," she said crying on her left side. "That was the name of my beloved son who died at fifteen in tragic circumstances." She sighed. "Jacques," she said smiling on her right side. "Aren't you the handsome hussar who spent a single night at my house, long enough to make me see stars?" Then she showed me her stocking suspenders which were of an ingenious make patented by a cabinet-maker who became an employee at Printemps. She asked me to accompany her home, and it was at that moment that her words became obscure and she started to put in doubt the land of dreams and the false Elizabeth.

Poor young man, who could you ask for advice? I've seen too much of it recently to know on which side good and evil were, something I've been told was a primordial and unique occupation of the Good Lord's creatures. So I followed the lady and rubbed my knees a bit in perplexity. As we came to a house of modest appearance, two buses racing through the boulevard at breakneck speed stopped at the corner of a street as though each wanted to let the other pass. The two vehicles moved aside and retreated, then elegantly wagged their tails. "Its quite alright," they paid their respects, "not at all," then rushed headlong with one bound together into rue Traversière, hustling each other energetically. "So kind." "Oh," murmured my companion, "Two buses that are so polite to each other – it's a bad sign." And then in a loud voice: "Enter, Jacques, and don't be surprised at anything."

★★★★★

first published in the collection *Robert Desnos* (Éditions de l'Herne)

★★★★★

ROBERT DESNOS (see volume one p 36)

MARCO RISTIĆ

An Example[1]

For a long time now the white tiger had been waiting for all the Babylonian waters to be transformed into a swelling colourless dream. But never before had his heart trembled with such expectation, never before had his eyes sunk with such a ruby-red scream into the night, for the sky had never glowed with such an air of promise. As if the most apparent laws were to break asunder in indisputable defiance of laws, as if all trains on all bridges were with one blow to lose their power to reach the other side. Meanwhile not a word the zoo-keeper had spoken indicated that the day had come when symbols will lose their sight, when all omens will begin to lose their way, wandering blind and helpless in an infinite desert amid ferns and lizards towards the Red Sea. Only the butterflies were lighter than ever before, only the crickets had changed their voices. Their song was the echo of wine and the soldier's mess, resounding like moon song on polar nights, cold as the glaciers at dawn, deep as the gaze of the star and the planet. The birth of new plants, the development of improbable new species in the plant world was similarly a mysterious, immeasurable omen. Finally the earth too prepared itself to plunge into that deepest music of its eternity and its destiny. People embraced on the ship's decks, on the terraces and on the

[1] This example of a surrealist style with no inclination towards beauty or intelligibility whatsoever is nothing more than the sheer documentation of a stream of thought which has no further application. It is a documentation of his play with images, in which symbolic meaning and the possibility of a poetic distortion of reality can only be found *a posteriori*, and in which, after rejecting critical examination, not a single word could be replaced.

streets. They proceeded on their way very slowly, but either hope or blind fear had misted up their eyes and widened their pupils in mad expectation. Necessary alterations, unconditional fears and self-confident phosphor in the sea – all these things told me that smiles do not differ, even at the poles. A sea-serpent, as long as the desolate song of sailors, strong as the desire of childhood, soft as speech before death, coiled around the ship three times after lashing together its flanks with the strength of an eminent cataclysm. The sponges which had sucked up the sea salt, heavy as the salt, together with several fish who had livened up with memories of their boyhood, began to fall from the ship's flanks as it shattered into pieces. The ship shakes the water off and, now dry, rises slowly and majestically into the air, while the sea-serpent loosens its grip with the unbearable but silent whistle – Danger – of locomotives in American films. The cinema was half-empty, but the ship's ascension on the screen filled their hearts with unanimous and delighted anticipation of Eternal New Life. This was such that the handful of spectators stood up, clambered onto their seats and bellowed out, so they too might be taken by the ship in the purple reflexes of lethargy and the blood of heaven from reality to reality, from dream to dream, through its image alone. The sea-serpent had meanwhile uncurled itself and lay in the grass of a pleasant valley. The pines, which had bent across the river in which the snake washed its fiery poison-tongue, smelt of honey.

*****

translated by Victoria Appelbe

*****

MARCO RISTIĆ (Belgrade, 1902 – Belgrade, 1984) founder of the short-lived but important Yugoslav Surrealist Group in 1925 (the first surrealist group outside France), Ristić wrote poetry and narrative work and was especially interested in the phenomenology of perception, writing, with Koca Popovič, the important *Projet pour un phenomenologie de l'irrationel* (1931). After the Second World War he was the first Yugoslav ambassador to France.

GEORGES RIBEMONT-DESSAIGNES

Carmen And Carmen

The great poet Germe died insane. He left two daughters which was enough to rank him among the more off-beat authors. They were two twins so identically similar, from head to toe, in the least detail, that the father himself, on his death bed, gave up trying to tell them apart. And he had probably already given up as soon as they had been born, since he gave them both the same name. The mind was no more able to differentiate them than the eye. Germe was also in the habit of saying: my daughter Carmen.

Their temperaments were as similar as their faces and their bodies. At least it was easier to imagine so: it would have been necessary to isolate them in separate cages and submit them to the pressure of identical circumstances to be quite sure about it. For the same reasons no one at school knew whether the homework of one was done better than that of the other. They themselves had difficulty in recognising their exercise books, and it is not certain that on numerous occasions they did not contribute to the confusion with some duplicity.

Relations and well-intentioned people strove repeatedly to artificially distinguish between the two sisters by attributing nicknames to them. It made no difference, as the same Carmen could accept both nicknames, or alternatively respond to the one that pleased her, and at worst not worry about either. Furthermore, Germe used to get violently angry. He had called his two twin girls Carmen in order than they might enjoy the dual existence of a single personality and did not intend anyone to minimise these advantages.

When their father died, the girls were left in poverty. Due to the one small mirror left to them, they quarrelled one day. Carmen Germe left for America, and the other Carmen Germe became smitten with an itinerant juggler who she thereafter followed blindly around travelling fairs. The separation lasted for two years. Tired of travelling, overseas Carmen returned to be near Carmen. The juggler, who went by the name of Mr Vladimir Tube, cried out with happiness at such a miraculous resemblance. In fact, the turns he invented, which involved the simultaneous or successive appearance of the two sisters at both ends of the hall, achieved great success. The operation worked wonderfully well, even more so with the help of a young negro called Arthur who was in charge of the extravagant interludes.

Carmen and Carmen, clad in the same costumes for the exercise of their profession, might easily have confused both the negro Arthur and Vladimir Tube, and the misunderstanding would in this case have approached incest, if an element of difference had not come to light. Carmen had brought a magpie from America, a pretty, tame magpie who knew how to pronounce his mistress' name. As soon as she appeared, the magpie would skip onto her shoulder, shake its wings and tail, and repeat twice: "Carmen, Carmen."

They soon realised that the bird was not taken in by appearances, and each of them gained the habit of consulting it – consequently they never doubted its abilities, and in the evening, after the performance, Vladimir Tube, in order to be certain of the identity of the woman who accompanied him into the bedroom of his caravan, did not fail to keep an eye on the reciprocal effusions of one of the Carmens and her faithful and discerning magpie. He would then be sure of having in his arms a loving woman, ignoring the cool existence of a double too similar to the beauty who murmured in the darkness: "My star, my heart, my little fusspot, my rainbow's end", or who slept a sweet angel's sleep at his side. And in the warmth of his own sighs, he drowned out all nagging doubt: The other, the other, what can she do?

Vladimir noticed that the handsome Arthur cast surreptitious and meaningful glances at the comings and goings of the two sisters – at one of the two sisters, but which? One evening, in the darkness surrounding the caravans, he thought he saw two shadows move apart at his approach. A few moments later, and by different routes, Arthur and one of the Carmens emerged into the light, while the other Carmen, with an ironical smile on her lips, loomed up to dispel Vladimir's concern: "You don't have to worry, darling. These two simplify things!" From then on each evening saw Carmen follow Vladimir, and Carmen follow Arthur. By force of habit, the magpie gave the signal, "Carmen, Carmen." And, perched on one shoulder which it tapped in a friendly way with flapping wings, went to sleep in the oddball's room.

The greatest harmony still prevailed between the two sisters, more united than ever by the intimate tenderness and the cares of each day. If tiredness caused one of them to become overly pale, then the other one would soon become a little pale in her turn. Applying lipstick was a doubly arduous task. They were so alike that they themselves were unable to distinguish between their photographs.

And yet this astonishing duality was to be dramatically torn apart one day. This coincided with the engagement of a musician who played the cornet with such virtuosity and feeling that all the flowers of the earth seemed to bloom in the artificial light and dark as soon as he broke into a melody. The stars fell or altered course, trees swayed like elephants' trunks and women. . . women seemed to lose their hearts, like chalices of blood perfumed with amber and musk into which dim-witted men with swollen veins inclined to drink in all the world's problems.

One evening a violent argument broke out between the two sisters in one of the bedrooms. Threats, entreaties, piercing cries, pleading tones. Tears, laughter and insults. Vladimir wanted to intervene. The door was locked. He knocked. A curtain behind the door was drawn and the shouting seemed further away. The earth started to spin frenetically. Tube staggered as he caught a few more distinct words which came pell mell on the night wind.

"Let me have him, let me have him, let me have him," said one of the two voices, as alike as the two mouths, the two tongues and the two throats.

"No, you rotten cow, no, you rotten cow," said the other.

"Not that, not him, let me have him."

"What difference is it to you, since he won't know it isn't you?"

"Let me have him, let me have him."

"Ah yes, I'll have him all, all of him, his eyes, his heart, his kisses. Everything. His soul in my ears, it will flow: he'll know everything, he'll know that it's me, I will drink him in, you hear, I will. . ."

"No! oh no! no. . ."

Tube became aware of Arthur's presence. He dared listen no more. Both of them turned their backs after exchanging a beady look. They were suddenly unsure of the truth.

. . .Tube woke in the morning. He had slept in the auditorium under the tent, and in front of the open door of the caravan he came across Arthur. They went in.

One Carmen, as pale as polar ice, eyes open and filled with the opaline mists of the Northern cape, was seated on the side of the bed, leaning to one side. Another Carmen was spread out on the ground with her head in her hands. She got up. She was alive, but was the colour of snow at night. A secret thought weighed upon her as though the force of the earth's gravity had increased a hundredfold. She had never before seen her sister in a mirror so clearly: she only knew her face as a reflection; her sister's she saw at that moment. And as blood abandons skin and flesh from the muscles, returning to the folds of her heart, she had suddenly become an enormous and shivering wineskin. "Dead, dead, dead. Am I not the one who is dead? They'll see me like this, and I, I will see nothing. I'll be, I'll be, a dead woman." A complicated chronometric mechanism whirred for a thousandth of a second in the brain. Carmen stretched forth her arms, her eyes sprang from her head, barely retained by the sockets.

"Murderers! Murderers!"

At this Vladimir and Arthur scrutinised each other. Who was the guilty one? They threatened one another. And who had the guilty one killed, his mistress or the other man's? And if she was the killer, who had she killed, Carmen Vladimir or Carmen Arthur? Should she be protected or torn apart?

"Who are you?" demanded Arthur.

"Oh, Oh! I'm not the one who did this," said Carmen, calm now that perfidious snakes lurked in all the dark corners. "Perhaps she committed suicide. . ."

"Who are you?"

Carmen saw Arthur's fearsome hands. She spoke simply in a little girl's voice lost in a poster.

"Vladimir Tube, I am not your wife, nor am I yours, Arthur. I belong to neither of you. This is not me."

A portcullis of lead descended around each person. But a small flower was born. The magpie entered chirpily. It took no notice on seeing Carmen. With a bound it leaped onto the shoulder of the cold Carmen.

"Carmen, Carmen."

Perched on top of the head, claws embedded in the hair, it repeated: "Carmen, Carmen."

Carmen, the remaining one, looked at her face framed in the mirror. She expected to see herself disintegrate. Her dead voice stammered out without knowing what it said:

"It's her: she alone was Carmen for both of you. Not me, oh no, not me!"

Then she uttered a shrill cry, jumped up, and fell down in a corner where she crouched and muttered as she incessantly shook her head:

It's in the eyes, in the eyes

That I look for it. . .

By now Vladimir and Arthur were at each other's throats, laying into one another with the boot. They rolled on the ground in common fury. Arthur finally gained the upper hand and gripped his adversary's windpipe, overwhelming him with fresh vigour. It was then that Vladimir, his eyes bulging, saw in the corner that the carefree magpie no longer perched on the dead woman, but on the trembling shoulder of the other.

"Carmen, Carmen."

One or the other one, now as always. It recognised neither the importance or the difference. It never had. Everything depended on how it felt. At the whim of whim.

Astounded, Vladimir loosened his grip. That's why Arthur strangled him.

It's in the eyes, in the eyes
That I look for it. . .

sang Carmen as Arthur scratched his chin uncomprehendingly.

*****

published in Georges Ribemont-Dessaignes *Dada 2* Paris: Champ Libre

*****

GEORGES RIBEMONT-DESSAIGNES (Montpellier 1884 – Saint-Helene 1976) One of the most amiable of the Parisian dadaists, Ribemont-Dessaignes had the sensibility of a surrealist, but not the temperament to accept the rough and tumble of group politics, and soon distanced himself from the group around Breton. "A bald man who isn't bald, a general who isn't a general, a seducer who isn't a seducer," as his 'judgement on himself', written in 1926, had it, Ribemont-Dessaignes's always incisive and perceptive writings remain for the most part scattered in inaccessible journals and out-of-print volumes. His novels are perhaps his most notable achievement.

GEORGES LIMBOUR

The Actor From Lancashire Or The Illustrious White Horse

Herodstar was an actor at the Dream's Theatre in London, a very poor stage on which the world's greatest masterpieces had been performed, although only a few people ever saw them. He lived with Pamela, who could more accurately be called his companion than his mistress, and they went in tattered clothes to the tops of monuments and the supreme shifts of history.

The evening the premiere of *The Famous White Horse* took place, Herodstar, who had to find a white horse for himself, noticed that the prompter's trap-door opened just above a mine, in such a way that one could slip into the shaft. Pamela and her friend Olga applauded this discovery. Olga said that she had been born of a convict father in the Siberian mines and that she was an ardent flame detached from the pyre, a will o' the wisp more dangerous than lightning going down the chimney into a room in which there would be someone reading his paper, and which would zigzag all over Europe. Then the little one let herself slip through the trap-door while Raingo took up his violin on the edge of the well to play such delightful music that those who descended underground never feared suffocation while the rhythm continued.

"During winter sunsets, standing on a promontory so I saw the scenic sea as a surface rather than a line and, as coal-boats appeared from all sides of the horizon, I thought that, as they opened their portholes, they would throw their coal onto this fire. They swarmed over the ocean like blowflies ready to devour the decomposed star, and the blank gesture of a cloud fanned them.

"Tear yourselves open, nordic mists, greenish masks in moistened cardboard leaning over these vessels which also bring the coffins of sensitive consumptives, sad fables in the bronchial tubes incrusted with black dust, sick realities throwing up small setting suns dusted with the mourning of badly burned dreams like the spitting of a coughing miner, greenish mists of phantoms that emerge from the absinthe, marvellous veils in which falsehood was draped! I am on my way to your land, Lancashire, knowing only a tiny quote from Shakespeare, a land in which ardent looks smoulder over a fire-thorn with black countenances. A few hermetic hearts, illuminated with blue or green gleams, pass through the firedamp of reality. On what rock face does your palms rest, Pamela, as you assume the indecisive and awkward gesture of repentance, afraid to reflect the image of sin on your dress, and you are amazed to discover inside your hands the shiny traces of a bouquet of absent ferns? You would be food for the encased lifts of Pogrom City, minute fantasies of tertiary arborescences, wings of fishes excavating a void of memory of the azure in the coal."

A majestic plunge was heard and far in the distance an echo unleashed an obscure avalanche.

"We're near the stables," thought the Actor.

He raised his lantern: on the walls a clumsy hand had drawn a battered heart which looked more like a leaf that an edenic hare had just started to gnaw. There were also some names engraved with a kitchen knife on the tedious hour of life: "These folks decorate their graves," said Pamela, "now they are dead."

They had reached the stables: the warden upset a glass of absinthe gleaming like his eyes and from which the wicked and mysterious balm of night was exhaled. This man, happy to have some visitors, recalled a trick executed on public squares and angry at not being able to grasp a man about the waist in order to throw him to the ground, cried: "Firedamp!" in order to challenge them. He filled his mouth with petrol and, as he struck his lighter, an immense flame was exhaled which, with a roaring of speed, drew towards it all the air of the reddened mine, from whose corners flew white bats and the remains of birds.

"Stop!" said the Actor, but the man laughed and drank a greenish draught from which this time he swallowed the flame.

"I've come to look for the White Horse."

"Look for him," said the coal-merchant. "He was the favourite of my illegitimate child: she bought him flowers on Sunday, the fool."

They found him lying down like a supply of shrouds. As they approached he got up and neighed. His eye was inflamed like that of Russian rabbits or the bloodshot eyes of coal-merchants delirious with drink. He inspired no pity since he was stronger than his destiny, his neck dignified with magnanimous blandishments, gracious and chivalrous flatteries which had not convinced him. Nevertheless, he wore small bells as ridiculous as the Engineers' jester, like dull eyes with resonant pupils. The blinker of darkness seemed to him more acceptable than the back of a white hand for his nostrils trembled. But Pamela gathered together the reins which fell from his mouth like a dribble of mourning, or those leather straps on a horse-guard's sabre hilt, in a bunch of tactile nerves by which the will of the horse died in her hand.

They climbed back onto the stage.

"We need to build him a stable behind the scenes," said Olga. "He will not go out but will have music, flowers and the pink sugar of electric light."

The clumsy cocks of theatres upset the beam behind the door of falsehood and three knocks signalled the dawning of night.

The curtain was raised and as the Actor wiped his dirty hands on his handkerchief he genuinely wished to announce his intentions to the audience with a prologue.

"I have come to cast flowers over a white catafalque and the tenacity of its anxieties.

"All the plagues of humanity: periods, pregnancy, cancers and ulcers, at once its repulsiveness and its beauty, distract it in the same way as parrots, monkeys and the white rats that some people love to feel run down their spines, but we still prefer exoticism to the tedious vibrancy of the morbid Marseilles heart. There are people who conserve pustules and viruses in order to avoid military service. Humanity is caught in the snares of clever playwrights. It is a strange wager not to find boredom behind these medical occupations or some banking additions, but, behind Appetite's tricks and the greasy craftiness of the Candidates, we have encountered Beauty, and that's why you will be able to appreciate events on which we will never insist, that attain a sensibility without offspring or business dealings and for whose benefit you are prepared – almost heartily! – for us to make a collection in the house, I mean for the RUSSIAN Famine! It is extraordinary that young rhetoricians and orators of youth clubs and boarding houses have not devoted holy representations of their Sundays to such charitable fellowship! It must be said, in their defence, that the impulse did not come from *on high*, and that they could not start a new type of theatre if Messrs Bernstein – *Yes!* – and Lenormand – *Yes!* – did not take the lead. That is why the small foetuses living in the tumescent bellies of negro children die on European steppes from the powerlessness of Art, to profit future schools of dancers whose perpetual hallucinations and atrocious memories would help them dance on tip-toe over innocent corpses."

At this point bouquets were thrown over the proscenium, and the crowd, the same one that had bellowed out the sentence on Jesus beneath Pilate's window, demanded their immediate sale for the benefit of the starving Russian masses, yelling out ridiculous bids. But these flowers, thrown with an extravagance to which we prove that we are oblivious only when faced with prostitution, the orator crushed them, trampled them, tore them to pieces, and the prompter in his box was heard spitting out the petals he had been forced to swallow.

"So I will tell you about our inventions, without opening the doors of the stables where we have kept – behind the scenes of our smile – the last chimeras.

"They deceive you by offering you the clinging MARVELLOUS, these market-dealers who hide in their sculleries a siren from the Red Sea! And these obscene and flaccid fables are the only ones to disturb the minds of schoolboys and their families. If the innkeepers on the quayside had (no, not the audacity!!) the stupidity to uphold such lies, it was a long time ago that the Chinese sailors, negroes and primitives, the most credulous of people, had thrown them, with shattered jaws, into the stinking box of their fish.

"But Chimeras couldn't care less about their native lands. The most formidable race does not leave them breathless, otherwise they would long ago have given themselves away by cutting the tongues that perpetually hang like beautiful masks of falsehood, red with irritability. For the sake of form, their wings resemble those of bats whose indentations suggest the curves of gulfs in which blue oceans breathe and one might think, seeing them fly, that the sea had sought to rise up from its depths. Opium, their dung no less precious than that of the creeks, speckles the grass of the Lymphatic Vale: they have lungs only for the perfumed spirit of breath and they breathe only for the elegance of coming to a halt.

"Enough of this! Here are my brothers and sisters:

"Pernsön, the Norwegian, who has taken a trip around the fjords more than a thousand times, his hands behind his back like a horse that has been broken in around the red post of the sun fixed in icy water, beneath trees where he was probably forbidden to ride a bicycle. Being born in one of these wooden chalets where – the Lord be praised! – men spend their lives, he will tell you about family life, river keepers, little rosy or sallow civil servants, his one comic monologue, if he has nothing better to talk about.

"Pamela is a young girl of eighteen, something young men prefer to experienced women of thirty since they are drawn to the arithmetic pass-mark of love, unless they have weak constitutions. It is particularly for this that some old men and worn-out naval officers pay attention to the hair which the comb each evening brushes away from matted eyes. Her father, who ran a filthy junk shop and gave her a mandolin as a gift, taught her how to ride a bike without tyres, to appraise forged paintings, broken jewellery and XVIIIth century armchairs with no seats. She escaped from the carriages through gaps in their floors. Her lilac pulse was never captive and brushing against the doctor's crew-cut never gave her a dread of the warm hair of bats squatting on her stomach. She dances carefully on the tightrope of youth, excited by no longer having to wave the handkerchief of childhood, but afraid to grasp the serious sunshade of maturity that a grotesque figure holds out to her with respect as if to say 'Madam'.

"There is no point in speaking about the others. All of them are in equally good health.

"After that, can we be surprised that the noble mouth of the poet throws up more venom than the toad, the slander that is sometimes pregnant with calumny? The dog to which the butcher's boy has cautiously thrown an ox gall goes to rend it open and spit it out in the public square. The calumny of people of the world escapes from their gob joylessly and without energy like the slobbering false confinement of the exhausted sick that they do not even wake. But the severity of the poet spares himself less than the sunken and spanked flesh of his cowardly companions, in spite of the fact that his healthy loves did not need to be flagellated: his whip is the weapon of his nobility. But that's enough of our friends who complain about having vices.

"We had promised nevertheless to say no more about it.

"How can we escape from it?

"We are going to introduce our legendary horse in order to see above reality.

"May your disparate occupations dissolve the dream for a few evenings, alkaline *Emperors of the Poor*!

"We recall that a Veronique, a little schoolgirl whose puberty dreamed of splendours, tried, in the midst of her friends, to dissolve false pearls in vinegar squeezed from the sponge of Christ."

The curtain rose and Pamela Amazone was seen on the horse. But no sooner had they appeared than a new uproar rose from the hall. The mine-owner had in fact recognised one of his horses and was scandalised that a beast of burden could be profaned under the hands of ham actors for the purpose of puerile wonders.

He accepted that many things could be mocked on an evening such as this when he granted his anxieties some doubtful 'intellectual relaxation', but not that the nobility of his business and life should be attacked by one of their presentations. But the reaction from the Gods was even worse: hundreds of miners had attended with their wives and children and they recognised the horse and some called him by name, while others demanded in the name of the law of the eight hour day that he be taken off the stage. Cries like 'the mine for the miners!' were heard. And the masks of Comedy and Tragedy and Drama on the balusters uttered political references.

The handsome director appeared like a man disturbed at his wedding feast and declared that, since this horse did not belong to him, he would be forced to conform to the wishes of its owner. At these words, a grand-duchess leaned out of her box and threw an enormous bouquet at the actress, saying "This will pay for the horse." Within a few moments the bouquet had been bought for a hundred dollars by a Spanish lord and the presentation could continue. Coins had showered down like a handful of American confetti into the owner's box.

The incontestable fact was that the woman riding the horse was extraordinarily beautiful, and the white gloves of knaves of gallantry were afraid to give proof of it, for they felt outraged by the presence of Pamela, who was beyond their means. But the bouquets mutilated by Herodstar among their torn white papers, and whose secretion ran down the length of the footlights as if there had been snails in the peoples' gifts, had the aspect of those corners in cemeteries where the faded debris from tombs had been discarded. It seemed to Pamela that she had just drunk from one of those bronze chalices placed like a gong on the granite where the rain dissolves infusoria in licorice water to ward off the evaporating sun and where children are sent for refills at verdigrised taps next to a mass of dried wreaths, scalps and rotten flowers. She held her hand to her waist hoping to find a tube of smelling salts there, but her fingers felt only a rose, an adorable leech which she threw under the horse's hooves. Feeling herself weaken, she went backstage.

The veil of dead lights immediately spread through the hall. Some people blamed destiny for acts devoid of meaning, but the strange lilac perfume on mornings when the earth is so black (it will be a rainy day), is emitted beside the celestial mechanism and please believe that Pamela's was too intelligent to be concerned with arguments defending God, free will or Reason. At the time she lived in a small room opening out on to the poisonous garden of logic the five geraniums of the universals filled the night with a bitter and mortal perfume in the dwelling from which she nearly did not waken.

When there was no longer anyone in the streets, Pamela's body was mounted on the horse and they left to find her a tomb. Olga suggested lowering the corpse right into the middle of the Second Pitt Avenue where a ditch had been dug to repair the water pipes which the workmen had started to fill in again. But Herodstar was afraid that flint sharper than the stars might penetrate the flesh and he preferred a well in an abandoned park in the North.

This eye of insomnia paralysed fixed dreams. The Actor rested Pamela on the grass: she had on her actress's dress.

On the body of the outstretched boxer there were marks showing where he had been beaten. Traces of blows appeared in each part of the body where Pamela's sensibility had just suffered its attack: the hips where the challenge had taken its hold, the kidneys which had held it back for a well-balanced vertical smile over her teeth, the shoulder which had maintained a secret, the waist where she had been gripped by death, the throat where her hand had begged him to be less clumsy, a line underlining her heart and such swooning kisses from her lover that the blood which had received them had no longer desired anything but death. These marks were as blue as Herodstar's eyes and they moved like their reflections and watched him. It seemed that before dawn rose, they would have devoured the corpse.

"Water will suit her better than earth. Hyacinths of immortality, I know into which element your roots reach forth."

Pamela was lowered down into the well. The perpetrators separated. Herodstar mounted the White Horse.

The hooves resounded haughtily in slumbering London town, tinder boxes of genius spattering the pavement with fire.

"You can't have expected, England, that this Great Horse would one day set foot on your rough virgin territory, suspicious and perfidious Albion I laugh at your colonising counting-house genius. The immortal monster, for which you would never find your Saint Helena, tramples on your heart and yet you sleep! The horses, whose sense of smell is generally keener than that of men, who have a presentiment of volcanic eruptions and earthquakes, storms, plagues and thieves, don't rear up against me as I approach through the back of the nocturnal stables.

"It's true: set your mind at rest. I would not give a ha'penny's worth for your trade, John Bull[1], faced with an

[1] Or John Bulldog. This is a character who is neither credulous or amusing and whose belly does not overflow with the common guts of humour. Married to the fisherwoman, he rests his spite sitting on

Aunt Sally who had wanted to ask for powder and compass from the Chinese, mortar from the Boulonnais, propellers from Anjou, steamers from a child, officers from Saint-Cyr to exterminate Corsair, seal and whale. You grow fat on adventure novelists and hockey players so we may believe in your boldness, but we know that your trudgen-stroke swimmers come from Australia and your tennis champions from New Zealand. Only your baby-blonds are beautiful and you don't eat them, but nurse them with decayed teeth, governess with metal feelings, you send them to become over-ripe at Oxbridge, this tender flesh delighted by the innocence of my caresses. Your captains of the Army Service Corps furnished beautiful models for illustrators of Epinal, but do you imagine that your bear-skin surpasses the beautiful hair curled and dishevelled in the Zulus' war fans? Where is Gladstone, the crafty old negotiator, sometimes more intelligent than I am, but his mind makes the thick canvas smell. Others[2] appear on the screen digging the ground and comparing themselves to Cincinnatus, but people don't go and smash their windows and disdain his stupid credulity to this extent. As for your daughters (on whose flayed bodies children would refuse to study anatomy), having, like dogs, sucked the oxalic acid of offices, they will relieve themselves at the foot of the Pyramids. But you consider yourself so great in this respect that you want to have two flags, one for the navy as well as the other one, rather than be content with one like everyone else. In the meantime I declare a perpetual war on you, race of pickpockets of empty matchboxes and furniture dealers of conspiracies and you can employ this means of patience rich in heroism which you call a Block-ade against me."

The Illustrious White Horse walked on with his imperial amble. At the crossroads of a closed-off avenue a few small red flags stirred here and there, safeguarded by workers,

---

pickled sardines which I would not recommend that you contemplate for too long.

[2] Lloyd George.

and labourers' belts hung down like ticket rolls, for these men have cold bellies and are afraid of the obesity of wrestlers. Noticing the works forsaken beneath the night, the Horse changed direction.

He found himself in front of the consulate of MY country. He turned around to face the offices and, mounting on his stirrups, the Actor called out 'Down with France!' The consul appeared on the balcony and saluted. Then he hastily sent the maid to close the shutters and use a mattress to create a barrier behind it. But Uncle Sam, his guest that evening, went down to the street and turned up his shirt sleeves, for this excentric (Barnum's spelling), this excentric (this is what we call people with tics and other slight nervous disorders, who have changed their meal times and are in a better or worse mood than ordinary imbeciles), this bachelor excentric, loved to mix it with hooligans and dockers. The highway whores had never come across playthings worth his goatee. He would be annoyed to be loved for himself. The great flirts of the Cinema – these Ladies – have rather fat buttocks in order not to feel his knees. Why does he unbutton himself, this imitation Satyr? He is sterile, to the point of impotence. He gives them a gift from Jules Verne and if there are poets, or even Great Lakes, in the vicinity, he stops up the women's ears with gobs of his chewing-gum. The seventeen candles in his peasant's handkerchief symbolise the independence of American snot.

So this man who hoped to do business with a common scoundrel had left his gin, his armchair, his cigar and his sentimental politics (i.e. national and matrimonial alliances) to go down into the street – with several brownings in his pockets just in case. But when he saw Herodstar on his horse, he was afraid even to flee and with that marvellously hypocritical smile assumed especially by opticians, he crossed the macadam and, taking off his top hat under the fresh chestnut trees, he greeted the Actor with a commercial platitude:

"How much is a hundred kilos worth?"

Herodstar did not move, and was rigid like an equestrian statue.

"Don't you want to break into the market? I won't insist."

Happy to extract himself so cheaply, Uncle Sam turned around and walked back turning his shirt sleeves down. Herodstar's scorn was merely the whispering of a smile which chilled the merchant and he went back into the corridor of the consulate with that trembling that characterises adolescents stepping over the threshold of a brothel for the first time.

"It's just as well," said the Actor, "this spot is degraded."

He continued on his way.

"In due course I'll go down to Italy, the resting place of English poets. Pamela, I will have left you frozen at the bottom of a Lancashire cistern and how long will your memory last?

"How I wish that there was only ever one woman on earth one could love. Pamela! For me you would have been that woman.

"But the ring of Fidelity is worn out from rubbing against the crystal of glasses (oh must I name mundane objects), and even from caresses, just as the Rainbow is worn out, as the fragile rainbow wears out under the lips of the breeze.

"Marvellous knowledge and loves, you pass through the intelligence and the heart, like those real swords used by Hindu magicians to cut up the body – without ever cutting it! Oceania, you were a handsome continent on the surface of the Indian ocean, but here you are submerged leaving only a few Polynesian islands. In the same way the Greek tongue was once a beautiful land of my adolescence, but here it has vanished under the waters of Memory. Pamela, remembrance, would your continent be built on more solid foundations in order not to be destroyed by underwater explosions?

"New worlds, and tomorrow's surprises, rise up within

me, corals! Like these false violet islands whose clouds drag the shadow over the sea, islands which will forget themselves and where imaginary Robinson Crusoes die."

The Actor, noticing a closed bookshop, dismounted from the horse which he tied to a street lamp. He woke up the bookseller and bought a Spanish grammar and dictionary.

He set out again across town, marvelling at the way the words of the foreign language were freshly gathered fruits and not old and dry. They touched the senses marvellously, new like young beggars who accost you, not yet words but the very things they designate, happily running naked before being clothed again in abstraction.

Three policemen loomed up. As they noticed (what professionals!) that the trousers the Actor wore were not riding breeches, they said: "What is that horse? It's not your's."[3]

Harton thought that if one squeezed humanity through a wine-press, its essence would flow out as drops of policemen.

The Great Battle was about to take place: from the summit of the moon ran white pyramids: a great light formed on the desert sand and while the ruffled Sphinx dreamed of reading 'The Man with the Broken Ear', the armies lined up on the Kheops plain.

Herodstar's side was a badly dressed group branded by the superintendent of police with the name of 'riff-raff', and included some youths who had escaped from special children's prisons, extraordinary inventors of mechanical toys exhibited on the asphalt of the streets, inspired beggars who sketched out paintings on London pavements that were too beautiful to be hung up in museums and which the women rubbed out with their Wilhelmine, acrobats and thieves, some from the heroic Bohemian races and women who had grown tired of killing the flabby flesh of

[3] in English in original [trans note].

husbands in sky-blue shirt sleeves who directly faced the mass in the uniform of old presbytery maids and puritan suffragettes looking for the opportunity to throw their ovaries and others still I would be unable to name.

Opposite Herodstar were lined up a considerable number of novelists led by Binet-Walmer with his wooden sword, accompanied by theatre and cinema people and journalists, and along with the world's police militia, missionaries of all religions, propagandists of anything you like, crowds from Lourdes and Aix-les-Bains, apocalyptic masses of the sick, the crippled and the scrofulous, the absurd spite of Young Royalists and highways commissions, and Franklin selling his red umbrella, the renovations in the manuals of the Will, the idiotic band of Kantian lifeboatmen, false heroes, all artists of revues and Pantheon, the troops of Valmy and Iena, and finally all that can do without the heroism of popular song in THE DREAM PASSES. ('Can you see them. . .')

At a distance from this battle the only neutrals were open-mouthed lovers with the eyes of molluscs in astrological glasses.

The Illustrious White Horse reared up. Herodstar raised his head and seeing some tourists at the top of the pyramids, cried out:

"Are those sick eagles that have shat on the peaks?"

"Herodstar, the foot of a virgin crushed the snake, but the weight of centuries and freestone does not crush vipers. They stretch out under these tombstones in rollers characteristic of ballistics and one could roll the great Pyramids over humanity's crimes in the sea to fill up the lagoons of Alexandria.

"Soldiers, the Touring-Club and commercialism will acclaim your undoing."

In London it was after midnight. A policeman drew his revolver.

"Don't miss the man, but don't catch the horse," said the Police Sergeant.

A rearing up saw him struck him down on the spot, dead. Herodstar grabbed the weapon and struck down the horse.

The Actor got away.

A crowd of party-goers surrounded the corpse.

Herodstar pushed open the door of the small room he had shared with Pamela. On the gas appliance he noticed his companion's curling-tongs – red-hot since she had forgotten to turn it off. He took it and set the six equal and gleaming fingers in motion which opened and contracted on a ghost of love. The Actor offered his jacket to them instead of his heart, where a red burn outlined the grip of an illusory hand.

Sterile electricity did not exist in Herodstar's dwelling.

Gas illumination of slums, your bad breath more stinking than that of the feverish is a sweet air to those about to die. Workers, don't disconnect these lead pipes, these rampant snakes in the thirsty plaster of ceilings, bent midway around a tongue which whistles a monotonous and desperate song, denuded of these captivating looks which charm the birds from the trees, but make sleeping eyelids fall over men's pupils. Herodstar took his penknife and pricked the reptile as it dreamed about the yellow canaries of the lady downstairs. He lay on his bed, and thought he would have a glossy black hearse like the formal dress under the white front of a bouquet.

He was sad,
then
he found that to die young was a fine thing.

Suddenly he heard a knock at the door. It was the porter who smelt gas as he was passing. He asked what was wrong.

"Nothing," said Herodstar (he laughed). "Can you believe it, my dear friend – my hands are full and I can't open the door – I am blowing up children's balloons, you know, green, yellow and red. Tomorrow I'm going to sell them at Victoria Square. Life is hard."

"Great heavens, you have some first-class schemes. But you'll regret it when the bill comes at the end of the month."

The chap went away and Herodstar felt his head lighten.

In fact the room was filled with balloons and the dying Herodstar watched them sail away one by one like an aerial legacy he had left to this uninhabited world.

The multicolored cloud filled the sky, attracted by the sun towards the whirlpool of stars. It was twilight and swallows with sharp cries had clusters of needles in their throats. Some balloons burst in the cloud and fell slowly down onto the lawns.

Others lasted long enough to travel through the night.

A Blue One fell in a Japanese basin wrinkled into a sheaf of blue feathers of which the swans were jealous.

A Red One rolled over the solitudes of the Pole, a drop of blood, with a distracted heart.

A Green One in the branches seemed to be a magical fruit of explorers and amused the monkeys in a wood for the whole morning.

But the last one, which lingered on the surface of the atmosphere, fell at dawn in a ball of silence into a sandstone court where the glory of Rome slumbered and made the geese of the Capitol bawl in a frightful way among a beating of wings.

*****

published in *Contes et propos* Paris: Gallimard

translated by Krzysztof Fijalkowski and Michael Richardson

*****

GEORGES LIMBOUR (see volume one p 45)

ANTONIN ARTAUD

The Astonishing Adventure Of The Poor Musician[1]

Hoichi, an excellent musician with the ill-luck to be blind had two beautiful ears that were red like a setting sun and which he lost one evening in old Japan. Here's how.

It all began one evening, a little after sunset in front of the gleaming door of the Danamosoura Temple where Hoichi, the forlorn musician, had been given shelter through charity. Hoichi did not see the twinkling of the sky nor the waters on whose banks the old temple had been built, but the unstable magic of the approaching night lent a rustling to the air like a sound of invisible presence, and the blind man sensed the flight of hidden demons, of the legendary Heike whose passing was communicated to his flesh with mysterious shudders. He was afraid. The empty temple slept. At times the waters breathed a sigh similar to that of the dead. Huddled in a ball, his biva pressed against his chest and huddled up against the frail wall, he waited. It was just then that the imperious voice of a Samurai, as though emitted by the essence of things, summoned him. It called him once, and then once more. And since Hoichi still did not respond, the invisible Samurai came closer. Hoichi felt a iron-clad hand grasp his own. The warrior seemed very powerful and well-armed. So he yielded.

"I have come," said the warrior, "I have come. . ."

[1] This story, Artaud's version of an old Japanese legend, was presumably drawn from Lafcadio Hearn's version, which is contained in his collection *Kwaidan* (translator's note)

And they continued to walk on amidst the silence of the stones.

Then booming, imperious and distant voice continued with the same sound of fractured music: ". . .on behalf of my master, on behalf of my master, to look for you."

And the stones started again to fall silent, and the leaves to whisper.

The road was of an incalculable length, but what alarmed the blind musician above all was the goal of this inexplicable journey, which he felt he would not have the strength of will to escape. Finally they arrived before an immense iron gate at whose foot his guide left him. "My master," he said to him, "hopes that you, oh most marvellous of the earth's musicians, will play a song on your biva that will be more beautiful than what you would sing to the greatest mikado on earth, since my master is greater than the greatest mikado." And silence again fell. The iron gate opened, there were hurried steps like those of an immense crowd shuffling on the spot, and they arrived in front of what the musician thought was a stairway. There were some boards that were drawn back, whispering that came down like a flight of wild geese with panting breath. A sensation of intense light touched the blind musicians's skin. He sensed he was in a very brightly lit palace. But the vertiginous terror which pricked his flesh caused him to stagger at each step he took.

"Sing to us, sing to us," came the piercing voice of the fully armed Samurai. "Sing about the marriage of the princess. . . the princess of our great mikado." The unfortunate bard felt that his vision had come back to him. It was as if he no longer had eyelids, as if his limbs had suddenly become glass. He had the impression of falling, and felt his fingers running along the strings of the human biva in accordance with the rhythm demanded by the poem, and images were traced all around, beautiful and marvellous like dreams dreamed at the bottom of the sea. He saw magnificent processions come and go, astonishing flowers fade and die, the legendary faces of virgins vanish in the flames of prodigious fires. And he felt himself spinning round. He fell backwards and wanted to die, he felt an intensity of emotion consuming his strength. With lightning speed, the Samurai had risen and cleared the space that separated the palace from the iron gate, had reached the open road – and he was following on behind. A little before dawn they found themselves again at the small temple by the water. Hoichi spun round three times and listened. Once more he was blind and alone. Then, for once, he dared look inside himself and asked: WHERE HAVE I BEEN?

The Buddhist priest who had given him sanctuary returned around dawn to take up his duties and was amazed that morning to find the musician lying against the temple wall in the same position and place as when he had left him the previous evening.

He neither spoke nor moved until evening twilight began to fall, and when they tugged at his arm, or shook him to make him eat or get him back on his feet, he again fell to the ground like a puppet, in such a way that the priest thought he was dead. He sought out bearers and mourners and sent messengers to the village as he began to keep vigil. The shadow of the trees became terrifying. Night spread over the earth. It was then that, called by some unnamable spirit from the other world, the blind musician got up. He walked like a somnambulist and, as if guided by an alien hand, did not seem conscious of his own movements. The little priest became breathless as he tried to keep up. Besides, he was very much afraid. He sometimes touched his mouth or eyes, and hoisted up his short robe which slipped from his fingers with each stride he took. In this way they arrived in front of the old iron gates of the town cemetery. The little priest recoiled. He fell to his knees in fear. He felt he had arrived at the extreme limit of life. The gates were open. He seemed to hear clashing armies. He heard the trumpeting of fantastic elephants. And the musician was lying on the slabs of the tomb, his face ecstatic as though present at the unfolding of mysterious wonders and he shook his biva with convulsive movements.

They met again a little before morning on the road leading to the remote temple. The exhausted musician, dragging his feet, had come to his senses, and the priest led him on. "You have been bewitched, Hoichi," he told him. "You have been bewitched. You have heard the summons of the spirits, Hoichi, you are. . . you are DEPARTING THIS LIFE. Take care not to completely succumb. They will torture you, my friend, and you will fade away in such torment." And they continued on their way, the musician dragging his feet, and the priest, the little priest, with mincing steps, accompanied him.

"But don't be afraid. This evening I will dress you in the robe-which-protects, the magical vestment that misleads spirits."

And so as evening came the priest, with the aid of a student, undressed the musician, and on his flesh they traced words of exorcism to repel the spirits. Covered with such inscriptions, he seemed to be dressed in a robe of black lace. They covered his face, his limbs, the whole of his body, and, as the hour drew nigh, they went on their way. Having become conscious, terror had once more taken hold of the musician and he huddled up and waited. Sombre birds brushed against his head. Distant junks quivered on the waters. He felt his head sink into his shoulders at each sound the night exhaled. He wished he was deaf. He wished he would lose consciousness. He wished he was dead. And all of a sudden the clanging metallic voice of the Samurai boomed out. He blanched, a long shiver shook him, and he felt the hairs of his skull stand on end. But the Samurai seemed uncertain. He whirled around like someone at the end of his tether. Then Hoichi heard him stamping around enraged. "Hoichi," he cried. "Hoichi, you are expected at the palace to sing the rest of the story for us. Hoichi, where are you Hoichi?" And suddenly he stopped. "By all the Gods," he cried. "If I am unable to see the musician, I can at least see his ears, so I will take them to my master to prove that I have fulfilled my mission." And so he came over to where the musician was lying, and where only his two ears were visible – and he tore them off.

The priest had forgotten to paint the protective versicles on his ears.

And that's how Hoichi, the forlorn musician, lost his ears.

*****

published in Antonin Artaud *Oeuvres complètes* Vol 1

translated by Paul Hammond and Michael Richardson

*****

ANTONIN ARTAUD (Marseilles 1896 – Ivry 1948) Joining the French Surrealist Group in 1924, Artaud was a central figure in the early years of the movement until his expulsion in 1927. His dramatic theories, conceptualised as the 'Theatre of Cruelty', have been of enormous importance to the contemporary theatre. Certified insane in 1937, and confined to mental institutions for the next nine years, his visionary writings remain as powerful evidence of a consciousness at the extreme of human experience.

DUŠAN MATIĆ

Sightless Illumination for Dragan Aleksić

As I went down Njegoš Street at midnight, it seemed to me that someone called out to me. I turned round, but saw no one. There was a second call – the same thing happened; the third time I still did not notice any one. I continued on my way. At once I beheld a stranger next to me who was brushing dust off his shoulders. So unexpected was his appearance beside me that I had the impression he had emerged from the wall of the house I passed by. He stared at me as if I were the one for whom he had been searching and as if he wished to say something to me, to be more precise, as if he wished to give me the answer to a question. But he changed his mind and walked past me. I turned round, but he was no longer there. I did not hear the answer to the question which I neither posed then, nor can now articulate. I cannot claim that this tormented me, but it was an open wound in me, admittedly a wound solely of my thoughts. Since then I have been living in a house without a roof, yet I have never seen the sky. I retraced my steps in order to look for this man, to seek, moreover, this answer. But I have never found it.

One evening I found myself near the Savina monastery and saw the very same man. He was standing on a flight of steps lit by electric light, leaning with a hat in his hand. But he did not so much as glance at me. My feeling was that he did not even have any eyes. And so it is that this undeciphered answer which lacks a question hangs over me, like the empty space drawing me away.

*****

translated by Victoria Appelbe

*****

DUŠAN MATIĆ (Cuprija, 1898 – Belgrade 1980) Founder member of the Yugoslav Surrealist Group, Matić was a translator from French and a poet and writer. Some of his theoretical texts have been translated into French, including his memoir of André Breton, *André Breton, Oblique*. He has also published a novel, *La Robe de bal d'Anna* (1956).

ROGER VITRAC

Consuella or meditations on the Gouffre de Padirac

In her timorous way Consuella went before me. She gave me a strange illumination, by which I mean that, invisible and white, she inhabited the whole of the silence with her whole voice trembling, or rather, and you must excuse me for such a foolishly honest preamble, I wished, as she had such great difficulty recognising herself, that she would blend in with this theatrical death, in short; for so little I would have pushed her into the vats of hell that I would describe if the large white butterfly whose proboscis whirled round my mind a hundred times did not stop me on the point of making a useless profanation. No, hell under the analytic ooze of deep dew and drop by drop measuring the permanence of night, compromised in a sinister way by electricity – apologies, for now, in evoking this professional sprite – no, hell stopped short at the single plastic analogy of a world where inoffensive and blind shrimps alone breathe. And for us, men in spite of our novice's gleaming hammers, we accomplished the ritual with less horror than curiosity. Consuella alone abandoned herself, necessarily, right to the core. I did not dream, as I do today, of bringing her back to the shadows of mimosas and offering her these dates which had been cruelly gathered up in the snow and marked by the inevitability which accounts for my always winning when I play no 11 in the lottery. I did not think of that. But a fine murder in this solitude where blood was lacking, in any case a colourless murder, would have tempted me, and also the sound of a fossil love in the underground river, of an eternally noisy ammonite and a passionate, lacerating interrogation.

"Here the road is 200 feet high," announced the guide.

Submissively, Consuella placed the town belfry there and a whole fauna from the shadow above which a thin limestone platform in direct sunlight bore a flock of sheep and goats. The twistings successfully arranged the sea and forest. Except the impenetrable moulding of the walls, the depth guiding us with strictness, we attained an increasingly light serenity, to the extent that Consuella affirmed to me that she was the very essence of marvel and confirmed my fears by laughing without my hearing her.

I thought that there could be no revolt against nature. I accepted the landscape without dreaming that, behind, there still prowled large skeletons without fur. With just one sign, I thought I was able to make them rise up outside their refuges, but I was worried about the terrors of Consuella, already surrounded by the ice-pack, still laughing silently at some horror or other. Sad ship, pressurised on every side by the amorous glacier, nourishing the nervure birds in a country where it was necessary to see this marvel: the diamond that gleamed without reflection. Doubtless the bedazzlement of multiples in the projected light, borne in the hand like a torch, propagating it scientifically, from coal to coal, but having the absolutely spiritual eye, the owl's eye which sees the marvel without aid of a lamp. Let all things pass away, Consuella, and let there reign here, by your abandon or your sacrifice, the aurora borealis which is one with the crystals. I scorn the swindle of the conqueror who comes with flame in his fist and whose fire is only a plaything beaming above appearances.

A visitor was amazed at the spurred crystalisations which brought a halt to the morphology of quartz. Ah! rather embark in the large ship of the floodwaters, submitting to the eddies of a phantom stem, and regret that our last gesture would not be traced on the pure figure of amazement.

*****

Here is the landing stage. We take our places in a flat boat and religiously leave the bank. The man rows soundlessly. He cultivates a silence he has been taught to respect. The idol shivers in a white stole. "Listen," he said, "Consuella has taken me by the waist and I clasp her too, I could. . . No, neither Venice, nor Amsterdam, but absolute immersion. The water sublimating itself and rejoining the solid element by means of the ladders of solitude. Matter in its coldest aspects is spreading out by harmony and joining with all the purity of men. Pen and dagger, carbon and poison, flowers and tears, ether and boredom, Christ and despair, avalanche and dream.

"Listen," said the guide. And the boat advances into a green harbour at the foot of an extinct volcano. And proud of this flower gathered from the very depths of his suddenly vitrified eye, the passer-by steps over the sacred landmark, responding by a clap of his oar to the incipient rumbling from the lake of Rain.

*****

Before the streaming organs where each vibration of the drop of water stirred up a cruel plant, these crown-shaped water-lilies that project the fleeting outline of an unconscious woman as far as the vault, Consuella still proposes the red oasis of a collapse. I reproached her for comparing the perfection of a palpable body to this dazzling misery. Rather than the sparkling richness of its gaze, which assumes purity, confessing that it is powerless to fulfil its metaphysical role even though the eye really draws inspiration from the diamonds that besiege us, I prefer by far those sovereign corners which erase all matter, and I accuse myself of weakness towards Consuella, of cowardice in the face of her indifference of a devoted creature.

It then occurred to me to propose the impossible. To create a lyrical drama in which each image would be *truly* translated into its immediate meaning. In other words that the Azure would, beyond its setting, become Azure in fact. I would refuse all concessions. If I spoke of an emerald river, free to gather all the emeralds on earth, I would like to see them all gleaming there on the stage. If Psyche was the heroine, it would be necessary to find her somewhere and Eros himself, even if he should turn out to be a Monster and illustrate the covers of all the world's magazines, must have wings of feather and flesh. When I glance at a gem as I lazily offer it up to the eyes of a mistress, apologising for a ridiculous compliment which brings them closer together as well as, at a moment's lapse of concentration, I know very well what distant or non-existent relation made me the dupe of bad poetry. And after all that, I still prefer her eyes to the diamond to which I compare them. Then, from the spectacle in which I am invited, despite the imaginary and yet still possible magnificence, I would leave miserable and disenchanted like those children imprisoned in the midst of treasure. But that I might write and announce that tomorrow at the Opera, Azure would preside over the meeting of Eros and Psyche on the bank of a river of real emeralds, for such is the will and extravagant power of the author that, I believe him, I would cross the seas to be there.

It is there that the power of poetry resides. It is through such barbarous marriages that modern thought is rejuvenated. I would covet the poet who would bring back from the unknowable an isolated means expressed in an unforeseeable language. But the greatest among them are still those who throw the highest bridges of the civilisation in which they live to the barbarity they experience, to qualify either of them in a passionate way. As for what remains, what is essential, you might as well ask the star to announce its presence before its movement of light arrives.

. . . .

*****

originally published in *La Revolution surréaliste* no 11 (1928)

republished in *Dès-lyre* Paris: Gallimard

*****

ROGER VITRAC (Pinsac, Lot 1889 – Paris, 1952) Founder member of the French Surrealist Group and the most important dramatist of surrealism, especially for his early plays *Les Mystères de l'amour* (1924) and *Victor, les enfants au pouvoir* (1928). His early prose experiments, explorations of alchemical transformation through the word, include the texts of *Dès-lyre*, and the novel *La connaissance du soir* (1926).

JACQUES PRÉVERT

The Adventures Of Footstool

1. Dog Stories

"Surname. First names. Address. Occupation?"

"Footstool," the man replied, causing the police inspector to scowl.

"We can't all be called Sedan-chair or Nicolas II. My name is Footstool, spelled just like the piece of furniture and pronounced in the same way, and if you want to know my first names they are Alpaca, Rover, Lucifer."

"These aren't saints' names," roared the inspector as he bared his yellowed teeth. "All very suspicious."

"Calm down," said Footstool. "There was certainly a Saint Thomas Aquinas, a Saint Peter and there is a Saint Pierre de Miquelon, not to mention all those druids and what have you, so why not a Saint Lucifer or a Saint Alpaca?

"Personally, I couldn't give a damn about names and numbers. I bet that if my name had been Saint Geneviève you wouldn't have given a toss."

But at that moment the policemen rolled up their sleeves and took to the warpath.

The police inspector discreetly pretended to be asleep and Footstool, aware that it was the crucial moment, put his cap on backwards and started to run around the station dragging his feet as he emitted a life-like imitation of the roar of a locomotive and the tinkling of the handbell shaken in restaurant-cars announcing the second sitting.

In general policemen don't expect the unexpected and these officers watched the train going past as attentively as they would have done in a meadow.

"Occupation, age?" and the inspector who had dropped off into a deep sleep came back to his senses.

After turning a bend, Footstool braked and came to a halt in front of the desk.

"You're asking too many questions, inspector. It's not a matter of questioning but of making suppositions. Do you know how to make suppositions, inspector?"

"I suppose so," the other said, caught unawares.

"Ah well, suppose that I'm in the street instead of being here, are you following my reasoning?

"I'm in the street sitting on a bench. A woman goes by, I get up and follow[1] her.

"Follow me? Right, so there I am, a man shadowing a woman. But if I'm the shadow of a woman I'm not a man. If my shadow is that of a woman then I'm a woman.

"Now follow carefully. . . I still shadow the woman; she stops, goes into her house, and leaves me at the door. No longer am I the shadow of a woman, but equally I can no longer be Footstool, since I'm not myself. Get it? Well, a dog then comes by, I slip in behind it, tailing the dog. We've established that I'm not a woman, and I can't simply be the tail of a dog: I must be the whole dog. And if I'm a dog then my place is not here but at the Dog's Home, and you've made a wrongful arrest.

"You can't get away with it. I shall bark you up to the highest court. Listen!"

Clambering onto a bench, Footstool held forth, barking and howling at death, at the inspector, at the sergeant and the whole bunch of those who were crushed into the police station like a herd of cows frightened by a large mad dog.

And, hidden underneath the desk was the real dog, which belonged to the police inspector. It trembled through its whole body and panted like a seal.

"That's the way it goes," said Footstool, getting off his

[1] Through the rest of his speech, Footstool is playing on the concordance between 'je suis = I follow' and 'je suis = I am'. It is of course impossible to retain this in English and Footstool's reasoning is therefore more tortuous than it is in the original. [trans note]

bench. "Dogs breathe like seals, Bulgarians are as robust as Turks, everyone's leaving for war and they all vie with each other to shed crocodile tears. Its such a dirty trick that it has to be changed, which is something we shall certainly look into."

He then left on tiptoe.

The police inspector and his animals stopped jostling and when a barrow-boy came in on the act, they jumped on him and tore off his ear.

2. Place Saint-Sulpice

It is a beautiful square, a little world unto itself devoid of grass and with water stagnating in a fountain, wheelbarrows tied to the bottom of trees, and some urinals which get moved from one corner to another every six months for no apparent reason.

There is also a Town Hall with a tricolour flag, a public convenience with a tricolour flag and a church which also has a tricolour flag at times, especially on mobilisation days.

There are also pigeons, cats, old bugs from the cathedral, and little girls going to their violin classes.

Sometimes a priest comes out of the church, crosses the square and goes into the public convenience; sometimes a priest comes out of the public convenience, crosses the square and goes into the church – sometimes it's the same one.

That day there were two little boys floating a bit of wood like a boat on the ornamental lake. They watched this bit of wood without saying anything as a middle-aged man dressed in a large rattan overcoat passed.

It was M. Petit-Buis, a collector of prints and a dealer in church ornaments.

He stopped, shook his head, and a tear appeared in his eye like a glob of snot as he cried out in a magisterially trembling voice:

"Aren't they great, the little beggars, having fun with

nothing!" And the toilet attendant stood agape on the threshold of the toilet waiting to hear the end of his speech, but the end never came because Footstool was there.

"Since you admit, sir. . ."

"Whom have I the honour of. . ." asked M. Petit-Buis

"Since you admit," continued Footstool without saying who he was. "That the little beggars, as you call them, are able to amuse themselves with nothing, you must also admit that they are able to amuse themselves with something if given half the chance."

"Why, of course, of course," said M. Petit-Buis as he smiled affably.

"This something," said Footstool, "is my foot up your arse and the palm of my hand across your chops. Here they are and I hope it gives them a laugh."

He did as he said and fled once he had done so, to howls from M. Petit-Buis, broad laughter from the two children, cries of indignation from the toilet attendant and of fear from his clients, together with the sound of bells which began to peal as the hour struck, all of which caused a quite frightful din that woke the police inspector with such a start that he grabbed his scarf and left like a shot along with his oxen, his dog and the whole fine crew went around the square several times before they discovered what was going on.

And as M. Petit-Buis watched them all he could do was repeat: "It's the end. There's no more discipline, no more fatherland, no more respect!"

He then went over to the paper-kiosk, bought *L'Action française*, shoved it in his pocket and returned to rue du Vieux-Colombier where the Petit-Buis house was to be found, with Road to Calvary scenes, visiting angels, Saint Christopher charms, sacks of earth from Lisieux and bits of the real cross in every style.

(to be continued[2])

[2] although it never appears to have been [trans note].

*****

originally published in *Spectateurs* 1 April 1932
reprinted in Jacques Prévert, *La Cinquième Saison*, 1984

*****

JACQUES PRÉVERT (Paris 1900 – Paris 1977) one of France's most popular poets, whose poems have been sung by some of France's greatest singers, and writer of some of the finest French films, including *Les Enfants du Paradis* (1946), Prévert had the wonderful quality of being able to capture the marvels of the everyday in accessible language. He was also one of the most interesting creators of collages in surrealism.

RENÉ MAGRITTE

Notes On Fantômas

"He is no longer the pretext for a story: the story itself renders him homage."

"The works of Fantômas can neither be destroyed nor accept modifications."

"His general staff is composed of young Tziganes. They obey a system, in spite of the rather brutal expectations with which they begin to burst into the annals of crime."

"Fantômas requires more of others than of himself."

"He is never completely invisible. His likeness can be see through his face."

"When memories pursue him, he follows his arms which carry him away. His movements are those of an automaton; any furniture or walls that happen to be in his path become displaced."

"His daughter speaks for a long time. She is not curious about his body. She admires his life."

"Fantômas's science is more precious than the word. It is not possible to guess it – and no one could doubt its power."

An unexpected event – Juve has been following the track of Fantômas for a long time. He crawls along the broken slabs of a mysterious corridor. His fingers touch the walls in order to guide him. A wisp of warm air suddenly strikes him in the face. He comes closer. . . His eyes have got used to the darkness. Juve makes out a door with disjointed boards a few feet ahead. He unfastens his cloak, coils it around his left arm and cocks his revolver. As he pushes the door wide open Juve sees that his precautions were pointless: Fantômas is near by, deep in sleep. Juve hastens to securely tie the sleeper up. Fantômas continues to dream probably about his disguises, as he tends to. Juve, at the height of joy, pronounces some unfortunate words. They have caused the prisoner to start. He wakes and, as he rouses himself, Fantômas ceases to be Juve's prisoner.

Once again Juve had failed. But to reach his aim there remains one course open: he must gain entrance into one of Fantômas's dreams: he will try to become one of the characters.
(1928)

*****

published in René Magritte, *Écrits complets* Paris: Flammarion

*****

RENÉ MAGRITTE (Lessines, 1898 – Brussels, 1967) The importance of Magritte's painting, exploring the paradoxes of visual languages, is now well acknowledged. His acerbic writings are less well known.

EMMY BRIDGEWATER

The Birds

One

He pulled the blanket over and she drew up the blind. The yellow mice rushed into their corners. The spiders ran behind the pictures. The lecture began on Christ the Forerunner. Only the very young mice sat still to listen. The blackbirds flying near the window passed the word to each other. "Come on! Here we may find something! Something to put our beaks into!" Snap went the window cord: down came the blind. The birds, disappointed, did the best they could. They flew nearer and nearer the window-pane. It was dangerous. It wasn't worth it. But they wanted to get the news – to be the first to know – to pass on the news. What had come to the lecture on Christ? Did one still lie under the blankets? The spiders laughed into their hands to think of the birds outside all twittering and over-anxious.

*

Two

As she walked into the garden the birds flew down to her pecking at her lips. "Don't do that" she cried. "It's mine. I'm alive you know." "Well why don't you wear colours?" She heard them talking. "Dead people walk, but they don't wear colours. They scream and they talk too." The bird went on chattering about dead people. They all perched up on the holly bush but they didn't peck the soft berries. They just stared down at her. All of them stared with their little black beady eyes. They were looking at her red lips.

★

Three

"Sing a song for the King. Come on, now Sing!" The child was shy to start, but her mother, standing behind her, gave her a little push which startled her into opening her mouth and she began, "Wasn't that a dirty dish to set before the king." "Begin again dear," whispered her mother, "at the first line." "OK ma," and she chanted, "Four and twenty Black. . .oooH" for a peacock had walked in front of her and spread out its tail and croaked "Frico. Frico." The little girl went very white. "Frico. Frico," she said. The birds, who had been sitting on the cornice as part of the decoration, flew down into the court and circled about the heads of the King and Courtiers, fluttering as close as possible. All the people flapped their hands helplessly. Suddenly the little girl pointed at the King. "You must get out of here," she said in a grown-up voice. "This is their Palace."

★★★★★

★★★★★

EMMY BRIDGEWATER (Birmingham, 1906) A painter and poet, Emmy Bridgewater participated in the activities of the English Surrealist Group from 1940 until its dissolution in 1947.

ANTÓNIO PEDRO

Just A Story

The River Minho has a tributary called the Coura, which rises like a thread of water amongst the stones. Along its banks stand distracted pine trees beneath a sky that is always blue and luminous; wolves and turtle doves quench their thirst in it. The water flows by with no time to gather up these images, fragmented into foam, from rock to rock. As it flows down the mountain slope it grows wider, why, no one knows, and then grows more serious as it descends and increases in volume. It starts life as a playful stream, home to a few frogs, and ends up being a whole landscape with romantic nooks where trees are reflected in the water and where trout, mullet and eel swim. In the midst of this crescendo is a system of sluices used to produce electricity, which, with their industrial air, look out of place amongst the shadows. Sometimes too there are natural rivulets that stagnate, by mistake, in a fold of the earth and others built for that purpose to irrigate the fields. And above all this bustle birds, flies and dragonflies. I believe that these things were established at the beginning of the world. It was a long time ago but, with the exception of the sluices, everything necessarily retains an air of having just begun. Alongside the riverbed are small areas of arable land built in terraces down to where the plain begins. There the planter was walking, through a field, up to his knees in the rich, black earth. It was pleasant to see him walking naked, the pink of his body contrasting with the colour of the turned clods of earth, scattering along the furrows bits of women which he was carrying in a bundle: the arms of queens, their hands still attached, fingers white and beringed, rosaries of eyes like variegated flowers full of moist, incalculable tendernesses as well as hatreds and stupidities, mitres and mushrooms, like anemones, that had been born and had died purely by chance, according to the comings and goings of the blood beneath the skin of some unknown person. Amongst the things he carried in his bundle there were also legs and mouths, small white bones and teeth, as well as hair. It was clearly a habit of his this way of sowing and, even if it wasn't, it seemed so, framed in the bucolic atmosphere of the evening which, in that part of the Minho, has all the charm of paradise.

When the day ended and the birds settled down for the night and stopped their singing and all the ducks and the cold-weather birds that fly so high and all the other birds of passage had crossed over into Spain, the planter lay down on the ground and lit the moon with a lamp to keep him company in his well-deserved rest. There were almost no stars and all would have been silence but for the barking of dogs that could be heard in the village nearby.

With the night, the romantic tone of this whole scene took on a magical quality, but a time came when all that romanticism grew unacceptable. The things he had sown rotted down into humus and the man woke up to find himself bound to the earth, like the trees near the water's edge, nourished by a sap to which he was unaccustomed. Thanks to that sap he grew as high as the sky, until he was taller even than the night.

Everything happened so fast that the height made him feel giddy and faint as he never had before. He felt as if his head were spinning. The sudden movement and the intense pain dislocated his neck. Then all his veins burst under the pressure of the altitude. It was as impressive as a waterfall and, given the colour, even more spectacular.

The inhabitants of the Minho are great ones for pilgrimages and firework displays. Everyone came to see the man's rise into the sky and that falling from above of red blood in cataracts that were reflected with the moonlight in the river. But it didn't last long. Once the sap had dried up his flesh was like straw and of no possible use. After a few weeks no one even noticed him, as if he were just some giant scarecrow. When the harvest was over they set fire to him as they did to the stubble. In his ashes cats peed and chickens pecked. Only the shadow he had cast on the ground remained, like a stain.

It was a dark green stain, broad as an open field. There were various discussions as to whether or not it should be removed from there because of the tourists and the good name of the locality. Some deemed it to be picturesque and others simply wanted things to be as they should. There was even one person who was convinced the shadow was a natural phenomenon. Finally, they rolled it up, as if it were a carpet, and carried it off for inspection by the members of the Academy.

It exuded such a powerful odour of sadness that the academicians were moved. So much so that each of them wrote a commemorative sonnet. That collection of superior literary outpourings became a book which was published and is now on sale and, of course, has nothing whatever to do with this true story.

The planter was called Adam, as you might have guessed. It's not true, however, that he was the first man. The savour of emptiness that fills the world with irremediable disquiet existed both before and after him.

*****

published in *Apenas una narrativa* (1942) Editora Minerva, Lisbon

Translated from the Portuguese by Margaret Jull Costa

*****

ANTÓNIO PEDRO (Cape Verde Islands, 1909 – Lisbon, 1966) Having become interested in surrealism during a stay in Paris in 1934, Pedro collaborated with the English Surrealist Group from 1942 to 1947, organising with E.L.T. Mesens the exhibition 'Surrealist Diversity' in 1945. On returning to Lisbon he helped organise the first Portuguese Surrealist Group (1947–49). He was a poet, a painter and a sculptor.

CLÉMENT MAGLOIRE-SAINT-AUDE

Fédor Rascalaub Or The Gods Of Stupre

> . . . The sons of God saw that the daughters of men were fair and took to wife such of them as they chose.
>
> ". . . For man is flesh."
>
> Genesis 6, 2, 3

I

And the mustachioed lip of the man moved.

He assumed the word, saying:

"Your soul, Fédor Rascalaub, is subject to concupiscent passions. . .

"Don't open your mouth, jackal, let me continue.

"Your soul," I said, "is subject to concupiscent passions.

"They emanate from your eyes, from your veiled eyes of an Oriental; and from your lips, your thick lips, unsatisfied with lust.

"The hands, unveiled throats, bellies and languorous nude bodies (and unveiled throats, bellies and hands) of Nescay women have been unable to satisfy you with their bitter and monotonous pleasures!

"And you dream, beast! You dream, absurd man! about bloody and sorrowful sensuality."

II

> Your naked foot stepped on my shadow.
>
> Rémy de Gourmont

The man was quiet.

Then, suddenly breaking the silence, he continued: "In the town of Igualabea lives a tainted humanity that had fallen from grace because of vice.

"Oh women of Igualabea! Your bodies are supple and the lines of your ochre-coloured nudity are harmonious and beautiful.

"But the harmonious and beautiful lines of your ochre-coloured nudity are, oh women of Igualabea! pock-marked with fistulas.

"And the women of Igualabea groan when evening comes.

"And their groans cause dread among males on heat.

"And the males depart with anger in their eyes and they fill the night with lugubrious soliloquies.

"But the gods, the libidinal and voracious gods, are hungry.

"They are intensely hungry for lascivious flesh and unknown lusts. . ."

III

The man started to laugh. Then was silent.

But his mustachioed lips still moved.

He said: "Fédor Rascalaub! The silence of Nabulon-Merevoye-the-dermatologist would be powerless to cure you of the horrible curses suffered by the women of Igualabea.

"However, you dread the vengeance of libidinal gods, who yell out, wild in appearance for they don't like your abstentions."

IV

So, do this.

Go to your room.
Take your beggar's wallet.

Arm yourself with your staff.
Put on your old slippers.
Wear your eliminated tunic.
And then go!

V

The Lord saw that the wickedness of man was great.
Genesis

Go along this desolate and long road.

It is strewn with pines, with fragments of broken bottles and with erygria
And, on both sides of the road, thatched cottages had been built.
Don't enter.
Men would appear on the threshold and would call out to you.
Shake your head as a sign of refusal.
Go on your way, and hurry!

VI

By the first stars, which are here, you will arrive at the gates of Malaubey town, weakened with thirst (as well as hunger), you clothes whitened with dust and your feet stained with blood.

Don't yet sample the delights of the kef.
Enter the town.

VII

The younger lay down with him.
Genesis

And satisfy the gods' hunger.

VIII

Omne animal post coitum triste.

Lucretius

But, oh contradiction!

Here you are speaking conciliatory words.
And you fear the anger of obscene gods!
The gods of concupiscence are not satisfied, Fédor
Rascalaub, and your flesh is an ardent brazier!

IX

Then do this.

With kadsura flowers quickly prepare a bouquet.
Be heroic.
Do not be afraid of suffering.
And experience Eupathy.

X

And then you will call the science of Merevoye-the-Dermatologist to the rescue.

★★★★★

published in *Les Griots* Vol 3, no 3, 1939

★★★★★

CLÉMENT MAGLOIRE-SAINT-AUDE (see volume one p 212)

PAUL COLINET

Homage To Raymond Roussel

The Moribihan Archaeological Society gave us access to an odd manuscript recently discovered in the middle section of the Bourd'Ach menhir in which the learned president of the illustrious society perceived, rightly or wrongly, a sort of homage *avant la lettre* to the author of *The Star on the Brow*.

The manuscript gave information about a rather original person. Is it the nature of this originality that caused the President of the Society to perceive a homage to the creator of Canterel? We don't believe so. We are rather inclined to think that the learned president's reasons lie in the complex singularities of the manuscript. Our readers can judge this from the complete text:

Manuscript Found in the Bourd'Ach Menhir

In the middle of the nineteenth century there lived, lurking in the vast woodland on the western coast of Finistere, among a population of fishermen for whom he was the object of veneration and terror, a very singular idler, who had no known name and who was subject to a propensity to fall periodically into a very protracted cataleptic trance, a state which gave the rather emaciated body of his person a rigidity and even a cutting edge that was similar to what could, through analysis, restore the essential properties of a metal blade.

During the months this catalepsy lasted, the idler living in the woodland had no other existence than to be an inert object.

The fishermen, always keen to keep their tools in good

working order, had quickly got into the habit of using this momentary object when they were led, after fruitful fishing, to decapitate some of those flat fishes from cold and temporate seas which, in Lunné classification, have been given the name of rays.

These involuntary but effective services rendered by the idler to the industrious plunders of the ocean, had inspired them with feelings of gratitude which perhaps could have reached the status of a barbarous cult, if strange elements of the idler's behaviour did not, outside the cataleptic periods, impress them in an unpleasant way and even cause them extreme irritation. On the one hand, the character in question was accused of concealing from public contemplation, through magic, a whole mountain range on his property which would, had it remained completely visible, have given to the desert-like and flat region of Finistere an unexpected attraction by which it would otherwise be unable to claim distinction. This invisible mountain system would have, had it been able to affect the sense of sight, a rather glowing colour, situated halfway between yellow and red. It was also known that its highest peak was called the Sub and was the object, on the part of the Atlantic winds, of a work of slow erosion which, after a few centuries, would give the Sub the form of a colossal eagle's nest.

Public rumour then attributed another pastime to the woodland hermit: he untiringly rubbed the side of this future eagle's nest with a kind of iron-grater to break up its regular and natural formation. Besides this Sisyphian exploit, the involuntary decapitator of ridges had consigned its meagre connexion into a kind of report making it the object of an opuscule distributed by its author, by boasting or provocation, to the population of the neighbourhood, and he amused himself by enriching each copy with a choice binding. Such practices intrigued the fishermen. But what annoyed them had a distinct seriousness. The woodland idler, when seasonal catalepsy did not transform him into an object of prime use for the valorous fishermen of enormous rays, became, through his frequently observed mysterious powers, a veritable plague for the inhabitants of the western coasts of Finistere. In fact he had the terrible faculty of rendering the earth infertile, of draining all character of fluidity from the water, making the solid earth mineral and transforming all nascent, smouldering or blazing fire into premature ash. It can be conceived, from that time, that this baneful man, in spite of his temporary contribution to the fishing industry, was the object of the anger of intrepid harpooners of the high seas. He inspired them particularly with a continual terror. Every one trembled when he passed and the unease communicated to the whole body by this dread was such that the clothes of those terrorised visibly became shredded. Besides, as he crossed the wild paths of the region, this exhausted the earth to the point of rendering every place the catastrophic idler's feet trod definitively chaotic, barely recognisable and sterile.

*****

published in Paul Colinet *Oeuvres* Vol 3, 1989 (Lebeer Hossman)

*****

PAUL COLINET (Arquennes, 1898 – Brussels, 1957) Member of the Belgian Surrealist Group from 1935, Colinet's idiosyncratic writings and drawings are collected in four volumes published by Lebeer Hossman.

GISÈLE PRASSINOS

Sondue

I

A dog ran into the street. In its mouth was a cherry stick between which were two slices of freshly cut and bleeding flesh. A woman ran after it, dragging her feetless legs covered in black velvet. She had long white hair which almost touched the ground and a pink blotting-paper hat that was like a bag covered her eyes. When the dog turned the street corner, she stopped and sat down on some stone steps. She took a small diary out of her pocket, tore out a few pages, and glued them to the palms of her hand. Finally, after taking off her hat, which she threw into the stream, she got up and went on her way.

For its part, the dog had stopped, out of breath, and tried to eat its booty. But at the first bite, the meat declined to be offered up. The dog did not lose heart and was about to start on the second piece when the sight of the woman caused it to take flight, forgetting its stick and its dinner.

Sondue – such was the woman's name – skipped up and caught the dog's prey which she quickly thrust into a newspaper she had brought with her. Then she made her way more slowly, making the sign of the cross to thank the Spirit of Goodness for having helped her to recover her property. She walked like that for a very long time and came to a large field filled with burned grass, in the middle of which was a small rectangular pond. Its water was slimy and it was covered with green spiders. Sondue went towards it and had a good idea which brought a grin to her face. She sat down on the bank, put down her things, and undressed. She shook her clothes, spreading them across a small cherry bush which watched her. Then she knelt down on the grass and plunged headfirst into the pond. Nothing more could be seen but the violet end of her inert legs and some of the white hairs of her skull. She remained at the bottom of the water until two in the evening, from time to time stretching out her arm to catch a fly to swallow. Finally the water stirred lightly and then more strongly, allowing Sondue to emerge soiled with green fibres, spiders' legs and blue confetti. She stitched up the sides of her navel which had become enlarged and dressed again, leaving her blouse on the bush.

Before leaving she raised her wet hair and fastened it up with one of the green threads that covered her body. She took to the road again and sat down on the same steps, taking the cherry stick from the paper. She took a few pieces of flesh between her fingers and slipped them one by one into her lip-less mouth. When her meal had ended, Sondue rose like a mad woman and started to run into the street yelling. She raced to the door of the church into which she vanished till morning.

At eight o'clock she was seen leaving with a prayer-stool on her head. She was laughing and singing hymns as she pointed at a little boy who had started to cry. But hardly had she taken a couple of steps than the Spirit of Badness rose up before her, covered with adorned and multicolored chamois leather. It flattened her with the bottom of its blue beard, the two halves of which were separated.

II

Sondue remained in this free posture for four hours. In other words till noon.

When the priest came to placate the angry God, he uprooted one of Sondue's long hairs, which immediately released her. But she forgot her prayer-stool and her cherry stick which would very soon rot.

Insulting everyone in her path she reached the door of a large shop where a small bearded man with a pot belly and flint-like calves stood. To hide the top of his bald head he had glued to it a piece of gold paper completely bristling with bride's pins. His name was Fluchon. Exasperated by Sondue's stony look, he sank back into his shop, causing the pipes above the door to ring. But Sondue took no notice and stationed herself in front of the counter that enticed women.

On the counter displaying kitchen utensils she noticed a large wooden tub placed against the wall. The tub was covered all over in holes. As she watched attentively, Sondue saw a blue eye at the bottom of the hole which seemed to be looking at her. She racked her brains to ascertain who this eye might rightfully belong to but she was unable to do so and concluded that it was an onion. Then, having become fed up with looking at the display case she went away because it was night. As she passed the small pond where she had spent the previous night, she thought it was a good idea to sleep there again. So she went into the field and, as she started to get undressed, her eyes were attracted by a small hole which had formed in the middle of the water. She bent down to look and saw a blue eye at the bottom of this hole which stared at her teeth. Somewhat amazed, she plunged into the pool in order to sleep there. As previously she stayed until ten o'clock but did not eat any flies.

Meanwhile, Fluchon was crying in the crockery corner deep in his shop.

Before having supper he wanted to draw a horse but was unable to see anything very clearly. He was very tired and went to his mother's house to get to the bottom of it. His mother was a well-educated woman and had anticipated the absence of one of his eyes. Poor Fluchon returned home in tears.

At the moment Sondue came out of the water like a nymph, Fluchon was desperately weeping for his fugitive eye. Soon the water dried up and he stopped shedding tears and got on with his horse.

III

Sondue came out of the water and, being unable to see the point of getting dressed, crossed the field.

The road in front of her was long and glorious in the midst of a phosphorescent sky.

As she walked she held her breath in order not to make a sound because something at the end of the street frightened her. It was a naked woman, whose stumps were violet and shrivelled. Her long white hair almost reached the ground and on her head she had a bag made of pink blotting paper which hid her eyes. A blue eye was joined to the end of the nose and stared at her.

In spite of her fear, Sondue continued to march forward in order to arrive more quickly and kill the apparition. She soon realised that the road had become narrower and the phantom was getting bigger. A few more steps were necessary to reach the end of the street and all of a sudden it became impossible to go any further: an invisible obstacle separated her from the woman she could not touch. She was so afraid that she felt her own body to make sure she existed. The horrible thing was that the woman facing her looked like her.

When she rubbed her nose, it seemed to be as humid as a moist duster. She pulled it, looked, and recognised the eye from the wooden tub and the pool of green spiders.

For at least ten minutes, she kept the eye in the hollow of her hand, not daring to look at it. Suddenly the phantom vanished and Sondue no longer saw anything. Only the blue eye served as a torch to light up the way. Touched by such a sign of good intent, she put the eye in her mouth, down at the bottom of her right cheek, in order to warm it up. But she was then rather amazed to no longer be able to see anything around her but darkness. Without thinking what she was doing, she started walking backwards with her eyes closed and cheek bulging. The sound of her legs recalled that of paper being crumpled up.

At one point she stumbled against something sticky which soaked the violet ends of her legs. Without giving her time to bend down, the thing in question stuck to her face. It was a piece of flesh with the form of a parallelepiped whose freshly-cut shorter sides dripped with blood. It came out of some indented steel points on which clots of black blood were hooked. The larger sides of this meat parallelepiped were covered in a fine and silky skin. One of the surfaces was perforated in the middle of its slashed navel from which a long, thin and dry intestine ran out. At the end of this sort of twine hung an enormous human head. Its brow was narrow with abundant black and stiff hair. In the depths of two hollowed-out holes a blue point swam in the transparent water of a tiny pool. Below, a few small and almost invisible holes could be made out which the air, as it surged forth, enlarged. Further down still a long bleeding gash revealed two or three old and viscous bone ends. The whole thing was wagging rather like the tail of a contented dog.

Sondue felt a sort of air hole inhale its brow. On its belly shook the upside-down skull whose eyes were gradually emptied.

After an hour, she decided she would try to walk because the blue eye at the bottom of her mouth was burning her. She took a few steps and noticed she could continue her way but by using one hand to hold the head which was being beaten by the guts.

In this way she reached Fluchon's shop. She entered with the piece of flesh on her face and the blue eye in her right cheek. Fluchon, busy drawing a knot in his horse's tail, noticed nothing. His siliceous calves alone shattered against the table leg.

Approaching soundlessly, Sondue pulled a needle from out of Fluchon's skull. Not surprisingly he felt a rather sharp pain. He turned round, turned over, looked around, and saw Sondue who smiled at him while hiding her right cheek. "Dudu, sweetheart!" "Here I am, my darling! as refined as the flower of one of the king's poulterers," said

Sondue. "So the mice didn't eat you?" asked Fluchon. Sondue remained standing at these words. She tore the blue eye out of her mouth and threw it in Fluchon's face. Chance had it that it fell right into his hole. Immediately, Fluchon saw himself borne away in the face of marvellous things. The leanness of his horse in flight became white light and the knot resembling the long hairs of his tail became a beautiful pink, a sublime pink that Fluchon adored. In his eyes Sondue herself attained a peerless beauty. Her white hair twisted out of shape and formed long silver curls. Her body was dressed in a golden tulle tunic and the violet ends of her legs changed into small shoes smelling of wood. But soon, as the blue eye got used to being back in its usual place, it became as grey and dirty as its neighbour. And at the same time the beauties that Fluchon admired became reality. As he got up and went straight over to Sondue to pull her hair out, he said: "The holiness of angels and the fear of God shall return wisdom to you." Then he left, crumpling up his horse to show how much his appetite had increased.

These words left Sondue in a state of paralysis. She slumped into the armchair where she had placed the plump parallelepiped and maternally held it on her lap. Shedding tears of bronze and warm ashes, she addressed this speech to what she held:

"How can I cut you up, the only being I venerate and love? Twice you have saved my life, you have borne me on your breast from the time of my youth and, in spite of your nudity, you have given me rubber to cover my eyes. Until I die, I will have your name on my tongue, that name I dare not pronounce as I don't yet know it! I will bear you on my knees as long as I live and, in order to repay me, you will buy me cherry sticks. You are my only consolation and I am sure that I'm the same for you, my beloved!" She slept, holding the being to whom she had spoken in her arms. While she slept, her eyes gradually opened and the light of day pervaded them.

She awoke crying out: "Vicrate! Vicrate! You are

Vicrate!" And she grasped the formless being to her heart and licked its body.

Finally she got up, placed Vicrate on the window ledge and sat cross-legged on the arm of their chair, awaiting Fluchon's arrival.

He entered a few moments later. He had replaced the pin missing from his head and was happy. In spite of himself he smiled at Vicrate whom he had cherished for a long time, kissed him, and, without even deigning to look at Sondue, went to sit in his shop window.

The fact that he did not move infuriated Sondue and she left, taking Vicrate under her arms. She passed before Fluchon as she walked on tip-toe and this caused a verruca to appear.

Sondue had taken with her a piece of gingerbread and a pencil. She went for a walk along the Seine quayside, holding Vicrate by the head. But she soon became tired and sat down on a milestone.

The river in front of her was black. She thought it contained many things.

Vicrate let out a small groan and wanted to run away. He tried to get down on his own but fell and broke his neck. In a panic, Sondue took the two pieces and returned to Fluchon's shop. As she went past it she lost one of the two halves. Fluchon, seeing something fall, looked closer and recognised Vicrate. He gathered up the part, which was his head, and vanished into his shop.

Sondue soon reappeared, holding a new Vicrate in her arms. Not having found the head of the first one, she had glued a lump of coal in its place. She seemed completely happy with this change and prepared to see Fluchon when he appeared at the window bearing Vicrate's head on his shoulders, to which he had affixed a feather cushion to represent the body. Each of them in their own way settled their own Vicrate down in the same armchair and decided they should be friends.

Sondue placed the head of her Vicrate, who will now be called Vicratone, into the mouth of Fluchon's, who will henceforth be Vicratwo.

But Vicratone struggled and got bitten by the ends of bones to be found in his neighbour's mouth. His poor head was cracked and he lost part of it. He told himself that he did not want to associate with such a monster. For his part, Vicratwo turned away and made it clear that he did not like meat.

Sondue and Fluchon were very annoyed and did not say another word. Each took their own Vicrate and they left without shaking hands.

Sondue went for a walk near the Champs-Elysées and took the opportunity to visit the President of the Republic. They greeted each other very tenderly and Sondue presented Vicratone to him: "He was born in 1689," she said. "His mother was a butcher's wife and his father grew lemons. They calculated how many years their child would live to give him the name Vicrate which really suits him marvellously well, except for the V at the start which brings a bunch of watercress to mind." "That can't be possible, since you haven't dressed him," the President replied.

While the two friends were talking, Vicratone crept under a chair. He closed his eyes and his lips moved as he emitted a few vulgar groans. Before Sondue rose to open the door, he started to get to his feet, straightened his neck, tore a piece off and, enlarging his gash, sang:

> He bore the fruit of his pain
> across the greasy vales
> for the water's first concern
> as it slipped across his face
> was the inconstant indulgence
> of crystalline souls
> and the charming sketch
> of the skilful bottle

This song was a continuation of plentiful and rugged cries

which desperately escaped from all the holes in his body. The President, who had a chalk-like nose incrusted with shells, slipped his index finger into one of his nostrils. He drew out a little white pearl stained with green and, with a more than presidential gesture, offered it to Vicratone, saying: "Poet of the Christian era, be blessed among the enchanted."

Vicratone grasped the object with his navel into which it completely vanished.

The President, whose appendix hurt, had a bloated stomach which he patted from time to time. He hit himself so hard that his stomach got bigger still and collapsed on Vicratone's head which split into two. Sondue became angry and left the corpulent President, dragging along the weeping Vicrate.

On the way, she complained that there was nowhere she could be in peace. She did not want to go back to the shop since Vicratone would be offended and his head would completely fall apart. He cried so much that he lost it on the way without Sondue noticing. She despaired. Fortunately she found an old pink pitcher in a stream filled with milk. She attached it to Vicratone's neck by the handle and once again he had a head.

Her intention was to go, accompanied by her protegé, to visit her old aunt who, she learned, had been ruined. She made for Avenue Richerand.

She entered the building, holding Vicratone's hand. When she reached the bottom of the stairs, she raised the little one on her head and went up to the third floor where her aunt lived. She drummed on the door and a young boy whose head touched the ceiling came to open it. He showed her into a round room without furniture. There was just a small mauve chest of drawers in the centre on which empty bottles of all sizes were set out.

In the four corners of the room, on the blue floor, there were twenty three beautiful bright red apples with large yellow leaves which hid them and, above, a plank of painted wood covered with Turkish rugs. From the very high ceiling hung long coloured threads to which were suspended tit-bits of food that could be unhooked at will.

Sondue and Vicratone had waited a long time. They were getting bored. So they amused themselves by moving the bottles on the chest of drawers around.

After an hour a fantastic noise shook the building. An enormous voice flattened the air and baffled the owner. Then everything went quiet.

Soon the door seemed to creak from all sides and opened up to let in a woman who was immense and had a head surmounted by a huge dry and broken rice cake. Her yellow hair was curly and fell on her massive shoulders. Her prominent chest was riddled with pink holes that had the form of daisies. She wore yellow slacks inlaid with different shaped sweets. This was undoubtedly her aunt, the mistress of the house. She went straight up to Sondue, who had squeezed under the chest of drawers with Vicratone between her legs, fell down on her face in order to grab her foot and got up again, holding Sondue at the end of her gigantic arms to get a better look at her.

After having raised her to the ceiling she put her back down on the floor. Then taking her up again, she sat her down among the bottles on the chest of drawers with Vicratone in her arms.

She settled herself down in the midst of the apples which did not move and began: "As-tu un crayon à me donner?"[1] Sondue looked at her strangely. "Really, my dear aunt, I don't have the time. A bit of embroidery but nothing more," she replied, scratching her knees. "Mais," continued her aunt. "Un crayon n'est pas la même chose. Si tu ne me donnes pas un petit morceau de bois, je suis incapable de faire une maison!"

Sondue no longer moved. She clasped poor Vicratone so tightly that the President's pearl burst out of his navel and

[1] This, like everything the aunt says, is in English in the original.

lodged in one of the multiple holes that appeared in her aunt's chest. As a result, her aunt fainted.

Vicratone, very annoyed at the loss of his treasure, hurled himself on the aunt's belly to fish it out. He put his index finger very deeply into the hole and drew the pearl out, followed by long and twisted but still living intestines which he immediately started to devour.

But the aunt did not move and one of her breasts, which Vicratone drained, had gone flat.

Sondue and her little companion furtively slipped away without daring to call the tall young man who opened the doors. They hurtled down three floors and were in the street, which had no light. Vicratone's pearl was shining and was therefore substituted for it. That was how they got back to the shop.

Sondue opened the door to allow Vicratone to enter and sent him to bed, while she herself went to sleep on the armchair.

The day after when she awoke it was daylight. The sun penetrated through the window panes and gave the objects on sale the appearance of a display. She got up and wanted to go into the room next door to wash her face. But she had barely opened the curtain than her eyes widened with horror:

Fluchon lay rolled up in the rug. Only his head projected out. It was open like a coconut and his brain was hanging out, gradually liquifying. Two hands and a foot floated in blood with veins and nerves which still twitched. Further on, wedged between two chairs, Vicratwo rolled fearful eyes. He had lost so much hair and the end bones of his mouth were on the ground, covered with blood. A sound escaped flutteringly from his body.

The entire room was strewn with steel feathers and boxes of spoiled matches. In a corner, a pair of open scissors still gripped a big toe.

In spite of her fear, Sondue rushed over first to Fluchon, pulled back the carpet, and rested him on the table. Then she released Vicratwo who let out lamentable cries. She took him over to the bed of Vicratone, who had woken with a start.

Soon, Doctor Fradimus made his appearance.

He was a rather small, thin man with very broad legs that were fat and shaky. His reddened moustache hung down on his shoulders, refined with a few pebbles. He had thrown across his back a yellow silk shawl with paper lace pricked with matches.

He went straight up to Sondue, who was twitching her nose with despair, and asked her to show him the wounded.

She took him to the table where Fluchon had been laid out. After having examined him, Fradimus declared: "This gentleman, who has pins in his head, is dead. They murdered him with quills. Whoever killed him is a nasty bit of work!"

He then went over to the bed on which Vicratwo was yawning. He picked up the head, pushed a kind of penholder deep up his nostrils and still said nothing. A few minutes later he tapped his gums and, showing Sondue an empty bobbin wrapped in silver paper, placed it against Vicratwo's neck, saying something like:

"The liquid feebleness of this young man serves as a great pulmonary advantage. He certainly had some basic gas but his health has such actuality that it sustains his ferruginous state."

Taking up his bobbin, he left like an arrow as the bottoms of his legs cracked.

IV

Vicratwo spent the whole night insulting the deceased Fluchon.

In the morning, around eight o'clock, he stopped shouting, raised his legs up to the lamp and finally fell asleep.

Later, two men entered the house. They had small red

skull caps on their heads and white bows on their shoes. They each held a large pair of pliers and a rectangle of cardboard from which they took bites in turn. Behind them came a large box wrapped in white paper and with golden nails. Together, they raised it up onto the table while murmuring prayers.

Soon, Fluchon appeared in the door. The two men quickly grasped him and aimed him at the bottom of the box which they covered over with gold paper. They had decorated the entry door with small climbing rose bushes and yellow daisies. Instead of kitchen utensils they had arranged prayer books with 'At Fluchon's place everything's fine' written in bold letters. So many people came, among them the President of the Republic and Sondue's aunt who had stopped up her holes with sand specially for the occasion. Sondue was kept busy going from one to another asking them for drinking water. Sometimes she encouraged Fluchon who made gestures from his box. Then she got up to see the Vicrates who were beating each other with door-mats.

Finally a new bell rang. Everyone got in line and a car with blue velvet ribbons entered the courtyard. The men in red skull caps slipped the box in which Fluchon was becoming irritable into a hole made in the back of the car.

Soon the cortege set off.

Sondue followed the car, holding Vicratone in one hand and a tooth mug in the other. She had put a few bits of gold paper and hazel nuts in her hair. Finding her mouth too narrow, she had stuffed two long, thin bits of wood there. Vicratone had arranged long threads of brown wool on his head so that it looked as if he had hair.

Behind them came a filthy couple who had been scorned by fate. The woman was naked to the waist and her enormous belly came out of holes in her skirt to reveal a box which served to confine her intestines. Her nose was joined to her chin by means of long cylindrical warts she had caught in the Colonies. The man wore a green alpaca with red stripes. His trousers were glued to his legs and came up to his knees. His thin legs were covered with neither flesh nor skin. They were bones that were cut open in places and eaten away by tapeworms which hollowed out their passageways. His head, which was a glowing coal, crackled furiously.

Then there was the Aunt who offered her generous arm to the President of the French Republic in a pink serge corset.

Then came another couple who were young and held each other close. The woman cut her husband's finger as she kissed him from head to toe. She was fashionably dressed, with a hat wound around with flowers that flapped in the wind, the folds of her dress rose up so that she had to put them back in place again and her nose, which had been freshly glued on, shook with humidity. Her husband opened his terrible eyes to adore her in silence. His trousers, clasped with a white ribbon at the ankle, rose up squeaking.

Finally, three yards on, walked a rotting man. He was dressed in a red linen shirt and woollen underpants. He had grey socks held up by a thread and square-toed shoes of mauve velvet. On his head a sort of wooden statue had been erected, magnified with an aureole of copper thread. A fantastic apparatus made of glass and rusty iron had been fitted on his sloping shoulders. The whole thing had the appearance of a tree with no leaves.

The cortege followed the car to the church. There they took Fluchon out of his box and spread him out on the stones of the master-altar. Doubtless he was woken by the cold as his legs kicked out at the priest who was in the process of blessing him. The more they performed in front of him, the more he cried out, saying that they were plotting his death. Sondue, sitting nearby, gave him wrapped up caramels to keep him quiet.

A bishop soon arrived, went straight up to Fluchon and said: "The soul of this man who has never stolen apples will remain on earth to do good and as an example to the wicked. It will rise to heaven when, feeling its end near, it will think about taking rest."

When the ceremony had ended and they wanted to put Fluchon into his box, he replied that he would like to walk beside Sondue in order to tease her. But the men with red skull-caps refused and laid him down again despite his excitement and wish to have done with it.

The priest's small garden which served also as a cemetery was two steps away from the church. Boxes of all sizes could be seen there, arranged against the brick wall. That is where the cortege went.

As they were placing Fluchon's box at the side of a large tin-plate box a great cry was heard in the crowd. It was Sondue, who had been overcome with emotion. Vicratone raced over to help and took her back to the shop. He put her down next to Vicratwo, who was very angry when he saw her.

At night, she sighed and repeated twenty times over that when all was said and done she very much loved that bloody Fluchon.

V

Sondue was woken at dawn by a sinister noise. She rose onto her bottom and saw Vicratwo in the middle of the room doing his physical training by skinning his calves. She told him off and ordered him to go and serve the customers.

She got up at noon and tried to walk but her legs no longer carried her. All the same she managed to go into the garden with the help of the Vicrates. There she sat on the stones and thought it would be a good idea to invite the President of the Republic for tea. She did so straightaway. But the President replied that he could not come because he had broken his back when he had returned from the cemetery. This upset her and she decided to pay him a visit.

And so, that afternoon, she put a ribbon in her hair and took out the Vicrates. The President received them very politely but did not greet Vicratone because he had been fond of the pearl he had taken. He offered them cakes and, as they left, kissed each of them ten times.

This cheered Sondue up a little.

She must have caught the typhoid microbe because she felt ill when she arrived back home and decided to go to bed.

It was six in the evening.

Sondue slept. The Vicrates played ludo.

At half past six, Sondue moved a little and murmured: "Vicratwo!" He immediately left his friend and went to her. She continued, her eyes closed: "Why did you kill Fluchon?" Vicratwo started to cry and said that he hadn't meant to. He decided to tell the whole story: "We were playing gentlemen and he told me that I was too stupid to be with him. I became angry and called him a snake. He became vexed in his turn and pulled my hair. Then, to defend myself, I looked for matches and beat him. He returned my blows and things continued like that till he died. After that he kicked me into the air and I fell on the ground, between two chairs."

He burst into tears as he quickly repeated that it was not his fault. Sondue took pity on him and sent him off to play. Then she thought that it was sad to be sick and that Fluchon was a good boy. Between her teeth she said a few incomprehensible things.

When supper time came, Sondue put a blanket over her head and went into the shop. She took all the saucepans she could find and put them in a circle. A customer entered and asked for nails. Sondue put him off by saying there was no one to serve him. After having closed the circle with saucepans, she called the Vicrates and told them to sit inside. The little ones obeyed without asking questions.

They amused themselves among the saucepans for an hour before they had had enough. Then they went into the bedroom where they found Sondue.

She was lying naked on the bed. Her hair had been flung back behind her and was full of big black snakes. Between her breasts a wide opening revealed her insides.

To begin with the Vicrates were afraid. They patted her cheeks so she would wake up. But she did not even move. They turned her over and found, attached to one of the long white locks of her hair, a cardboard rectangle on which these words were written: "I am dead."

They looked at one another at the same time and automatically went out to call the doctor.

He came. He took off his shawl and, to respect decency, covered Sondue with it. He took a long band of blue Chinese crepe and folded her hands inside: "That's to snatch her away from the Devil," he said.

Soon he took off the silk band which had not worked and left without saying anything but in a very angry mood.

Not knowing what to do, the poor Vicrates took Sondue's body in their arms and left, locking up the shop.

Their burden caused them to walk slowly. As it had become night, they did not have a very clear idea of where they were going. They scampered along the road without saying a word.

Soon they reached a large field full of grass in the middle of which something gleamed. They approached and saw that it was a small pond where green spiders swarmed. They placed Sondue beside the water and rested for a few moments. When the deceased cried out, they got up, held her in their arms and, with a great bound, threw her into the middle of the pond.

The body floated for a moment, then gradually sank. Feet first, then the trunk, then the arms. . .

There remained only the head, which was completely white. The Vicrates looked at it and, despairingly, left.

They again found the road that had brought them there and took it. The moon illuminated their two monstrous small forms which swayed side by side.

The head of one of them bent over and rolled into the stream. A dog gathered it up and fled.

The other one stooped down into the shadow and vanished.

*****

published in Gisèle Prassinos *Trouver sans chercher*

*****

GISÈLE PRASSINOS. (see volume one p 127–8)

UNIKA ZÜRN

It Is Such A Beautiful Day

On the sand path stood a woman and a man.

They stared down at a line drawn in front of their feet with a sharp spade.

The men who had cut these lines into the sand were lying asleep.

They were lying, red-cheeked, and they slept.

"They are not sleeping soundly enough for us to escape. They are not sleeping soundly enough for us to dare duck down behind the hedge, leap over the enclosure, rush through the grazing cattle to the shelter between the first walls . . . they are sleeping . . . alas, they are not sleeping soundly enough."

The man and woman stood motionless, and their thoughts, leaden and heavy, dragged beneath their brows – they could not be fulfilled, they could not be translated into action.

"One day this sleep too will come to an end. They will then wake up and stretch out contentedly – these blond men with their friendly child's eyes. They might then draw up their knees and yawn, perhaps eat a morsel of bread or take a sip from the bottle – and then stand up – might lift their arms up high into the spring sunlight and – eventually – they will come and command with a single word: "Dig!"

The man and woman thought minutes ahead, foreseeing what was to come and they remained quite still, their foreheads bent down, the tips of their feet grazing the line cut sharply into the sand.

"Dig –", – the sound echoed far and wide – "Dig! – dig deeper – that's not deep enough yet – deeper – further –

you must move more earth and sand – the spades are good and sharp – dig . . ."

They no longer merely think about these men waking and approaching. Now they really are coming!

The man and woman can already feel the smooth, round handles of the spades in their hands which their fingers clasp tightly. It is like a support.

"Dig! –", – now it really was happening!

The youngest, barely 19, carefully begins drawing a long rectangle of the necessary size, like a child intently painting. The men stand around idly, smoking.

Their guns lie abandoned in the sand, the gun straps curving upwards.

The men stand there, hands in their pockets, chatting.

They do not force the man and the woman to hurry. Who cares how soon it is finished! It will be finished one day. As the man strikes into the sand which, mixed with lime, slips so easily from the spade, he glances from time to time at his wife's hair as it hangs tousled across her forehead. Her face is white. They do not speak to each other. Now, when their eyes meet, they both pause for breath. All is swiftly past and forgotten when they look at each other. As they do so their spades almost fall from their hands.
"Dig – ", says one of the men amiably.

For a few minutes they forget the purpose of their work and take pains over it. They carefully mark off the edges. Finally they climb down and cast the sand upwards from the depths. Their digging and breathing responds to the same rhythm. Close together in the pit they work. From time to time their shoulders touch, then they gaze at each other once again.

The men step up to the edge of the pit and look down. They gesture sharply with their hands: "Enough!"

"I would like to sing once more", says the man to himself. He brushes aside the offer of a cigarette. But the woman thirstily takes one more sip from the bottle held out to her.

"I would like to sing once more", says the man loudly, staring past the men across the fields.

It is a very beautiful day.

The woman looks around and thinks: "There cannot ever have been a spring more beautiful than this. I did not know until now that clouds could be like this. I did not know that the sky is a sea and that clouds are the souls of happy ships, sunk long ago. I did not know that the wind could be tender, like hands as they caress – *what* did I know – until now –?"

The men, even-tempered, nod their permission to the man. They stand in a semicircle around the grave and he stands beyond the grave, leaning on his spade.

He raises his head and his eyes see into the distance – far ahead. His hair is white, his face is tanned and lined with many wrinkles. The wind strokes his brow warmly while he sings. In the semicircle the men's eyes soften and they gaze dreamily across the wide country. The woman alone turns her gaze inwards. While he sings, she concentrates her thoughts on the clouds passing above her: they are mutable – light as feathers and like wandering dreams. His voice is warm and deep. His singing is both departure and rebirth.

He stands with raised hands and those who watch him have already ceased to be part of him. His song becomes like the endless circle closing tightly around life and death, around departure and return.

To him it is as if the sky's blue light had gradually darkened and become like an upper circle which curves in a majestic arc about him. There are a thousand heads – the silent, the listeners and the entranced.

A deep sigh escapes from the breast of the youngest man standing in the semicircle. He casts a shy glance at his companions. He bites his lip and looks sadly at the ground.

The older men observe the singer with pious, attentive faces. They are thinking of their homeland, of the wide green plains of a distant country where women and children still live and wait – where there is harvesting and singing – where there is dancing and whispering, and the sound of metal being sharpened rings out behind the barns in the evening, when people stand at the well talking.

The singer lets his arms fall to his sides and closes his eyes – he stands somewhat distanced from the woman, so the eldest man takes him gently by the shoulder and draws him closer to the edge.

The woman grips his hand. Behind their backs the men step together; the carefully prepared grave is before their feet.

High above them larks plunge far into the infinite blueness voicing eerily high-pitched sounds of joy.

Six guns are primed and slowly take precise aim at the two backs. In pain, explosion and plummeting, the sky's dome spins around the fallen couple in a rush of flight – they plummet with their eyes into the deep blue, and, solemnly, before the singer's face – a heavy, purple curtain slowly closes.

★★★★★

originally published in *Der Sozialdemokrat* (1949)
reprinted in Unika Zürn, *Gesamtausgabe* (edited by Günter Bose) Berlin: Brinkmann, Brinkmann und Bose

Translated by Victoria Appelbe

★★★★★

UNIKA ZÜRN (Berlin-Grünewald, 1916 – Paris, 1970)
Unika Zürn came into contact with surrealism after she met Hans Bellmer. Marked by emotional turmoil, her drawings and writings bear witness to a tortured yet indomitable sensibility.

EUGENIO F. GRANELL

The Bridge Of Fire[1]

Tupinamba the Indian kept walking along narrow streets that led him back again and again to a small cobbled square in which, by a fountain adorned by the thinnest of dripping threads of water, a mule train stood dozing. You could still hear the faint sound of weary celebration. What Tupinamba the Indian wanted was to be alone, to be still: in silence. Sleepily, he dragged his feet through the ever more labyrinthine network of steep streets. He reached the outskirts and the glitter of a path gave him the nudge his feet needed, drawing him towards solitude.

He followed the path, little more than a line of dust – a serpentine line immersed in night and sleep – plunging into it up to his heart, to the very marrow of his soul, until his eyelids were his whole body. In the shadows he could just make out a rough, ghostly wall that stood out in the pitch darkness. As if drawn by an irresistible black beacon, he slowly advanced, step by step, towards that incandescent wall of shale. Far off, the city was vanishing into the air. The fiesta disappeared somewhere beyond his eyelids.

The wall was increasing in size, growing amidst a mixture of shadows and sparks. It was a wall of smoke from which sprouted candles that resembled asteroids. In fact, it was not one wall but two. Two tall, crackling walls, silently burning.

But it wasn't two burning walls either. It was, in fact, a street.

It was a pale street, smeared with soot, covered in

[1] This is a chapter from *La novela del Indio Tupinamba*, a novel in which the Tupinamba Indian wanders through a European landscape marked by the experiences of the Spanish Civil War.

cinders and embers, a street in which night was constantly falling. A grey street, smoke-filled, stinking of rotten wood, studded with sewers and street corners limed with dense clouds of yellowish gas, foam boiling in the corrugated zinc gutters full of holes, the edges crumbling into rusty fringes. It was a street ripped open by sword-sharp winds down to the dripping clay rock base, a street that was dark as a night of wolves.

There were two funeral parlours in this street. Before, when there had been only one – which its former owner had bequeathed to his eldest son – the youngest son, the disinherited one, was in the habit of drowning his rage in drink and, as night fell, going over to the funeral parlour with every intention of setting fire to it. The flames of the fire would curl and mingle with the invisible flames from the black, yellow, blue and pink coffins and the whole conflagration would be accompanied by the heartrending cries and extravagant vomitings of wine that would emerge from the now-repentant incendiary's night-dark mouth and help to extinguish the bonfire of pine sarcophagi and wreaths made out of tin foil and paper.

When the two brothers set up rival establishments, they each built a bridge out of myrtles, dead leaves and wire, each reaching across like a long, lingering, lethal lance to the funeral parlour opposite. The bridges were woven out of branches of trees and bits of string, rising above the brown, livid street, heavy with a silent disquiet that presaged death. Then it was the bridge or, rather, the two bridges that were set on fire each evening, releasing into the air a diadem of embers that produced thick clouds of soot. As they burned, the abundant resin and turpentine contained in the branches of the trees – mainly birches and pines – crackled and spat. The two scorched, fratricidal undertaker brothers hurled insults at each other and gestured wildly, flapping their hands at the thick smoke between them, kindling fires, scattering sparks and, at the same time, dancing tremulously on the swaying bridge stirred by the air, the vibrant air wrapped in a thick winding sheet of flame. The brothers, equally afire, each promised to make for the other the narrowest of coffins, its interior studded with sharp, protruding, rusty nails. The bridges became one when the two met and fires and foliage intermingled. It took on colossal proportions, obscuring the mineral landscape and the mountains and the trees. At one point, the bridge was a forest of pines, bundles of tree trunks transformed into a smoking bridge, a bridge belching forth smoke and hot ashes, swaying between the two funeral parlours, fused into one by fire, covered in dry ivy and handfuls of pine cones and willow twigs and tiled with scabby bark, the bark like pustules on the scorched wooden bridge, the bridge condemned to die in flames, packed with wood intended for coffins that would rot before they were even made and even before the fire devoured them, gulping them down in its dry, crackling greed.

The whole neighbourhood participated in the building of the bridge of pines between the two funeral parlours. The neighbours on the right, who lived in the row of houses with even numbers, took the part of one undertaker and the neighbours on the left, whose houses were now without chimneys, became the allies of the other. The two brothers captained their respective bandage-swathed armies, both hating each other like poison, estranged tribes who bore on their own bare backs endless quantities of pine trees, ancient and new, dwarf and giant, as well as the water and earth needed to reinforce their part of the bridge against the constant onslaught from the other side. Each party was convinced that their only guarantee of peace and of their own continued existence was the disappearance of the rival funeral parlour. Each side believed that the destruction of the other offending coffin shop, along with its owner, his family, neighbours and supporters, was vital if they were ever to recover true happiness and the joy of living, even though they had long since forgotten whether these qualities were naturally occurring species in some kingdom somewhere or merely simple beliefs from ages past. They were all absolutely convinced of the need to conquer life with fire, sleep with smoke, and thus no one cast doubt on the idea that the longed-for horizon would only be glimpsed once each faction had managed to achieve the total destruction of the row of houses allied to the rival funeral parlour that concealed the fire beneath a dress suit of flaming bridges. It was also true that the original undertakers had died long before. But the hostilities continued, because the sense of wounded pride continued, the reason why it had all started; thus too the duties and endeavours demanded by the bridge continued unabated, as did the fires and the blazing row amongst the ardent inhabitants.

The forest suspended between the two funeral parlours had become a mountain of fire, full of birds and creatures of all kinds, patrolled by vigilant teams of forest rangers, not that their vigilance served much purpose amidst the choking, asphyxiating smoke. Secondary fires would break out here and there and burning coffins and flaming wreaths would leap into the air along with large numbers of singed locals emitting hair-raising screams that only added to the deafening density of the victory cries with which each impassioned band urged itself on, firm in the knowledge that victory would one day be theirs.

The bridge was rebuilt again and again on top of piles of blackened bones, embers, brands made from the legs of tables and chairs, products both natural and man-made all burned to a crisp: tree trunks, branches, feathers, animal skins and, last but not least, forest rangers, leaving behind only their broad leather bandoliers and their enormous brass oval badges bearing the municipal arms and stamped with their number. Little piles of ashes punctuated the vast fratricidal barbecue. Not even the mayor could do anything. That was the blunt truth. That's why the mayor, just like any other neighbour, carried branches of pine wood which he lit with his rustic lighter or participated in the transportation of a whole tree or spent entire days and freezing cold winter nights scratching about amongst the dead and that ragbag of incinerated remains, struggling to tie knots in burning rope in order to secure the branches one to the other and thus make indestructible the part of the bridge to which he had, at that moment, allied himself. The mayor was just one more villager, one amongst many, just like all the rest, absorbed in the task of setting fire to the bridge and stoking that fire, of piling up flammable material, of feeding the fire with pines and the pines with fire as well as cultivating forests in order to build the bridge, in order to continue the war of flames and smoke, in order to achieve the destruction of the other side, blackened by burns, covered in scars, pustules, wounds, in order to consume, melt and scorch the hated enemy, the funeral parlour opposite, and to free themselves from the unbearable threat posed by its existence.

By then, the houses were nothing more than a memory, apart from the occasional bit of vine trellis still clinging to square granite pillars. The stone bases, black with smoke and dried blood, were scarred by traces of metal window frames and fragments of charred kitchen utensils. There were no more staircases or chimneys or balconies or roofs, no more cosy corners, only the faintest of ash-grey murmurings. Only the ignescent foundations, down below, in the dun-coloured pit of the dark precipice roofed by sombre smoke from the burning forest, like a fiery walkway through the clouds.

Far beneath, all you could see was the ash-strewn street, narrow, stagnant, a thick, meandering river of flames, in which, very occasionally, an ember throwing out fleeting sparks glinted feebly, almost imperceptibly, as crushed boulders plunged into its burning lava, mingling with the dust of skeletons, the wreckage of shattered coffins and the withered corpses of humans and animals and misshapen, stinking, colourless flowers, whilst above, walled in by the flaming forest, the locals battled on amidst the fire, barricaded against the enemy behind wormeaten coffins made out of precious woods and bronze and pine, with their phosphorescent bones fanning the air, now perhaps little more than fodder for the damp and the woodworm, the dense flames.

The battle continued amidst the agonised cries of burns, amidst the slender bonfires of gashes, amidst the stigmata of wounds; and the multitudinous clearing of the tinder-dry throats, muffled or dumb, of the charred, tumultuous pines underlined the random nature of the fire. Each and every inhabitant spent long periods without noticing the train pass, without counting the quarters of the moon, without harvesting their crops, without finding the halter now lost forever, entrenched in their coffins rapidly being consumed by a scorching mould, coffins that flowered, sprouted mushrooms, brandished splinters, softened knotty fibres, became intertwined with tendons and muscles, with weeds and parasites, all part of the heaving carrion pierced by the interminable, corrugated rains threading their sudden cold cracklings onto embers like fleeting constellations in the smoking sky of the forest-become-bridge encrusted with clouds like stones.

Tupinamba the Indian could understand the rationale behind making a sacrifice to something, but what he couldn't comprehend was making a sacrifice to a sacrifice. He lit a cigar on the crimson point of a blazing nail and went to queue up at the telegraph office: "My dear little Carmen," that was how he intended to begin his brief message.

*****

published in *La Novela del Indio Tupinamba* (1959) Mexico: Costa Amic

Translated by Margaret Jull Costa

*****

EUGENIO F. GRANELL (La Coruña, 1912) A militant during the Spanish Civil War, when he met Benjamin Péret and started to participate in surrealism, after the war Granell was exiled and lived in the Dominican Republic and in New York until returning to Madrid recently. His wide-ranging interests in history, anthropology and geography are apparent in his painting as much as in his writings.

He is the author of one of the finest of all novels written by surrealists, *La novela del Indio Tupinamba*, from which the above extract is drawn.

BERNARD ROGER

Melius Spe Licebat

The world we are born into has raised walls between eyes and eyes. It has constructed steel doors for the ears and of rigid poly vinyl chloride gloves for the hands. Forewarned in this way against 'homo sapiens' and 'homo faber', it would finally be able – nothing left seemed to stop it – to stifle its old enemy, its ancient sire, the red demon of its sleepless nights, present everywhere and invisible, the guardian of all powers hidden in the deepest forests, in the hollows of old oaks and under the lively springs: it is the terrestrial receptacle of the rays of all the stars, the scandalous *savage heart*.

The coincidence could not fail to be noted that it was precisely in the first days of May, at the time of each year when the 'Dew of the Sky' bestows strength on all of nature, that among those whose social structuring had so far been unable to extinguish all hope of life, surging forth from the spear head that the world we are born into has reached and from which it will not be released.

Towards those whose gaze was gleaming so clearly in the street – 'Young red women, still more beautiful' – the world we are born into has turned its empty eyes, its old man's face, to obscene sneering. It was no more than a hollowed out and dried bark. They were the morning star, the madmen dressed in leaves, green vitriol, the mysterious place where vibration becomes body. The spirit of life was in them: death can do nothing against the dawning light; death is but a cardboard mask soon consumed by fire.

Behind the black flag – which is nothing other than an *anti-flag* – the garden of all possibilities is hidden, opening out infinitely to the sea.

The old world's sneering will be its last shudder of existence – for how many more days?

Certainly 'it was acceptable to hope for better'. Nonetheless, the solar tree has pushed forth its first buds towards every part of the earth. Hidden in the 'forest of the nymph Venus', it already bears fruit which will soon ripen: your poison and your natural solvent, senile world, your everyday food, a 'golden age' so natural because gold is encountered only among the stones of the path.

14th July 1968

*****

*****

BERNARD ROGER (Troyes, 1924) An architect who has participated in surrealist activities since 1951, Bernard Roger is especially interested in alchemy, having studied with René Alleau, and has edited and translated ancient alchemical texts as will as writing extensively on the subject. His *A la Découverte de l'alchimie* was published in 1988.

JULIEN GRACQ

The Path

It was, as far as I remember, ten days after we had crossed the Crest that we reached the entrance of the Retaining wall, the narrow paved way leading hundreds of leagues from the edge of the Borderlands to the passes of Mont-Harbré – the last lifeline, cut off and then put back together again twenty times over, which every now and then linked up the Realm with the encircled and faraway Mountain.

What a strange, disquieting path! The only *highway* I have ever followed whose windings (even though everything about its encounters and dangers – its crepuscular copses and sense of dread – fades away) would, like a diamond point on a pane of glass, still etch its trace in my memory. One embarks upon this road as if on a sea voyage. Through three hundred leagues of indistinct countryside – unfurling on its own, without fetters or bonds, a thin thread, stretched, blanched by sunlight and rotten with dead leaves – the phosphorescent track of a footpath on which my feet groped among the weeds on a moonlit night unfolds in my memory as if between the banks of its night. I had followed it from one end to the other through an interminable black wood.

It began in a strange fashion (rather like those fragments of Roman road that begin and end, for no apparent reason, in the middle of a field, as though a ruler had been dropped across a chessboard) in the very heart of a grassy glade, and fitted into the gap formed by the fringes of two forests impatient to join together. Wherever its bedrock had remained intact it gave, despite its narrowness, every sign of having been carefully constructed: a compact masonry of small angular blocks – or, sometimes, near the river beds, rounded shingle – congealed in a kind of concrete, on which a pavement of large flat slabs had been smoothed and repointed. The general effect rather brought to mind the top of a narrow dike levelled out at ground level. Its resonance, dull and without echo under the hooves of horses, was that of a wall. Although it was just about wide enough for the wheels of a cart, it was apparent that the track must have been first and foremost a bridlepath, for the paving-stones of the surface retained traces of ruts which ate into the rock like a worn-away gutter, now incrusted with grey lichen, and these signs of ancient traffic graphically suggested the idea of an uninterrupted flow, an energetic life that must, long ago, have animated the path from one end to the other. This only served to emphasise the impression of extreme dilapidation it now had. It was a fossilised path: the will which had cut this gash out of these solitary places so that the blood and the sap would flow there was long since dead – and dead too were the circumstances which had guided this will. A whitish and indurated scar remained, gradually gnawed away at by the earth like a flesh that heals itself, yet its direction was still vaguely cut into the horizon; a languid and crepuscular sign rather than a way forward – a worn-out lifeline which still vegetated through the fallow land as it does on the palm of a hand. It was so old that, since it had been constructed, the very configuration of the land must have changed imperceptibly: here and there the substructure of the causeway had become embankment dominating the grasslands of the valleys, revealing a damp-course of bare blocks that bristled up – elsewhere, the submerged paving plunged down over quite long distances and became lost under the retrieved earth. And yet it was never completely lost from sight, or rather – even when submerged beneath a mass of debris or immersed in high grass – like a horse that insists on testing the stony bed of the ford with its hoof, one retained a sort of singular contact with it, for the trace of man's track takes longer to efface from the earth than the mark made by a branding iron: straight ahead of us is a clear breach in the thickets, at an unexpectedly more severe alignment of far-off trees, what still extant suggestion of *direction*, the Path, now and then disembodied, continued to offer us signs, like those enigmatic angels on the paths of the Bible who, far ahead, signal for us to follow them with just one raised finger, without even deigning to look round. It resembled those rivers in arid lands which cease to flow during the dry season and fragment into a succession of pools between which a thread of water still sometimes gurgles amid the pebbles. Blood had long since ceased to beat from one end to the other, but one could sense, from passages marked with fresher traces of wheels and hooves, that once the meaning and even the very idea of a long journey was lost, sleep had not descended over it in one fell swoop: it had continued to steal a march here and there, in a discontinuous way, and over short distances, like a labourer who feels his cart jolt on a section of Roman road that crosses his field – but then this was a trifling and wholly domestic haulage, such as might trundle along the alleys of small market towns between the millstones and drinking troughs – herds of small livestock led to pasture or to market, the comings and goings of the charcoal burners or woodcutters, peddlars who ventured forth from the edge of the Borderlands. Besides, the further one penetrated into the confused solitudes, even this slight human crackling on the hollow path died away, and after the great white emptiness of the day, in the twilight of dusk, it was wild animals which assumed the final tenure, for this clearing in the woods seemed both familiar and accommodating to them, especially to those who travel and go a long way. Often, beyond the next turning, footfalls of a herd galloping across stone were heard, or further in the distance, with reassuring grunts, a wild boar could be seen trotting with steady stride along the edge of the road with her sow and a whole procession of young in tow. And then one's heart beat faster upon advancing a little into the subtle light: one might have said that the path had suddenly become wild, thick with grass, its dark paving-slabs engulfed by nettles, blackthorn and sloe, so that it mingled up time past rather than crossing countryside, and that perhaps it was going to issue forth, in the chiaroscuro of thicket smelling of moistened down and fresh grass, into one of those glades where animals spoke to men.

To defend itself unaided in this way against the assault of trees, animals and wild plants – through long periods when men had ceased to circulate over its stony bed – the Retaining wall must have radically adjusted itself: the fine and strict proportions of the path, which had crossed this land like a foreigner, had come apart. Like those conquerors who one way or another adapt to the conquered land by assuming its customs and dress it had – passing from the fallow lands to the forest country, the swamps, and the stony hills – incorporated something of the very substance of the land it crossed, to the extent that it became almost unrecognisable, and if we sometimes cursed it in its malicious moods, there was still a charm in finding it so varied and changeable, wholly impregnated with the profundity of solitude, causing vague and encroaching daydreams of the high road, the smell of plants and the sounds of animals to flow successively within us, allowing moist branches to whip across our faces as we passed through the woods, or the dust of the sandy plains to completely whiten us. In the chalky fields its clear paving, under the slight trembling of dry umbels which swayed along the joins in the paving, preserved a distinctness of well-cut ribbon, flowing straight through the expanse. In front of us, on the ridge of the ground's surge, the talon mark of its clear trace was seen undulating far away into the distance. Those days, its dry and musty clarity, its reassuring and straight path, as it promised an easy day's journey, added something to the blueness of the fine weather. At the side of the gorges, cut from fallen rock, dislocated by landslides, oftimes split open to the lacerating rubble of its foundations, it was often no more than the bed of a dry stream, a poor pebbly track where horses stumbled. But this lost path was especially pleasing to me when, sometimes for whole days, it meandered into the forests. Here the paving had long since vanished beneath a hummus of yellowing leaves, a fine black compost into which the feet sank without a sound. Beneath the green vaults horses' hooves were stifled as unexpectedly as when one passed from sunlight to shade. We crept along in Indian file into the abrupt silence, under the fresh and soft rain of the moist undergrowth. This lost forest track, under its fine grass that was sometimes reddened with strawberries, with its traces of animals, its puddles of black water, its smell of humid moss and fresh mushroom, appeared so abandoned, so completely reclaimed by the wildness of the woods that one struggled with difficulty against the impression that at any moment it would come to a dead-end, that the trees would again close over its narrow crevice, but the stone embankment, the invisible wall that had been driven beneath the track into the ground, had obstinately contained the forest's assault, and the Path plunged on indefinitely, amiable and vaguely enchanted, filtering its calm and reassuring light through the undergrowth, step by step separating the curtain of branches ahead of us as a hand might.

I retain an unsettled image of the lands it crossed, similar to what the memory might retain of, for example, a cloudy sky (with its confused and indistinct masses, its slow drift as the hours pass and portents of approaching storms mount, together with the rapid way it has of completely turning from light to dark) rather than of terra firma, with all the phrase implies of precision, measurability and delimitation. When it became visible in the distance, from high on a hill, it was arranged in large stains with frayed edges which thinned out and dissolved towards the horizon in indistinct layers, finally mingled into a darker ring which cuts off the view: stained gloomily in the forests, more brightly in the grasslands, smoky-grey and quivering with moisture in the swamps: as a whole it gave a haunting impression of heavy stagnation. Even so, it was not so much of wildness it made one think, as of a return to wildness. One might at times have said it was a sand-bank that had been saturated by the tide, inundating recently begun earth works. All trace of life was not absent from it, especially along the Path we had followed, but the hold of man over this glacis situated between the pacified land of the Realm and the barbarous countries was visibly relaxed, to the extent that the waves of invasion had become more frequent. Signs of fire, looting and violent death were not lacking. Here and there redoubts of very recently felled trees cut the track, the black termite nest of a burnt-out pyre reared up, or else, in the midst of the empty rectangle of a clearing already consumed by thistles and nettles, the shell of a burned-out farm could be seen looming up. But such encounters retained the character, rather, of isolated accidents, to which the eye was not resigned in advance, as when one has assumed, once and for all, that one is passing through a land 'laid waste by war'. These coal-black ruins still stood out sharply and ominously from the intact landscape, like a herd or a barn burned to ashes by lightning in the midst of the greenness of June. One would sometimes have believed that rather than a land ransacked by invasion, one was passing through a country with unusually stormy summers. No, what numbed these fields peopled with bad dreams was not the oppressive grip of a plague, but rather an ailing retreat, a sort of sad widowhood. Man had started to subdue these vacant expanses, then had grown weary of eating into it, and now even the desire to preserve what had been claimed had perished. He had established everywhere an ebb, a sorrowful withdrawal. His cuttings into the forest, which were seen at long intervals, had lost their hard edges, their distinct notches: now a thick brushwood had driven its sabbath into the broad daylight of the glades, hiding the naked trunks as high as their lowest branches. The cultivated spots were being reabsorbed like a pool emptied from the bottom, abandoning around them the old fences sinking into the high grass, and a whole rippling ring of wild plants, studded with white mullein and red poppies. Of the small clusters of humble thatched cottages crowding together at long intervals in the waste-land, flanked by their cow-sheds and hay lofts, one could no longer see anything more than the roofs or rather their sodden rafters still smeared with rotting straw. The tide of fleecy and lustreless plants thriving in the rubble had already overrun them to the eaves. Nothing was more heart rending, in once enclosed and worked land, where little islets of apple-trees, the fringes of their crowns now resting on the seething wild grass, than the servile riot of these dust-coloured plants, leprous, shaggy and thorny, that thrive on human waste and are kept at bay in walled and weeded gardens. Now they hold sway, along with snails and snakes, over well, oven and wash-house, blowing an unwholesome chill of the cellar into the cracked walls. Sometimes, when we passed within sight of one of these wrecks that had already foundered in eddies of green foam, a sad curiosity diverted us momentarily from the Path and, through the vacant windows, we cast a glance into the empty rooms. A sinister white light fell through the staved-in roofs, making the desecrated cave of the depths of the peasant dwelling blink like a night bird, a house with its poverty-stricken secrets, the timorous vaulting of its alcove, its caches of provisions, with the sweat of its smoky walls, rubbed dull by human skin, the long thread of cold soot in the fireplace, and, in the red tiled outhouse, the broken milk jugs still hanging from their hooks over the rotten churn. It was no longer, as when we crossed the countryside of the Realm, the feeling of incurable old age which saddened us there: in this land of deaf and dumb roofs, with no sound of a dog's bark, without the early morning jolting carts, there was a physical malaise at once diffuse and violent, the feeling of having completely strayed in dream into a land which rises inexplicably late.

In spite of the shelter they might still sometimes afford, we never liked to camp near such forbidding places. I recall that one evening we made a halt in one of these vacated hamlets set with their backs against the edge of the woods. Three or four giant elms stamped their shadows over the small triangular square. Between the trunks a few banks of slate still parted the high grasses like tombstones – in one corner a roller had remained toppled in the shadow, buried up to its raised shafts (we saw these heavy stone-rollers everywhere with their arms held high above the grass in the farmyard, which people had given up trying to take away, since they were a millstone around their necks). With our horses shackled, we took a few indecisive steps into the rancid hay that came up to our chests, undecided whether we should light a fire, since we felt ill-at-ease under the stare of the bereft windows which followed us in the shadow of their carboniferous sockets, then, without even consulting one another, we took to the saddle once again and plunged into the forest.

Nevertheless, as obvious as were the signs of abandon, man had not completely vacated these solitudes. As happens when confidence slips away, he has merely made a change in his domicile and its appearance, giving to any encounter an ambiguous, somewhat disturbing, character. The signs of former activity that still marked out the route – enclosed parcels of land, sheep-farms, mills and abandoned villages – were all abrasions, still luminous with the trace of man, from which we took our bearings, and yet, for the singular race with which we occasionally crossed paths, all that had come to be as suspect as are the tracks and the dung of a forest creature to one of another species. When smoke was seen to rise it was always at some considerable distance from the Path – sometimes leagues away – on the tops of bare rocks or on hills whose shoulders rose behind the forests, in places where one generally sees the camp fires of hunters or the bonfires of charcoal-burners. This enigmatic smoke that rose at eventide above high places hardly suggested freshly-made beds and hot soup, and we watched for a long time considering how far away and where they were, before choosing the location to make camp. Even during the day we never overcame the feeling that we were defilading between two lines of invisible look-outs. The outlines we sometimes saw silhouetted on the path in the distance or threading their way through the undergrowth did not conjure up the impression of travellers on their way. Their indecisive and furtive appearance, and their antipathy to being approached, rather evoked a marauding tribe on the edges of its territory, or those people who roam the length of sea-shores. Hal, who felt an affinity with these distant idlers of the forest, had the gift of often being able to gain their confidence. Sometimes they felt bold enough to sit for a while at our camp fire, and we were able to gain some crumbs of information about the scattered life that lurked all around us. Set apart, a very mixed store of people had formed – nomads cut off from their main band who had entrenched themselves in clearings comprising consanguinous groups of a few families (although they had assumed the language of the Realm and scraps of its customs, they could be recognised by their round wooden huts with conical shingle roofs, and which were only billet tents), militia men from the Borderlands who had never received the evacuation order in their small forlorn forts, fiefdoms that dominated the small communities of trappers, clog-makers and horse thieves who had come to seek shelter behind their wooden palisades – also youths from the freed peasant-holdings who had succumbed to wanderlust and, rather than follow their elders into the old country which maintained its land-registers so exactly, had got out their rifles and taken to the forest. When we established contact with these small tribes which sprang up here and there like rank plants – half-hunters, half-pilferers – we were surprised to sense from their conversation how little regret they felt at having left behind the old and assured life and now revelled in the open air, a little giddy with their freedom, on freshly hallowed ground. Here the earth had become verdant again and preened itself, its coat fresh, completely clear of the abrasions of its old slackened girths, and mankind had also been rejuvenated, released into the haze of grass like a stallion, enlivened to be able to stride across an earth that is as unwrinkled as a beach from which the sea has only just retreated.

The attitude of the detachments which passed at long intervals along the course of the Path was neither hostile nor vindictive, but was that of plunderers in relation to any obstacle they might encounter: intact, a very well armed and provisioned troop, sure of its way, could believe it was merely crossing a solitude that abounded in game, but one that had lost its way and was short of supplies or had been held up by an accident, would fear the worst, for the scent of blood here, as in the sea, travelled a long way. Powder and shot, clothing and horses were the object of tremendous covetousness, and the life of the traveller was worth about as much as what he carried with him. What ordinarily hinders the corpse is the tangle of beliefs it brings in its wake: like those cork floats attached to fishing-nets that, if touched, would bring mesh after mesh to the surface, such a swarming as would capsize the boat. Here, where the moorings had been cut, the corks danced, and death no longer asked questions: from time to time, stretched out at the side of the road, one came across a small pile of stones to which the custom of the Path was simply to add a pebble upon passing, a gesture of distracted absolution which released the dead man of his memory and the murderer of his motives. This little man-made moraine which gradually formed along the track did not weigh in the memory as does the earth of cemeteries and it did not provide food for thought. Along the Path it gave off a murmuring of the unconstrained wind and water, like boats moored at the quayside, and where it extended into the trees, one could sit down to collect one's thoughts or get one's bearings. There was a calm in these faint burrows that rendered life at ease and in a way that was so unimposing as to be neither testimony nor evidence.

★

We sometimes encountered women along the Retaining wall. They travelled in twos or threes – almost never alone and almost always on horseback – although we once passed two who were on foot: two black and delicate silhouettes, far ahead of us on the way, whose cumbersome travelling boots made them appear to be hopping like small lame birds. They entwined fingers without speaking and – I recall that it was Easter time – they nibbled at a branch in flower: in the mist of yellow foliage the woods were full of cuckoo calls, but it was from these lonely gourmets all of a sudden on a road full of pot-holes and fresh water that we learned that the earth blossomed. The Path, on which they lived in the wake of the long voyage, had gradually given them a sort of uniform – almost all wore thick boots folded at the ankles, with laced up breeches, a small dagger, and a leather corslet which enclosed them severely from waist to wrist, but they travelled bare-headed and with their hair loose, a heavy abundant mane which fell down to their loins, full of thorns and wild odours. There was nothing mean or vulgar about these encounters; often they had come from far away, having heard about the travellers who passed along the route, not in order to live off them (since they asked for nothing and even gifts were only ever accepted on odd whims, or rather according to unspoken rules, which bore witness to a fierce integrity) but to live with them, or more accurately near them and at their fancy, in the sort of active wake that was the Path and where one breathed as nowhere else: sometimes we thought of those sea birds which hang for a moment on the slip-steam of ships, but abandon one of them for another, as though it is the fresh seething wake of travel itself, not the particular traveller, that captivates them. Almost all of them were beautiful, with a heavy and rather overwhelming beauty. They resembled those peasant girls – with eyes bold at nightfall – who could be seen riding horses bareback on their way home from the watering-hole, but the Path had matured them, or perhaps its summons had plumbed to the depths of these earthy lands only what could still flow of an altogether thinner blood. Their contempt for the race in bondage to the land, those who each evening cuddled up in their musty beds with their beasts of burden, knew no bounds: it was a contempt of an almost spiritual kind for the wretched mush of the soil, and a little of the arrogance of the nobleman's servitor who has chosen to breathe the emanation of the elect the whole day long. They spoke little and they were not fearful but had wise and subtle counsel on the dangers of the way, and it was possible, if one wished, to treat these alert and taciturn little companions in leather boots, who knew how to bridle an animal and swear through their teeth like men, as comrades, as travelling hosts for a day. But sometimes, at a halting-place, when night had thickened around the bed of red embers – the only coquetry they displayed was that it was always they who would *choose* – a mouth sought your mouth in the darkness with the stubborn confidence of the friendly animal which tries to read its master's face, and suddenly this was wholly a woman, warm and unleashed like rain, heavy like an exhausted night, allowing herself to founder in your arms. Along our way, chastity was not the rule and we accepted whatever sudden windfalls the road offered us. Sometimes since then I have thought – for there was in these encounters something at once incomplete, awkward and tender, that was tenaciously held in the memory that never retained anything impure about them – that these wanderers with soft tumbling hair perhaps offered themselves – even if it is a strange thing to say – *for want of anything better*, embarrassed by this female body which they offered in the darkness with a sort of humble submission, always determined to understand things only through its warm mass. What they sought, and what they wanted in a clumsy way to rediscover, what kept them awake at night with such dogged patience, was not those who passed along the Path, but was perhaps a reflection they bore, which had been passionately gleaned from things more distant – perhaps simply of wherever the Path was taking them. Woman responds quicker than man to the importance of what is occurring in certain murmurs that rise from the earth, but the warm mystery of her body weighs upon her and it may be that her impatience with how it prevents complete clarity within her causes her to give it in the same way one decides to take a short cut. It seems to me that no one ever completely failed to recognise this, and that even the coarsest person emerged from these chance embraces touched for a moment with a sort of harsh delicacy. As the moment of parting came in the morning, one treated them not as women but as campfire companions and as loyal comrades. They never tried to delay us or hold us back, and, when morning came, they served their friend of one night as he harnessed his horse with a page's skill and with completely dignified gestures allowing of no uneasy familiarity, since they knew that what is appropriate in bed and what is, for man, of a quite different order, and they resolutely followed the male in his repugnance at mixing the two.

I dream about them sometimes – it's odd, at times they were so close to us and so fraternal – with a kind of grave tenderness. Doubtless they still wander the intersections of the Path where no one goes any more, these unpacified bacchantes in whom desire sought to articulate another language – half-courtesans, half-sibyls, they had become forever unfit to partake of banal existence and their wide-open eyes were as proud and sad as an exhausted well on the deserted road – bearing the regret and widowhood of this small society of women, a fragile one, momentarily interrupted and modelling itself on the male order in places where he lives, only to close back on itself in the most austere way, and which in its way also blossoms – sterile though it may be – into strange qualities, with a potent and tenacious odour. In order to be able to touch and fully attain it, they gave, humbly. Lay sisters of the long journey, they were resigned to the most wretched tasks, but were incapable of soiling their hands and mouths with what did not carnally touch upon a certain order of which their hearts had a pre-sentiment. I recall their grave eyes and their faces strangely raised towards the kiss as if towards something which might have illuminated it – and the motion of kissing them on the brow still comes to me, as it came to us when we left them, with a kind of wild and pitiful tenderness.

*****

first published in Julien Gracq, *La Presqu'île* Paris: José Corti

*****

JULIEN GRACQ (see volume one p 221)

LOUIS SCUTENAIRE

The Life And Work Of Alfred Jarry And Isidore Ducasse

Since everyone knows this story they would without any doubt love to hear it re-told once more. So much more so in that it presents such strange aspects of cruelty which, if they were not supported with the most meticulous historical evidence, would have been dismissed as fantastic and completely unbelievable.

Alfred JARRY was born at Laval, the capital of Mayenne département, at the time of the Third Republic, on 8th September 1873 to be exact. His father, who maintained hedges and ditches, brought him up to continue this onerous profession. But, having little taste for this sort of work and, with a love of dissipation, he left home with a friend of similar disposition whose name was Isidore Ducasse. They retreated together into the wilderness, making their home on the coast, in a cave about a mile long and of remarkable breadth which was so close to the sea that it was often inundated with the tide to a depth of more than a thousand yards.

The entrance to the cave constituted a kind of labyrinth full of winds and turns by which it was necessary to creep along to reach the deepest part of the underground domain which was, literally, the scene of extreme atrocities.

As soon as JARRY and his friend had retired there they began the long sequence of crimes which completely permeated the rest of their lives. To prevent disclosure they murdered anyone they robbed and, being unable to obtain any proper food, resolved to live from human flesh. In consequence, when they had cut the throat of a man, woman or child, they would carry the body into their wild lair, quarter it, cure it and marinate the organs, drying them for their food. They lived like this for a long time, robbing and killing until they had a numerous family of eight boys and six girls, who gave them by incest and metagenesis, thirty-two grand children, eighteen boys and fourteen girls.

Even though there were so many of them, they often had more provisions than they could use, so many victims did they slaughter. When that happened, they travelled by night to somewhere far from where they lived and threw pickled and dried legs, arms and bits of human bodies into the ocean.

Under the iodising and reconstituting effects of sea water, a veritable broth of seaweed, some of the remains came back to life and combined into new forms. This was the origin of the manatees, seals and penguins that are sometimes encountered on French coasts without anyone being able to understand how these creatures had accomplished the impossible voyage from their natal solitudes to the coasts of our country.

Other pieces were often thrown up onto the beach by the tide and gathered by the local people. Every time that happened, consternation and fear spread through the population in whose neighbourhood relations, friends or neighbours had fallen into the hands of the cave-dwellers without anyone being able to discover what had become of them and their possessions.

As JARRY's group got larger each of its members took part in the murders as soon as they were strong enough. In such a way they could attack four or six men on foot, but never more than two on horseback, bicycle or in a car. In order to prevent any means of escape, they lay in wait all around so that if they got away from the first assailants, they could be attacked by others with a new fury and inevitably they were killed. Thus the prey never slipped through their fingers and nor were they discovered.

Finally such exploits roused the inhabitants of the land who thoroughly searched the woods and anywhere else men might hide. But though the peasants again and again went past the opening of the cave, they never had the idea of going inside since they were unable to conceive that any human beings could live there. In this state of doubt concerning the authors of such frequent murders, several innocent travellers and inn-keepers were arrested on suspicion just because people who had disappeared and were not found again had either been seen a little earlier with the former or had stayed overnight with the latter. Following these severe measures and the execution of these innocents the majority of hoteliers in the region left their profession, which created great difficulties for those travellers who still ventured there.

And the land became depopulated.

But one evening an event occurred which served to put an end to the terror. A man and his wife, both mounted on the same horse, were returning from a neighbourhood fair and were attacked by the elusive bandits. The husband put up vigorous resistance. Even so, his wife was dragged from behind him, taken a few steps and had her guts torn out under his eyes. Desperate and overwhelmed with horror, he redoubled his efforts to avoid succumbing in his turn. He knocked down some of his attackers, who were trampled beneath his horse. Fortunately for him, twenty or thirty mounted people, returning from the same fair, happened to pass at that very moment. At their approach, JARRY and his kin ran off into a thick forest and thence back to their lair.

The man who managed to escape, the first person blessed with such good fortune, recounted what had happened to the new arrivals and showed them his wife's mutilated body lying a few feet away, since the bandits had not had time to carry it off. Overwhelmed with amazement, the travellers at once took the body to Paris and related the adventure to the Public Prosecutor, who wrote to the President of the Republic to inform him about it.

A few days later, the Public Prosecutor himself, along with four hundred men-at-arms, began the search for the bandits. The husband of the woman who had been disembowelled acted as their guide. In addition they had a pack of bloodhounds in order to find, by any imaginable means, even the cruellest, the bandits' hide out. The band thoroughly searched possible shelters, scouring and examining the coast. They passed in front of the cave but did not tarry there since they still retained the conviction that no one could inhabit that dark and frightful hole.

Some of the bloodhounds nonetheless ventured inside and started to bark as if they were on the point of seizing their prey. Responsive to their barks, the Public Prosecutor and his followers retraced their steps, but, in spite of the signs, they could barely convince themselves that any living beings could exist in such a profoundly dark place, the access to which was so difficult and constricted. But the barking of the mastiffs became still more pronounced and they would not return, so all of them felt it was right to explore the abyss to the bottom. They obtained torches, let the dogs advance, and a large number of men scoured all the bends in the black and terrifying maze. Finally they reached the mysterious living quarters of those they were pursuing.

The scouts and the others in the group following were overwhelmed with amazement at the sight of the spectacle offered to their eyes, a spectacle unique in France and that had probably never been seen anywhere else in the world: row upon row of legs, thighs, hands and feet of men, women and children hanging like cuts of salted beef; and moreover soaking in brine were organs and other lumps of human meat. There were also piles of gold and silver coins, watches, earrings and clothes of wool, linen or dimity, together with a vast quantity of other objects accumulated and hanging completely mixed-up on both sides of the cave. The inner surfaces of the rock that were still visible had been painted with large frescoes representing maps, lines, geometrical forms or fancies, coloured red, green, yellow and white. In fact, the artists of the depths used only humours distilled from the bodies of their victims as colours, for example, red from their blood, green from their bile and gold from their piss.

The whole group of bandits, numbering forty-eight individuals, were arrested, the human flesh was buried in the sand of the sea shore, while the hired cops contended for the enormous booty. And the Public Prosecutor conveyed the brigands to Paris.

This procession, at once so sad and novel, strongly excited the curiosity of the city inhabitants who raced from everywhere to see the murderers pass by. They were all held in the Santé, where a large guard was set up, and the following day they were taken for punishment to Boulevard Arago. They were executed without being tried. Whether it was considered that ordinary forms of justice were pointless, or it was feared they would be pestered with perhaps cogent apologies from the wretched defendants.

They were forced to submit whilst still alive to the same ill-treatment they had inflicted on their dead victims. Their arms and legs were cut off and men, women and children were left to die like this. Far from expressing regret or repenting, they vomited out, right until their final spasms, the most horrible curses against the spectators and those who had helped to deliver them to the violence of the executioners.

But, during the night following the tortures, JARRY, DUCASSE and their friends went in search of their dispersed bones and gathered them together. Each of them, helped by the others, reconstituted his own skeleton, hung his inner parts on it (for the torturers had torn them out) and then gave substance to muscles, flesh and reconstituted skin. They went on the run and swindled, killed, pickled and consumed worse than ever.

Soon they had more provisions than they could use, so many victims did they slaughter. They travelled by night to somewhere far from where they lived and threw pickled and dried legs and arms of human bodies into the ocean, mixed with distressing forms made from ordinary objects.

*****

published in *Les Deux Soeurs* no 2 (Brussels 1946)

*****

LOUIS SCUTENAIRE (Ollignies, 1905 – Brussels, 1987) Participated in surrealist activities from 1927, when he joined the Belgian Surrealist Group one summer's night. Particularly known for his aphorisms collected in *Mes Inscriptions*, he is also the author of a novel, *Les Vacances d'un enfant* (1947).

JEAN-PIERRE DUPREY

Solution H Or About The Second Imaginary Journey Of Mr H

Traced in chalk, on a cube of air solidified in contact with the eyes, was this inscription: "HERE LIES, in the same place as a bone transformed into the clapper of a bell, the body – of Mr H – indefinitely rotating around itself like a whirlwind which will see its end only when it experiences itself transformed into the potent but invisible mass of a sphere that is full inside and devoid of its contours, something that is only a supposition."

. . .And, behind the window pane of appearances-suppositions, the thread (then representing Mr H's mind) was stretched from top to bottom, with a weight at the end, through the space contained between the void and its hollow appearance. And the bat, covered with cat's fur, sought to land there. . . Seen from behind, it closely resembled 7 yards of arms sewn together from octopus-men because, owing to its shadow, it appeared to be relatively long. Somewhere there was a star which was none other than a lack of star and it was there, and there alone, that things happened. . .

Mr H, under the skin without light of the Character-of-the-Night, followed the uniformly stiff path of a diving board inclined to the side. – And down below my rather flat skull rippled so as to look like a rarely combed sea. – The Other Sea was really somewhere, but we did not know where; this was why we concluded that it did not exist. . . At that moment, Mr H, raven-perched-on-the-tree recounted something like this to us:

"Fellow passengers,

"36 nights do not exist; in spite of this I have known

around a hundred of them and it is in the one hundredth, then called night-matter, that I vanished. It was the right one. . .

. . .THE SKULL-OF-NIGHT was a vase opened on a dark background but hermetically closed as far as the eyes were concerned. Some organs (such as a brain re-composed back to front) forming a passage, entered into a landscape from which the cats did not return, while the heart-of-temples beat in a way that resembled the applause of death – that was all I KNEW about it. . .

There was a moment of general consternation, in other words: the black was rather black, as has often been noted, and for a moment I believed that, under my nocturnal clothing, I was the night. . . I sought in the thickness of my terrestrial skull for the owl's eyes which would have served as cold blades for lightning flashes. I uncovered a bone from which I made my cane. . . After that, inside me, I proceeded silently for a period which should have corresponded with my days numbered by chance and whose number was not fixed. I passed an eternity there which I calculated with a watch which did not work very well; then I reached myself. But my appearance remained unknown to me. . .

Then, I opened my hands to discover that they were empty. . .

And in front of it, I told myself:

That this skull, seen close-up, was probably that of J.-P. Duprey. . .

That I will see three corpses come out of it into the shadow and which will embrace me. . .

That diamonds will not quench my thirst for air and for water. . .

That my life emanated within me to leave me here facing myself without being able to regain possession of myself. . .

That my veins had traced around me the waistband, definitively buckled, of a Woman who passes in each life with a sound of a torn dress. . .

That the Ruby-Bloodstone was not smelted within me. . .

And I heard:

". . .There is no longer sky, no longer sun, no longer night," said a voice, "no longer light and the windows resemble sewn-up mouths that are black, but toothless. There are no more friends and those who love you think you are leaving them; your soul – something that is only a supposition – will no longer comprise a body and no longer have a sky to drink; there will be no ground under your feet and the roof of your home will open like an empty hand or a bag with no fastening which loses its treasures that have no existence into the air."

Then the voice became a murmur and my mouth was rent asunder in four white lips to utter these words:

"In the absolute light, I recognised absolute darkness and the deepest silence was that of the heart which cried with the sound of a warm shower watering the sea. I sought a vase to enclose this heart, and the vase was a hollow flame. . .

"The water-of-the-wind will become white like the flitting of eyes visited by a sleep of snow. . .

"The Purple Flower will furnish its fire itself.

"Tears will thaw the face of crystal. . .

"Then, before that, I will close my mouth with a pocket handkerchief!"

And it is in a similar way that things happened, after the sea had been drowned and the earth buried and, the fire having been burned, the air vanished into the smoke of the new fire reborn from all these things.

. . .Then the day entered into earth as into a station; the Stations-of-the-Day and the Stations-of-the-Night became indistinguishable from one another in the sonorous fragments of a train in motion and the running of trains mimicked in its wheels the incoherent accent of a sentence repeated a hundred times by the squalls of wind and lit up in the fine linen of a fire, a sentence of which only one word (identified as being the most substantial) was retained: ETERNITY.

Between Parentheses

. . .And the gentleman of eternity, called the Eternal-Father and, equipped with a pair of incombustible antennae, now expresses the internal folds of his Eye to pull out one by one the imaginary members of his brain's family.

. . .One by one they will come out and the curtain of the Eye will fall as fast as a fall that has none of the conditions of time. . .

. . .The form the skull takes is that of a crab. – And only its shell mounted on rusty and broken axles is noticed. – But a circle of hair crowning the whole rather brings to mind a crown of white moss and this is why we can no longer have any doubt about the existence of a crab with a soap-bubble-head.

. . .The inside of the head can doubtless be compared, without risk of error, with the inside of a drum, although the cerebral resonance would not be particularly strong when a drumstick, thrown from the earth, seeks to create a sound, and the echo of reasonings of this cranial family sometimes leave much to be desired – they are not infallible. . .

The wind, burdened with wounds, caused the united heads of Doublestrome and the double of Mr H, to descend into its hole, in order to grasp the whirlwind with their soft hair. The elasticity of the earth did not cause the hollow sound of a cash box full of emptiness, but after its subterranean waters had been evacuated as far as the neck of the Great-Bottle-that-is-Blue, only by means of the pipe-shaft that is not enlarged but multiplied length of depth; thus the earth afterwards grew its daughters on its dry surface – a thousand and one joined to another thousand squared, if not cubed, and so on – its daughters, the carnivorous plants, in other words the legs of a gigantic spider it gave birth to, in the same way as the plants, which I call the unique-and-underground-spider-earth-in-the-stomach

. . .Inside, Mr H is called the colour of darkness taken to its full intensity; but the one who travelled into the skull of J.-P. Duprey bears the same name.

On the imaginary screen which is nothing more than the top of a decapitated general's cap – a screen cut out in a D shape – Mr. H, a sorcerer without sorcery, but also the celestial captain of the mystery-ship (it was possible to see him here navigating in the film without actors), was well-prepared to present to you some circus scenes in which he will be neither the knowing donkey nor the buffoon-acrobat. . .

First and Only Scene

First clown (with a pointed nose):

"Clowns in life, clowns in the night, overflowing with chalk on the blackboard. . . Nettle gloves and there is protection for tusk-like hands; elephant stature with stomach reinforced with scraps of paper; legs of twine unbuttoned down to the last knots for freedom of movement: this evening an actor will twist thunderclaps within the springs of his eyes, reddening until it was beyond his blood, and his image will newly rekindle old lamps in front of the bannister of his anguish, his laughter and his destruction, will say amen to the expectant crowd, subsisting in this way in the continuous and funereal dance step. . ."

Second clown (with a pointed hat):

"For clowns what is comical is the pike of anguish which gives its taste to the well-known farce. It is the wound which allows a pink tear to pass through the undergrowth of white flour with which Pipo's elegant partner, a motive-force actor, covers his face. . . That's the serious thing. . ."

Third clown (to Turlututu's tune):

"Serenity tells lies in the resting hand. Safety is maintained in a glass thread extended high and cutting the fastening of the isosceles trapeze. Clowns are the twins of forced laughter, of the laughter which is a wrinkle contracted between the lips of the Character-with-tears or the man of crystal. . . And now that people have laughed, this is what everything returns to. . . Let the three hammer blows cause the scenery to be burst asunder!. . ."

. . .And the fountain-pen with sea-water ink belonging to the Nameless gentleman, in other words Mr H., intercepted this passage cut from a conversation between male and female wolves:

"Have you seen my heart, Ghost, my heart reigning over the whistlings of the night and woken by the stars?"

"I've seen a heart under a red sky. . ."

"What is the sky?"

"It is the sea seen twice by raising its head and which sometimes weeps."

"My heart is an island. Where do islands come from?"

"They do not come. . ."

"And what do they say?"

"They speak of a sea with neither bank nor wrinkle at the bottom of which a sun inhabits two completely new eyes, two pilot-light-eyes of the morning. And I saw a heart explode, like the detonation of an eye, from the sun which is the mountain of fire and which rises down there (he points at what does not exist), in the knots of the veins of the person who was the author of the days and nights of Mr H. I was told his name: Lavella. He is red but I'll stick at that.

"As for you, you might be called Wolf, for black is your colour!"

"Lavella, I love you in myself. . . You are the second person of my verb. Exist in the present tense and I have designated you to be the burning space of my night. . . From you I have awaited the Thing. My heart has been beating so much in place of yours!"

"But soon, you see, I shall go back to sleep. . . The night will absorb me as though my body was suddenly found cut up from porous mouths that are soft and dark, awaiting the kiss that bears thirst. Nevertheless you will no longer be aware of me. . . And already my nails dig up a piece of coal which gives my hands their colour of dry ash. My wolf-head seeks ceaselessly for the place of the roots of my presence here. . ."

"And my eyes, my eyes, you know that they have been stolen from me! You know that they have drowned them! And no matter what I might do, my head has been taken along. And the bowl of spilled water has in this way restored three corpses of suicides to the earth, three drowned people, the two smallest of whom almost resembled beach pebbles considerably more soldered in place, symmetrical on either side of an overhanging ridge, at the bottom of the sockets of a rock face. . .

"There is one thing I can tell you: two eyes taken aside are equivalent to a fire which splits into two in order to consolidate unity. . . As for your body, to be able to understand it, it would be necessary to have seen it in the form of a cloth bag. . . But your hair resists weaving due to its scanty roots and still uncertain existence, and the cloth remains vacant. . ."

"Even so, I did have a shell!"

"And also the skin of your skull, but I scalped it!. . . And now the spaces contract and this soul of filth, which filled up the bottom, takes on all forms dreamed of by the flesh, thus satisfying the sinuosities of the void. . ."

And so on. . . and so on. . . As far as everything else is concerned, Mr H., whose journey inside-out either developed or did not develop, was able to communicate to us only the final scene of the last act, a scene then reduced to its lowest point which is a single word (without precedent in the said play) that one could see evoked on the screen decorated with two ears of two half-donkeys which are the sum-total of one; in the mouth (toothed according to the number and the forms of the letters of the alphabet) of the invented actors; and in the readers' eyes – the latter bearing a double question-mark, in an unknown style, where ordinarily the nose would be – And the Word of the play was inscribed in capital letters on the bolted door of gentleman H.'s apartments, and it is in this way that we read, in four letters devoid of any special significance, the word: END.

Letter-conclusion

. . .To be added to page minus one so the Voyage, ending at the beginning may start again indefinitely and veer in that way, like a wheel or a spiral, around the self having become everything: a sufficient and necessary condition for it to become ABSOLUTE. . .

Gentlemen:

I am in great difficulty, but this is nothing compared to what awaits us. . . That said, you can imagine the worst!. . .

The given (of time problematised) being given, I have slowed down, around my inside, the speed of the worlds that believed they were meteors; the sky that seemed to me to be a wide-open umbrella, but the rips and tears in it, without any special form, let it be guessed that nothing was there and the water of the sea, where I dissolved my inseparable person, was a slate placed on itself. (I will look carefully for a roof but this riddle will remain without possible answer. . .) The one who claimed to be the YEUR DE FOL then told me that he possessed, as his one eye, the colourless sex of the Great Admiral of the depths with a double meaning: as far as I am concerned, I know he was wrong or that he was blind, since the situation seemed to me confused. . .

I opened the sepulchre decorated as a nuptial chamber and saw:

A corpse imitating the radiance of the egg without a shell in its lunar whiteness – although the centre of the egg remained yoke despite everything. . .

A couple formed from a woman and the one she would have liked to be – The couple did not utter the word DEATH. . .

A ball of emptiness was tied to the ceiling by a thread and might have been the sun held as a prisoner. . .

A sea-storm and what followed after. . .

Mystery in embryonic form.

And the YEUR DE FOL told me: "To reach the point we are at, I have ascended the high mountain of the universe, but, when I came to the summit, I knew then that the tip of your heart was steered downwards. Still, you will tell your name, for we need to realise PERFECT CONSENSUS."

And perfect consensus was declared: hand to hand undoing. Or: fairy-like. Or better still: HAND TO HAND IS A FACT (and it is everything).

. . .Then, to express himself, the Y. de F. invented an unknown language and the situation seemed to me more and more perplexing. I shall refrain from defining it. . .

Postscript

a) The Yeur de Fol was a man of medium height wearing a monocle. His distinguishing feature was to have one leg short and the other so long that it seemed double. What's more he went about completely naked, but remained within the bounds of elementary decency in so far as his relation with nature was concerned. . .

b) The Sea-storm, seen in the nuptial chamber, was caused by the panting breath of the bridegroom losing a virgin-heart with a tear-water that drenched him. . .

c) The Voyage, which had started at the beginning of time, was completed well before the first hour of time, but I still continue. . .

d) And for those who would not have realised it, I shall recall that my name is Mr H., or No-one.

(February 1949)

*****

first published in Jean-Pierre Duprey *Derrière son double*
(1950) Paris: Soleil Noir

reprinted in his *Oeuvres complètes* Paris: Christian Bourgois

translated by Michael Richardson and Peter Wood

*****

JEAN-PIERRE DUPREY (Rouen, 1930 – Paris, 1959)
A sculptor, poet and dramatist particularly interested in the relationship between language and being (both in plastic and written form) at the edge of experience, Duprey killed himself soon after having been released from a mental institution, to which he had been confined after having been beaten up by the police for having pissed on the flame of the Unknown Soldier in an apparent unmotivated protest against the Algerian War.

HENDRIK CRAMER

The Moment

The only protection the widow had was a little bird, a poor sparrow with lifeless eyes, an invalid from the western wind: the last cry of her dead son lay upon it. The house in which she was not secure (as the mistress of the house is secure in her house) did not understand her and did not know her. This house was constructed with a hardened paste made from an alien powder brought in sacks, and it held itself up upright in an arid country between two ranges of hills. There was no cross nor any other sign to protect it in hours of risk. In the triangle of its space, the vulture appeared during the day, the worm during the night. This house was an eye consumed beneath the sky, an ear dried in the plain.

The things the widow did not have at hand (as the mistress of the house has things at hand) were adverse to her. Objects were made from the scum of metals and furniture from sick wood. A few carpets whose fabric had been eaten away by their own flowers and mirrors filled with the emptiness of days and nights.

The animals, a dog and a cat, which did not know her thoroughly, soured their saliva against her.

As she went for walks around the rooms – her life which did not live her and had not lived her – the widow placed her hand against her heart and said in a loud voice in order to be understood:

"I am not this throbbing, this throbbing is another."

The little bird, questioned later on, objected to the vanity of these words.

The plants in the garden – the aloes, the almond-tree, the rose-tree and the iris – were afraid of her. The flowers withered under her breath and the touch of her hands was leprous for the leaves. The plants whose growth is belief, whose breathing is hope, whose immobility is confidence and whose calyx is prayer, the plants which kept watch into the night, hated this woman with the secret force of stars.

On the anniversary of her son's death, the widow found an unpleasant weed – as tender as her child's skin – attached to a wall-flower. She tore it up and threw it on a stone so that the sun would consume it. But she regretted the action of her hands as though, through it, she had cast herself out for all Eternity.

She bent down to gather up the little plant. When she rose, she heard the voice of a dream which told her:

"I pity the wrinkles on your brow."

She took the plant inside the house and placed it in a pot with some moist earth, giving it a place where daylight could reach it.

And straightaway the plant started to grow.

The widow whose eyes were opened by the miracle saw how the stalks, the buds and the leaves were created in the image of a thought which thought itself and remained confined within itself, in such a way that nothing else could think it.

And seeing with the same eyes with which she had seen this, her own hands and the soaring of her hands, she said gratefully:

"I am these hands, yes, I am myself these hands."

Around her was the furniture, the animals, the plants, the house, the triangle of the space, and they listened to the woman who owned them.

Now her body also woke. A breath passed through her loins and her breasts and her lips and each of her senses interpreted this breath according to the grace of its passion: for sight it was the flame of a beloved face; for hearing it was the sweetness of a well-known voice; for taste and smell it was the saliva and the breath of a forever desired mouth; for touch it was the caress of what the days and years had announced.

Opening the window wide, the widow stood before the arid plain. She closed her eyes for a moment as if this sight had overwhelmed her. Then she spoke with an entreating voice, saying:

"Hard and wintry earth."

With a gesture of her hand she scattered a skin of fresh herbs sprinkled with daisies to the left and right over the naked back of the two hills. From the palm of her right hand, unfurled as far as the eye could see, an avenue of plane-trees; from the palm of her left hand, a filigree of paths and tracks, in the links of which burst forth, with the rapidity of a glance, flower-beds, rose-gardens, lawns, clusters of eucalyptus, magnolias, mimosas and cedars. When her right and left hands again joined, they created cradles; when they extended, ponds; and when they were raised, fountains. The space responded in a language of miracles to the loving hands which caressed it.

The widow allowed her calm eye to wander over the revived valley, as alluring and glorious as herself, under the depth of the sky's azure and there where her gaze came to rest guinea-fowl, doves and blackbirds stirred.

Then she opened the cage of the little blind bird, took it in her hand and said to it:

"See, how a ray of pure light has blessed us with the riches of countless years."

But a moment later she murmured: "I'm tired," and she lay down on the settee.

It was in that moment of somnolence that, as her eyes were closed, the plant betrayed the one who had gathered and cultivated it.

The widow was awakened by the sound of breaking glass. A storm of wind and rain overran the room. The windows gave way under the pressure of an enormous climbing plant whose mass of comose arms and spongy foliage had raised the roof. The widow tried to stand up, but her loins would no longer obey her and a weakness more unbearable than pain overwhelmed her body. She raised her hand with difficulty. She let out a cry. It was the dry and tanned hand of a very old woman that clasped the dried remains of a little bird.

*****

originally published in Hendrik Cramer, *Vizioen en Geboorte* Mastricht: A. A. M. Stols, Maastricht, 1940

*****

HENDRIK CRAMER (see volume one p 214)

FLORIANO MARTINS

Ashes Of The Sun

They talk to me about God or about History. I laugh at the thought of having to go to such lengths to find an explanation for the hunger devouring me, the hunger to live as the sun lives, in the grace of the air, eternally.

Gonzalo Rojas

For Lilia

(The title of this small book of stories was suggested to me by a passage in *Arcane 17* by André Breton. F.M.)

Alone with Lilia

The deeper I go into myself the more I realise that I am my own enemy. These are the most recent signs I have received: Georges' writings. All that laughter ripping through the grasses of my soul. The terror of being alone. Not even the shadow of a single tree in which to rest my solitude. Alone amongst my own shadows I feel crushed. I protect myself by refusing to know myself. However, Georges' words leave me stunned. They would like me to be satisfied with my own failure. To exhaust myself with being whilst simultaneously destroying myself. I'm afraid of this game that announces the coming of night like an infinite feeling of nausea. I am my own end. I fill myself up with pain.

Lazarus

I leave you, disorder installed inside your body. A single gesture evokes the decline of your existence. The times are gripped by torpor. My one hope is to kill you. I cross the streets, dodging bombs. The planet has a thousand ghettos that butcher it. It's absurd to say that I will rise again from the dust of your blood. We live in the hope that life will be different. Just a little more substance perhaps in the intrinsic frailty of the days. Such resignation frightens me. Between gunshots I get drunk. In secret, all knowledge becomes anxiety. I leave you: an arrow fired at random.

Angela's book

You lay your body on mine: fragments of the infinite. A glass of brandy while I re-read notes about our days together. I scribble something. Confronted by the silence, I feel cold. The challenge of creation reduces us to the inevitable. Our lives are full of tiny disasters. I am conscious of your death in every tremor of your body. Pleasure robs me of the key to new sufferings. I am your consecration. Your language that disappears with every word I write. The night too suppresses the simplicity of bodies seeking refuge in its ark. If you agree with me, there's an end to it.

Evocations of Antonio

Never cease asking questions. Interrogate the void. To what extent does the spirit retain in itself its essence? What other truth can man offer against God? Free from his arms I can order Fate according to my desire. The evidence is blinding. What is the purpose of such a position? The more provisional the lucidity the more it warns one against the vanity of existence. Ideals make reason inaccessible. Is recourse to order ingenuous? To duplicate meanings is to isolate the consciousness. Desire is carnal. Its source the overcoming of the senses. What challenge will cause it to renounce its gifts? Negation is the condition of being. I am an observer.

Gabriel laughing at himself

One by one I touched the errors of my suffering. The point of imbalance that I could not exalt. My limits lead me to ruin. I rush into a desert that wounds me. That requires of me defects beyond my own poor rigour. Everything enters me like a death that burns. Like David's fiery words. The blind force of elements subject to an eternal falling. Images of my suffering fragment silently before me. A laughable ecstasy. I am driven by visions of the horror that torments me. Nothing answers to the secret catastrophe of my days. Only the wild beatitude laying waste to me.

Diana's nightmares

The enormity of my fear made me touch your skin. Helpless amongst the ashes I could barely control the violent sequence of my actions. Your startled cry is like a wounded she-wolf in the pitch black. I will hurl your fear into the abyss of your pleasure. My tongue in your blood. The she-wolf recovering her hypnotic gaze. Two females abandoned to the fury of fate. The swooning drunkenness of our destinies. I bite your fingers. You help me to be alone, to forget who I am. Amidst much weeping, life continues in the wounds I inflict upon you. I try not to imagine anything. Until your cry floods me. A she-wolf circling in the night of my fear.

Sculptor

A constant human error: to believe in an end to one's fantasies. Our daydreams are the measure of our unreachable truth. The secret of all things lies in the emptiness of the formulae that guard them. Miguel used to sculpt stones. Extravagant blocks of granite carved out of his own vanity. One of God's small animals ate from his hand. When he felt himself to be in the grip of darkness he would reveal his clay heart. Danger was the weight of stones crashing down upon his hands. The stone divinities which his sacrifice exalted. Abandoned to the absolute, Miguel seemed almost imbecilic. There is a point at which all catastrophe is natural.

Charcoal sketches by Eduardo

I contemplate the mask of his actions. The inconceivable countenance on which his dead betray the traces of a fleeting artifice. Faces always talk too much. One line and all their plans are revealed. Madness plants mirrors in the desert. I find the means frightening. Our strategy of permanence in the uterus of chaos. Nothing terrifies me more than the poverty of our work on Earth. Undesirable, as are all occupations. We will never know the moral behind all these faces. We recognise with our whole body the places we have visited. All essence bleeds. Like the wounds of the absurd. We draw on the face the scars left by accidents. The death mask that demands of us an elementary beauty.

Letters from Adrian

I got your letters. We transform life from enchantment into delusion. The relative happiness of the world is pure impotence. I walk through the streets as if I were burning in some eternal bonfire. Your words echo in my spirit. You were beautiful and through you I breathed in the sweetness of the abyss. I remember how we used to love each other, quite without torment. The falling of bodies has meant we've spent our whole lives picking up the pieces. We wore ourselves out in this task. Death is limitless once the laughter stops. My body sees nothing. I live as if dragged along by memory. No answers. Like your letters.

David's agony

Tonight I rewrote the final pages. The hand of Hecate on the open book. The utter nakedness of the dark enraged me. A nakedness capable of killing a god. Around it the glorious architecture of the disasters that form the basis of all human existence. The bleeding soul of the world. Hecate's gaze points me to the abyss where I must live out my days. An avid void where passion and horror bring forth creatures laden with hatred. I re-read every page of her satisfied body. Her nakedness mingled playfulness and innocence. I had to shout out. With all the brilliance of an abyss reinventing itself: a single thread of blind light and the book, a vast compendium of the lies that are as essential to life as they are to love.

A flower in Lilia's hair

There comes a time when all that remains for us to do is to surrender to the idiosyncrasies of our nature. We love in a different way. Desire disguises itself as total abandon. It is possible to touch the face of the abyss. I tremble when I think of the ineffable tenderness of that moment. The light of a candle in the room. Death is the fall of a dream. I shout into the abyss that I am not who I am. His kisses leave me naked. He will never believe in me. He denies me as, in life, my children did. His passion for me is my ruin. Now all I want is to stroke the flower in my hair.

One of Erzsébet's maids

Her stone face aroused the lust of a goddess. I whispered her name amongst the tall grass and mixed the blood of other young girls in her cup. I am her most random occurrence. I love the madness of this strange woman who kills us one by one. In the bath, Amy hears her mistress say: these small creatures bleed from me like stars from a sky. The flesh opens itself like a smile. The fever of a woman who cannot contain herself. Amy furtive in the midst of Erzsébet's extreme cruelty. The proof is the wretchedness of all beings. I serve her the scarlet cup every morning before she takes her bath.

One last drink with Lilia

The body seduced by an intoxicating inertia. There is no way I can avoid thinking about the kind of world I belong to. The abuse of utopias disfigures everything. God is a book I can no longer read. Today all truth seems false to me. Someone sighing in the darkness. Lurking behind all pride a huge lizard with a voluptuous tongue. Something tells me that immortality is monstrous. The dialectic of every crime lies in the laughter directed at its victim. I dyed my hair throughout my latter years. I believed I could suppress death. My head resting against the sky is my final comment on the comedy of our lives. Only God would adore his own death.

*****

published as *Cinzas do Sol* (1991) Nova Friburgo: Mundo Manual Edições

Translated by Margaret Jull Costa

*****

FLORIANO MARTINS (Fortaleza, Ceará, 1957) is a poet, translator and essayist who has published several volumes of poetry and a study, *El corazón del infinito* (Toledo, 1992). He is a member of the Brazilian Surrealist Group.

MERET OPPENHEIM

Like Being Awake Sleeping And Hearing Seeing

Astor saw him hearing in his sleep. He watched him for some time with his eyes – so he could lie down even more swiftly in the wind beneath the rosebush, so swiftly in fact that he only saw his artificial ears coming towards him from the opposite direction some time later. He did not hold it against them though, and, after brief consideration, affixed them to his mother's last letter or to the gnarled trunk of the Rockefeller Building. When he raised his eyes he saw that a few windows had leant out of the house and were signalling to him. Although he knew that the hedgehog inside the house was growing ever fatter and that its bristles were beginning to scratch the dear child's skin, he had until now believed that it would recoil from hunting the windows into the desert and into the open jaws of Mount Etna. There – the first drops were already falling, and one window after the other shuffled off its mortal coil, leaving behind at least one ship's load of bird droppings. Astor covered himself with a transparent molehill and made his way unseen to the scene of the disaster.
Viravorabilis:[1] Lost in thought, Astor neared home. He lay down and soon fell asleep. When he awoke the following day, he was suspended from an unknown clothes' hanger. In his pocket he found a visiting card, on which his new name was printed: Caroline.

[1] Translator's note: "Viravorabilis" may be a play on the Latin words "vira" meaning "woman" and the verb "voro-", which means "to eat greedily".

*****

published in *Husch, husch, der schönste Vokal entleert sich*

translated by Victoria Appelbe

*****

MERET OPPENHEIM (Berlin, 1913 – Paris, 1985) Participated in surrealist activities from the early thirties and is especially noted for her witty and acerbic objects and paintings.

VĚRA LINHARTOVÁ

The Room

A persistent headache settled at the nape of her neck and, dividing into distinctly defined strips, assailed her temples. It worsened in the course of the night and abated towards morning. Otherwise Sophie felt almost nothing, except that it was becoming increasingly difficult to walk and talk, but since she had never gone out or spoken to people except when absolutely necessary, she paid this no heed. It was fatigue, an insistent, total fatigue, and nothing more. Sophie thought it would not matter unless there came a time when she wanted to be among people. It calmed her that she could, but such a wish never really entered her mind. She spent the days in bed or in a chair just a few steps away.

Her landlady came in, but only to bring meals or do the cleaning. She said nothing to Sophie, but disapproved of this way of living and pondered possible reasons for it. Being naturally talkative herself, she couldn't grasp why Sophie generally replied with just a smile, why she never spoke, and took it for airs and graces. So she came to Sophie's room as infrequently as possible, leaving as soon as she had finished her tasks. And because of this Sophie never dared ask for help, although she could now walk only with something to aid her, as she made her way around in circuitous and difficult tours of the room, hanging on to walls, furniture, the door, or the window frame, until her landlady, not believing her to really be ill and suspecting it be laziness, told her in no uncertain terms that on consideration it was her duty that if Sophie was really ill she would call a doctor, or, if it wasn't so serious, she would write to her parents to prevent anything foolish Sophie might have in mind.

Since Sophie thought there was no need to worry her family, and since her landlady insisted, she agreed to the doctor's visit. He examined her and said: "Get up!" Sophie would certainly have done so, but she could only sit up with difficulty. The doctor put his arm around her shoulders and helped her to stand. She couldn't walk. She was standing unsupported in the middle of the room and couldn't take a step.

Under the doctor's watchful eye, all the expression drained from her face and finally from her eyes, and the next thing she felt was a deepening sense of detachment until everything Sophie saw or heard seemed no longer to hit the surface but instead melted into unbearable emptiness. The doctor realised she would soon be beyond speech and, if he couldn't stop her, she would escape him; if he couldn't tear her from this state, he would never get through to her again. Taking her by the shoulders he shook her, and said: "Say something!" Sophie's eyes focused and fixed on him. "It's a kind of room," she said with difficulty, "and I'm completely alone, and it's otherwise quite empty; the walls are not flat but porous so you can walk through them, where you will. But I'm not going anywhere, I never even go near the walls, they're always at a distance; the ceiling's dark and the floor is pale, as though upside down. It's here, around this room, but isn't this one. . ."

If the doctor had wanted to speak he would have said: "You mustn't think you're a special case. There are many other patients like you, all believing they're different, lying in their rooms without moving. But to me they're all the same. As I do my rounds I can't tell one from another. And they all talk the same way. If they suffer the same distress, of course, they have to speak the same words." But he was tired and just said: "I don't know what's wrong. I doubt there is an effective remedy. I can just do what I can to ensure nothing more happens to you." Even so, his unspoken words remained behind after he had gone so that, without consciously knowing every word, they enlightened some as yet unformed part of Sophie's mind. All she could assimilate was what she already knew, and outside forces made no impression; they simply became tangible from out of darkness.

If she wanted to go to bed she still had to make the journey across the room; she felt the objects within reach with both hands, moved forward one step at a time. She didn't dare speculate how far she had gone, having to pause after every step and check how much the room changed when seen from a different point, and how the furniture and objects in the room moved. She learned it not just by sight, but by touch as well, and above all, learned the dimensions, the distance between objects, and how much those objects could be used to lean on during her journey. She wasn't sure of reaching her destination; she just knew she had to keep going.

Her bedroom was spacious, a square room with one small window, so high up that all she could see from it were the roofs of the houses opposite and a segment of sky. She could tell if it was day or night, what the weather was like, and the sounds she heard hinted at what was happening in the street, but she couldn't see people and the only movement was that of the clouds drifting by. The view from the window, with a few predictable changes, remained always the same. When the light was turned off and all was dark and quiet, the smallness of the window frightened her. Such a big room and just one tiny window, high up. In the daytime, while it was light, it didn't worry her, since the light penetrating from outside (which remained the same inside as outside) connected the room to the street. But inside the darkness was far greater; outside it was never as dark and the window was a rectangle of light in the wall of the room.

In the meantime she was falling asleep, still conscious of dozing, until sleep enveloped her. It had been a long journey and Sophie had to be on her way, but something still held her back, there was an errand she had to do for someone, or she had forgotten something absolutely essential; somehow she kept going, but she had already forgotten where she was going. In her dream, each of the people assembled around her looked like several others, whom she recognised, only they weren't gradually transformed from one into the other, but each of them seemed to be inside the others simultaneously and one of them shone through another. And something else was inside them as well, something unexplainable which wasn't within any of them, whose sum total they appeared to be, and this was what fascinated her above all.

She woke when some visitors, who occasionally visited the landlady, and were unaware even that Sophie was in her room, on the other side of that partition, rang the doorbell and she heard the landlady open the door followed by conversations and footsteps in the hall. The post was delivered too, but Sophie expected and received practically no letters, and even when an envelope in her name did arrive, the landlady brought it to Sophie in her room. The letter would lie on the table for a long time until the landlady insisted that Sophie open it:

Not having been given the reasons for your prolonged absence within the due period, we must inform you that you are suspended from further study at our faculty. The closing date for appeal is. . .

But another letter also arrived; just as with the first she made no reply.

Dear Sophie, wrote her mother, I think of you and worry a lot about you. All of us at home are so proud of you and hope with all our hearts that your studies enable you to achieve what was denied to us. That is why we save all we can, I don't wish to reproach you, it's just that you should remember it and not cause us unnecessary suffering. I know you often feel troubled, but someone who never worries has hardly begun to think about themselves. But at least try not to think so much about it that it stops you studying; think also of your obligations, just as I, your father, and everybody has to. Especially concentrate on finishing your studies, and if you ever think they're a waste of time, just consider what you would do instead. I can't sleep for thinking of you. You worry me so much. . .

The landlady insisted that she appeal against her expulsion and especially to tell her family, who were giving up so much for her, that she was ill and might not even complete her studies. Sophie tried to find an answer but had none to give, merely smiling to show at least that she had been listening. Losing patience, the landlady told her what she thought about it: that as it was she didn't believe in this pretend illness, which was just the result of laziness.

Sophie didn't have to walk because everything was done for her, so it was enough for her to sit and read, or even just sit and stare at nothing. Because her existence was so easy she could allow herself such an illness; forced to look after herself, she'd have soon recovered. Moreover, the landlady emphasised, even if it was nothing to do with her, she should at least consider her family. They were worrying themselves to death, and she wasn't even concerned because she was heartless. And the landlady practically burst into tears at the effort of moving such a stony heart.

Then she regretted have let herself get carried away, but Sophie's lack of interest in what she was saying was so plain it put her into a helpless rage. She complained to the doctor, giving him her opinion of Sophie's illness. The hardest thing to accept, she felt, was that according to the doctor Sophie was able to walk, something she could not reconcile with the doctor's diagnosis that she did not walk as she couldn't. But instead of admitting she didn't understand and doing her best to account for this double assertion, she just bolstered up her own view, and, rejecting any explanation she couldn't understand, cancelled them out by reference to the other one: 'she can either walk or she can't!' Her opinion was subject to careful consideration by the doctor, for whom a total picture was gradually forming, initially sketchy, but then becoming clearer.

He had been able to see from the start that there was no

physical reason for Sophie's illness, that there was nothing noxious that could be found and removed, but that it had a negative basis, responding to a lack of something, a vacuum. He knew she didn't walk because she didn't feel it was necessary. And she didn't have to leave the room because nothing awaited her outside which was not already inside; that to her the room was part of a whole, more precisely a small part of a larger part. What was contained within these four walls sufficed for her. And when walking becomes unnecessary, the ability to do it slips away. He compared his theory to the landlady's opinion and realised that, both actually said the same thing, only the landlady didn't believe in Sophie's illness while he strove to explain it scientifically. With a sad sense of envy, he realised Sophie was better off than either of them, for her illness was just a detail in an existence she lived without doubts or explanations.

There almost seemed no point in visiting; he could do nothing for her. Yet he recognised this as one of those cases which most interested him, in fact it was only these sorts of cases that really did interest him. At the same time such patients were precisely the ones who didn't need him, unlike all the others who came to him with their colds and minor injuries. And yet he never ceased to believe there would be a change in her condition, although he couldn't imagine what sort of improvement it might be.

In fact, Sophie's illness did not change. The symptoms remained what they had been to begin with; merely becoming more concentrated, intense and deep seated. Sophie had plenty of time to inspect the room. External sounds rose up to the top floor, and as indistinct as they were Sophie had an idea of what was happening outside. She knew what usually happened in the street; it followed the same course each day from morning till evening, and so without seeing the people, without mingling with them, their presence constantly invaded the room. Everything happening round about seeped into the room, reconstituting it in the same way as the light affected it, diffused in different positions, modified by the weather or the season. But it was always her room, there was always a guaranteed, if not immutable, arrangement of furnishings, and any changes, whether within or projected from outside, were tiny compared with what was enduring and familiar within, and with what remained.

The one visible movement inside was that of a stork, a glass toy based on an endless clash between an evaporating liquid and a little air: the substance ran down the throat's narrow tube and, when it reached parity, the bird always stopped moving for an instant, hesitated and then, at the last moment, rocked back one way or the other. It could hold Sophie – staring through it so she saw it only as an indistinct whole – enthralled for hours. She wasn't thinking of anything; her thoughts became mixed up, sometimes covering themselves up or fusing together. Some reached her consciousness, others put on a shell and passed through her. It was pure thought, with no sound and just thoughts, a whirling stream which turned and drifted as one current. But Sophie couldn't grasp any of them but had to let them flow past her, because whenever she tried, the only thing left would be fragments and splinters from which it was impossible to recreate the original picture. So keen was she to hear them that she didn't dare to think about anything in general, not even about herself or the things around her. There she lay lost in herself listening.

In the morning when the landlady came in, she had every reason to burst into tears and say: "Miss Sophie's gone crazy!" The doctor could see it was not so serious and nothing had really changed except for having become worse and having crossed a threshold. But even he, although he must have had a far better idea of Sophie's actual condition than the landlady and tried to explain it to her, finally had to agree, simply because they were both, as he ruefully thought, sensible people.

One evening just before falling asleep Sophie imagined rather than dreamed that the squares on the wall were moving. Someone else had rented the room before her and where her bed now was there had been a child's cot above which, at about head height, had been painted on the grey wall several large squares of various sizes. It appeared as though someone had thrown some building blocks against it, which had remained and then been absorbed by the wall. She always knew no one would believe this, but she never thought of trying to convince anyone of it. First, because she was afraid they would misunderstand her and so spoil her enjoyment, and also because she really didn't like to tell people, to reveal to them something she thought of as her very own, besides which she couldn't be sure that wouldn't disturb everything.

The darkness helped the wall and other things to grow, getting rid of the cramped space between door and window, and between floor and ceiling, which belonged to her during the day and spread itself around in a dense grey fog. Sophie groped around in it and lost her way; she could find no recognisable point to help her. The squares became blocks and bumped into one other in the fog. She could not decide whether they were all alike or if they were of different sizes. She could see that some were larger and some smaller on the face of the wall, but she now knew they were spaced apart – it was apparent before but she hadn't noticed it – but, however, against the effect of the surrounding grey, the distances grew ever larger. They moved slowly; if she watched one of them, the movement was nearly imperceptible, she couldn't make it out on its own until it neared another block. Then they came together, not with a loud, violent bump – Sophie had unnecessarily put her hands over her ears so as not to hear it – the blocks drew near to each other, held together for a moment, although the impact made no noise, and then bounced apart and, without losing speed, continued on their way, only changing their direction.

Some of them gave out a cold light, the mist around them shone, but the brighter they were the less Sophie could make out about their surfaces. Of those which were completely dark she could see only the surfaces, and even if sometimes after a silent collision they disintegrated, they always broke into smaller blocks, and it was still only the surface which appeared, although now it was the inner surface.

Sometimes a kind of shadow came through the fog. It was the shadow of something outside and Sophie thought about it constantly, sure she had to discover whatever cast that shadow, and where it came from. But not only did her memory fail her, the shadow often appeared quite unexpectedly, whenever she felt great distress, like a reminder of some uncompleted duty. Equally she noticed that it never fell over the blocks, because their paths never met it. All the same, when it did happen, as it occasionally had, that the one reached the other, then the block began to break up, not into increasingly smaller blocks, but into quite uneven pieces which then flew off into the fog, where the sound of them crashing into each other was all that could be heard. However, provided they avoided the shadow, the blocks could move in absolutely any direction.

For Sophie the six square sides of her room marked the boundary she could not go beyond. She thought at first that it would be easier to understand those dark unlit blocks whose edges were more clearly defined etched against the fog, because, as she thought, the light shining on them, which made them appear like spheres, would not interfere. But the more clearly she saw the surfaces, and the greater the detail (she even noticed different planes on some), the less she understood what lay behind them, and they became ever stranger to her, more complex bodies, never distinguished from the rest of the fog. In contrast, the blocks from which light shone were the most distinct. Their surfaces disappeared in the light, so that whatever was inside shone out, and that wasn't all: the brighter the light was, the more they merged with the fog, penetrating into it so that one could no longer make out where they began and ended, being nothing but light blazing up within the fog that surrounded it. Sophie herself knew, once she had studied them long enough, that she could walk among these – while the dark ones only hurt her with their sharp edges when they struck her – and so she could enter the light and dissolve into the fog.

But this didn't last long, for the shadow was coming closer once more and Sophie could not avoid it because she didn't know which way to go. As soon as it was all around her, she stood alone in the fog once more, and the blocks too, which she could now see, were moving about by themselves, each on its own course, but so sturdy that they could resist the shadow. She now remembered that somewhere outside the fog were things she was aware of but whose dimensions were a mystery to her; she couldn't explain them and they seemed pointless. And these things cast their shadows into the fog which at any moment might cover her again. Then it occurred to her that she could play with the blocks, that it was enough to see them and to want them to move faster or slower, in one or another direction, and this utterly distracted her.

If somebody had looked into the room, they would not have been sure if Sophie was lying in bed or not. But they might have supposed that, probably after a bad dream, she might have pulled the blanket over her head to ward off the phantoms of the dark which scared her. The street lamp, buffeted by the wind, cast a moving shadow – of a small white wickerwork chair – on the wall above the bed. "But who would claim that by discovering the reason for a sign, it ceases to be a sign?"

*****

published in *Povídky o čemkoliv* Prague: 1964

translated by Krzysztof Fijalkowski and Eva Gabriel

*****

VĚRA LINHARTOVÁ (Brno, 1938) Close to the Czech Surrealist Group during the 1960's. A writer and art historian, she has published *Dada et Surréalisme au Japon* (1986).

ROBERT LEBEL

The Treasure

A man a few steps ahead of me stopped suddenly. I was about to bump into him when he spoke sharply:

"Look," he whispered, pointing at the ground.

"I can't see anything," I replied as I leaned forward.

"Ah, you don't see anything," he exclaimed in a low voice laden with reproach. "Then look closer, my friend, and closer still. I assure you it's worth it."

I had enough curiosity to lean over further, but as I still could see nothing, I was determined to cut short such a futile conversation. The man gripped me firmly by the arm.

"Go on, look," he insisted, exasperated by my indifference. "What I am showing you is unique and you devote no more than a distracted glance at it. What apathy! Does the unexpected not interest you? At your age, are you already so blase about all the extraordinary surprises that existence saves up for us? Even though I am much older than you, I seek them constantly, you know, these surprises, and my attention never wavers, I am ceaselessly on the hunt for anything out of the ordinary. I watch out for the least strangeness, the tiniest anomaly, and each time I am awestruck, but a phenomenon like this – so stupefying and exceptional – my only wish would be to be fortunate enough to witness it one day."

"What phenomenon?" I asked, starting to think that I had got involved with a drunkard or a madman.

Such a simple question calmed him and he started to lecture me in an almost paternal way.

"Do you see on the pavement," he said, assuming a patient air. "Do you see this bit of asphalt at my feet, whose total surface is about a square yard and shaded a little darker than the rest?"

"Yes," I had to admit.

"Good. That's a start. For the moment concentrate on this fragment of asphalt which seems isolated in the middle of the pavement. Examine it fixedly and unremittingly with all the concentration you can muster. Do you begin to make out the folds, the wrinkles and the striations where first it had appeared, I presume, to be completely smooth?"

"Yes," I again had to admit.

"Good. We're getting somewhere. It by such prudent methods, born from establishing links between apparently innocuous perceptions, that true scientific deductions are made. For hours, days, months and years, observation seems to mark time but it no less marches on. It needs to be tireless but also collective. On his own a researcher may delude himself. Lacking a group of people, we are at least two. That is why I insist on your testimony since chance had it that you came along at the same time as I did. I can't let you leave without asking you to compare your observations with mine. My mental equilibrium depends on it. Your confirmation is indispensable to me, do you understand?"

"Yes," I again had to confess.

"Good. You seem less reticent now. Kindly try again, even if it is difficult for you. Don't take your eyes off this bit of asphalt and tell me if, in the course of time, you don't perceive a sort of undulation spreading across it."

"Yes," I affirmed, this time somewhat captivated.

"Good. Then be kind enough to describe what you see very exactly. Be especially careful not to go to the opposite extreme. Don't exaggerate anything. Express yourself, I entreat you, with meticulous precision and with the sobriety of words of the scientist facing his test-tube. Be conscious of the fact that one error of interpretation will be enough to distort everything."

What I saw on the asphalt was barely discernible yet was

present to the eye. It reminded me of a very thin sheet of water running over sand. The surface seemed to tremble with a light bubbling rather than being shaken by it. Some fine grooves appeared and developed their tracery with extreme torpor. The movement this established remained, in any case, infinitesimal.

My companion appeared satisfied with my report. "What is essential," he said, "is that you recognise that a process of disintegration is taking place. Be it only in the preliminary state, it is undeniable and is fortunate for us. Since we have been the first to recognise it, we alone will be the beneficiaries of it."

"How so?" I asked, more and more amazed. I still did not understand how this phenomenon concerned us to such an extent.

"Listen carefully," he explained after having mastered the annoyance my naivety aroused in him. "If this fragment of the pavement differs in colour and appearance from the surrounding asphalt, if it is clearly separated from it by an outline, it is because it was not originally part of it. It was added later, like an enclave or a foreign body whose integration to the whole was organically impossible. It that clear?"

"Yes," I took up the thread. "And that explains why this added fragment is cracking. Technically, this may be of interest, but what is so extraordinary about it? Streets are constantly being dug up, for all sorts of restoration works, with holes which must obviously be filled in later."

"Believe me," interrupted the man with a restrained passion, "this repair has certainly not been made by professionals. That is what immediately caught my eye. It is something that does not deceive an eye like mine since I have wide experience of public works. The actual condition of this stretch of asphalt denotes a gross error of calculation and it has been applied in a very unskilful way. Consequently those who put it here have probably done so clandestinely in order to hide something. It is clear that the process was done on two different occasions. They first dug up the pavement with pickaxes, traces of which remain here. Then the new bed of asphalt did not completely cover the hole since, here and there, the lips of the crack remain apparent. This is a crude job done by amateurs."

I had to agree and he continued: "But to be fair, as hasty and awkward as it was, this work can not entirely be the reason for the imminent subsidence. There is another element at work and, in my opinion, emanations coming from the sub-soil impregnated the poorly mixed, and thus porous, tar which is starting to melt."

"Whatever caused it to start would therefore be normal," I ventured. "Perhaps we are the spectators of a miniature earthquake."

"Normal?" he cried. We're hardly standing on volcanic terrain. Have you no idea about geology to imagine that a seismic shaking could raise the pavement? If that was the case, everything would be completely topsy-turvy instead of being circumscribed within these narrow limits. The emanations I have referred to do not issue from an erupting underground water-table, but from the after-effects of explosives which they must have used to excavate a hiding place."

"What do you mean to imply?" I finally asked. "Are you claiming that a treasure is buried beneath this piece of asphalt?"

"I don't claim it, I am sure of it," he replied calmly. "Do you not know that all buried treasures were, without exception, discovered in identical circumstances when the earthwork that concealed them was disturbed or collapsed of itself, or when its heterogeneity was observed by seekers who were a little shrewder than others?"

There was no reply to that. "Then what do you intend to do?" I enquired.

"Wait, and I strongly advise you to wait with me."

"For how long?"

"For as long as it takes."

"Without moving?"

"Quite. Don't expect to go home for meals or sleep.

The process that has been set in motion will not obey an official timetable. Everything may unfold in a few moments, in a fortnight, or in three months, but we will certainly not get any warning about it in advance."

"Won't there be premonitory signs, like a progressive enlargement of the faults?"

"Not necessarily. One unforeseeable factor might suddenly provoke, by retraction of matter, a sudden yawning gap."

Looking at the pavement, I saw him succumb to the same minimal thrill, the same slight stiffening, without anything in his appearance having altered. We had been there for over an hour.

"Why not get a pickaxe and dig it up?" I suggested. "We'd soon get to the truth of it."

He shrugged his shoulders: "You would also be behaving like an amateur. What you propose would not only be useless but also harmful. The reason is that a mechanical alteration, intervening in a continuous organic process, would probably be equivalent to putting an end to it and we would be at the mercy of a disastrous reaction which we would not be able to arrest. What's more, it would be unworthy. When one has the good fortune to assist in a spontaneous phenomenon of this sort, one has no right to fall back on the methods of a wretched handyman. Let's be equal to the situation. For me this is a matter of honour."

I couldn't have given the impression of sharing his scruples since he added: "From the practical point of view, your solution is otherwise worthless. To even admit we could obtain a pickaxe and dig up the asphalt, which is no easy matter, would risk attracting the attention of the neighbourhood and of the police. We are on a public road, don't forget. Besides, the removal of the asphalt, brought into violent contact with long contained emanations, could cause a catastrophic explosion. The object of our investigation would be annihilated, and we would risk losing our lives."

"I have a principle," he continued as he noticed my disappointment. "I never abandon a scent before knowing where it may lead me. I have to follow my instincts no matter what the cost. I am going to settle down in one of the thickets in the waste ground at the side of the road as, once settled, I don't want passers-by to suspect me and spy on me. If you stay with me, everything would be straightforward. We could take turns going for the things we need. One of us would take a rest while the other watched and our surveillance would be uninterrupted. I can't imagine a more splendid adventure. Stay!" he beseeched me almost piteously.

"I'm sorry," I said, "but I really have to go. I have an urgent appointment, for which I am very late. But if you like, I'll come by later to see how you're getting on."

"If you leave, I forbid you to return," he shouted out ardently. "I warn you that any absence, however brief, would mean you lose all the rights I was ready to concede to you in this discovery."

I felt no desire to stay. He realised it and, preferring to get rid of me unequivocally, declared, as he turned his back on me: "Since you are incapable of exposing yourself to the slightest risk of discomfort, since the course of your banal everyday routine is so much more important to you than a miracle, I prefer to say goodbye." And he made for the embankment.

"I'll bring you some food," I shouted to exonerate myself.

"No," he proclaimed without raising his eyes. "Go away. We do not speak the same language. I will no longer accept anything from you."

Incredibly, I was suddenly ashamed of leaving him, but at the moment I was about to rejoin him, he shook his fist, beside himself with anger: "You want the treasure?" he stormed. "Well, then, here it is, scoundrel." He then picked up a large stone and threw it at me with all his strength. It hit me on the leg and I hobbled away as fast as I could.

*****

*****

ROBERT LEBEL (Paris, 1904 – Paris, 1984) participated in surrealist activities from the forties. Critic and storyteller, his book on Marcel Duchamp is particularly notable.

ROGER CAILLOIS

A Mannequin On The Pavement

to Aléna, who was first to notice the mannequin

On the pavement, dominating the second-hand dealer's display, a mannequin stood out from afar because of its vivid colouring. Someone, whether playfully or through indolence, in the hope of gaining a little money or to dispel a gloomy mood or express a barely defined feeling, had used its surface to paint an all but empty landscape which would have been entirely sky had a tall isolated house not been placed right in the foreground.

Wearied by such curiosities in an age in which such things were all the rage, passers-by barely paid attention to the strange object. Nonetheless, it caught the eye immediately with a persuasive charm that from the start distinguished it from the usual booby traps.

I bore the object away. It was not a complete mannequin with an articulated head, arms and legs, such as might be seen in a window display, but one of those work tools that, reduced to a trunk, once served not only couturiers but also servant-girls who might make their own dresses. They could be adjusted to the correct height with a sliding foot. The decapitated neck terminated in a piece of turned wood, sometimes of cast-bronze, resembling an enormous chesspiece. Circular bosses, also of turned wood, replaced the absent arms at the shoulder.

The idea came to me to try and analyse the fascination exerted by this banal object now given a novel function. The painting, strangely and as if to create an initial uncertainty, does not occupy the whole useable surface of the mannequin. Blue paint outlines a low-cut bodice, which corresponds closely to the form rather than floating somewhat as it would have done had it been real. The neckline descends down to the hollow of the breast. Its tip is ornamented with a red pendant having the form of a pear or a tear, as baroque pearls frequently do. A white highlight illuminates it. A second *trompe-l'oeil* is congruent with the first: the dress takes the form of a radiant azure sky. The few almost transparent cotton-wool clouds are peaceably dispersed. The house is a suburban coffee bar, but set adrift in open countryside, in uncultivated land in which scattered puddles of water reflect a beautiful sky. Just one storey. Two well-appointed dormer-windows in a zinc roof. One of them is closed, the other open (as are the corresponding windows of the single storey, one of which is closed, the other half-open) in such a way that half the house seems condemned. On the ground floor, to the right, a tall and narrow brown door doubtless gives access to a stairwell, since there is barely space enough for a room. The cafe itself occupies, in fact, almost the whole frontage.

This time the doorway, narrow and almost as tall as the other one, is more than open: it is entirely absent. A black hole, as if the door panel had been removed or never put in place. In several places the plaster has fallen away. The whole establishment, upon which a mysterious menace indubitably weighs, is abandoned. The inhabitants have left without claiming what was due to them, and not so long since, as a box of nasturtium in blossom at the base of the left-hand window bears witness. They will not return. The building is gloomy and rather ghostly. It is painted on the right side of the mannequin's breast. The landscape runs uninterruptedly around the base of the image. It is continuous and infinite. Anyone can go all round it or make it turn in front of them without ever finding the end. The cyclical repetition of the dwelling adds to the impression of nightmare.

At long intervals, no less sinister, a large solitary leaf the size of a tree stands erect on its stem. At least to itself it is a tree. It veins make up its branches. This inconceivable vegetation constitutes the one fantastic element in the painting. At least, the only one immediately apparent. For if the whole thing is bathed in a radiant light, this radiance has no source. What is more, neither the house nor the leaf-tree cast a shadow. The thin black smudge beneath neither merits such a designation nor suggests it. We know it is the same for the light in dreams. Perhaps it is fitting to take literally the cafe sign, whose yellow capital letters catch the eye:

DREAM CAFE

The mannequin's curves modify the shapes of things. Also they serve to give lustre to a colour: a cloud on the slightly swollen left breast reflects a clarity which enunciates it more than its unobtrusive relief. The side wall of the house vanishes around the waist and merges with the nascent pelvis, but it only deceives our vision from one angle: the eye immediately corrects the anamorphosis. In the same way, if we observe the canvas torso from the side, the rise of the throat brushes against the roof. A slight rotation is nevertheless sufficient to reconstitute its normal inclination.

On the whole, it is nothing but an ordinary and stable structure on a disorienting and bounded expanse. I will now return to the blouse painted on the mannequin: by necessity it coincides with it so conspicuously that one thinks of it less as a piece of clothing than as an extended tattoo, most especially those Japanese tattoos called *irezumi* which cover almost the entire body of those unstable and scorned (frequently criminal) individuals, the *Yakuza*. The pride they take in them is proportional to the surface treated, for it is thought to measure the extent of their resistance to pain. The pattern wrought by the agonizing needles stops at the nape of the neck, the elbow and the knees. It has the appearance of a sometimes open tunic or a skin-tight polychrome garment, illustrated with dragons and peonies, with goddesses and leaves, with pellicular human bodies superimposed on that of the subject.

I have seen nothing comparable in Western art apart

from the inexplicable, but in other respects quite different, *Salomé tattooed* by Gustave Moreau. In this connexion I wonder, if only in passing, whether the indelible ornamentation that man inscribes upon his own epidermis does not respond to a nostalgia for the universal internally generated colouring of corollas, furs, shells, carapaces and wings. For man it has been necessary to create both works and tools outside of himself. But it may be that he retains an obscure nostalgia to create them on his own body, to make them a part of it, rather than projecting them outwards onto an independent surface, where he is free to retouch them as he sees fit, which is precisely what painting and art are.

I would like to underline one difference from the example that concerns me. The *irezumi* tattoo encloses its wearer in a totalising painting that isolates and circumscribes him, whereas the imitation landscape dissolves the mannequin, effacing it in a panorama where boundaries disappear, where the gaze is drawn, duped by an illusion of vastness.

In this way, the body which remains present behind the mirage, the corset which starts to conceal it but immediately fans out into a limitless horizon, introduces and sustains a back-and-forth shuttling movement, an incessant coming and going between three concurrent and continuous levels, of which each, ultimately, is as insidious and fanciful as the others. However all three contribute to a similar potent and perhaps fertile misunderstanding.

I am starting to understand why such a mannequin, contoured as required by the age of corsets and waspwaisters, was necessary and how it participates in the intentions of the work, rendering them palpable or even creating them through the effect of a kind of retroactive magic. Fashion then imposed constraints which prevented any form from developing. It constrained the chest, imprisoned the hips, and accentuated the variations of angle. The elongation of the body took on the appearance of a spindle and an utilitarian frame which reflected this canon again underlined an obsession with the vertical, since its only aim was to offer the professional or amateur worker a convenient support so the garment would hang well. The mannequin thus depicted a torso that seemed flattened and slippery, neither bony nor plump, almost asexual, as no woman could ever be, but which at the same time is a model of a quintessential femininity, freed from maternity and nurturing, a supple and evasive body, with sea-lion shoulders and weasel loins. The abstract effigy merely consists of impersonal curves devoid of function; it omits the face and ends just above the organs of pleasure and fecundation. Modest and available, neither statue nor doll, seemingly destined for neither splendour nor shop window displays, a simple instrument for a menial who perhaps experiences shame and who, having tacked the hem and adjusted the lines, hastens to return it to its cubby hole. This incomplete and simplified figure might simply fade from consciousness without being completely forgotten and serve as a springboard – not at all neutral but active – that is complicitous in a complementary vertigo.

To sum up. The mannequin: a truncated appearance, deprived of attributes essential to seduction and generation; the landscape: a shadowless infertile expanse with trees of a single sham leaf, of painted sheet metal, and finally the forsaken cafe with cracked walls and, right at the top, in the cleavage of the corsage, speckled flesh, marked with irregular brown and greenish stains, the colour of pus, whose confused touches go from the blurry to the washed-out: everything here confirms a feeling of deceived hopes or false joy. What can be more desolate than the vast summer horizon adorned with a wayward cafe located amidst the spreading of compost and bogs, and whose worn-out masonry, beyond an initial delusion, took the place of a scaly and gangrenous skin which attested to a similar senility?

In the space left uncovered by an illusory blouse where the sky and all of space stretches out, the likeness of the epidermis and the wall reminds us that the epithet 'leprous' is perhaps the only one that can be readily applied to both living tissue and the surface constructed to signify its shared and rapid decay.

The artist, who for the moment I am inclined to consider more perceptive than ingenuous, has been careful to inscribe above the hovel's entrance – and it is the only stable indication he has provided – a reference devoting it to the dream. Did he mean to hint that the illusion brings even greater and more precipitate disappointment than sordid reality?

This brings to mind the tapestry, famous above all others, on which, on the fronton of a pavilion of brocade, flanked by heraldic animals, a lord's splendid motto is inscribed: 'To my one and only desire'. At its most modest, the rapid sketch of the suburb belies the presumptuous affirmation. The dream clouds drift by, unravelling above the sterile earth and the deserted cafe. The pavilion woven with silver and gold might not claim a different destiny.

I still remember the samurai in *Trophées*. He declined to blink in the face of the sun and, in order not to lose face and seem to abdicate before the blinding star, he spread out in front of his eyes, not a lash of which flickered the whole time,

> '. . .his iron fan
> on whose white satin a red sun rises'

I still see the ornamental – or battle – helmet of a barbarian prince, the pride of the Damas Museum. The silver visor reproduces its owner's expression and features. As he lowered it, his vulnerable face was given the protection of an immortal mask.

I suspect that art has often made use of such ruses, I mean to deny those rebuffs and terrors not within man's power to overcome by his own strength and to do so he must have recourse to the subterfuges he draws from his ingenuity. They are his revenge over the ineluctable. It is not displeasing to me that a pavement artist should spontaneously have given new meaning to such a fundamental step.

Neither the tool covered with images nor the tinkerer who takes pleasure in giving it a new purpose, are separable from a civilisation of dubious conquests and from a turbulent phase in the history of art. Indeed, it is, first and foremost, a matter of the felicitous encounter of an abnormally sophisticated outline of the female body, of a structure of artisanal use made from some sort of esparto pressed and glued together, with an ancillary inspiration in its bias towards aesthetic fancy, trivial or knowing, suspended in the ambience of the times. It is not difficult to identify them: they range from the painted pebbles habitually sold as souvenirs in gift shops at the beach to many of the concerns of contemporary art.

The absence of shadows, the corsage which is the sky, the leaves that for themselves are trees, all serve to evoke Magritte's clever and monotonous ambiguities. The use of *this type* of mannequin as the frame for a painting also evokes the identical ones sometimes haunting de Chirico's canvases, notwithstanding that the meaning of the illusion here is inverted. At the same time it adds the couturier's accessory to the list of everyday objects to which a Marcel Duchamp assigned, as they are or slightly modified, an unexpected, if not usurped, future. In this particular case, one must admit that the conjunction possesses a singular efficacy. The superficial or puerile boldness from which it proceeds attracted the attention by its power to challenge. Today such powers no longer astonish anyone, for few surprises are lasting. What's more, they are violent and brief, without prolongation or complications.

The mannequin, given its nature as a naked mannequin, and by the metaphors added to it that go counter to or multiply its already significant message, offers in response a series of failures, correspondences and reflections, which tie together the entangled relations. Reverie gets lost there but is then unfailingly brought back to its pivot, not only by the multiple interferences of the image, but also by the key phrase that can be read in the centre of the composition. Such happy results are very much contingent. Doubtless they rely on chance more than on expertise or genius. Calculated intent, which would consequently be too cerebral and so run the risk of becoming distanced from a certain necessary simplicity, has less of a role here than obscurely registered impressions that have ripened in the shadowy depths of the heart. They surge forth at last, disturbing in that they illustrate the initially enigmatic aspect, which holds back and soon excites, since it visibly portrays a theme rich in resources and because it has been able to derive from it a clarity with many implications: I recently recognised the same thing in *The Menials of Jumièges*, a work which, once examined, possesses it to a high degree. A similar original fascination, distinct from its strictly pictorial qualities, which never coincides with them, even though it often gives them the benefit of its particular seduction, in the same way that, inversely, plastic qualities add a supplementary attraction to the enchantment it provokes.

The two categories are not in competition: they frequently co-exist, as numerous paintings demonstrate. But one of the sides leads to the work of art properly speaking, where the subject counts less than plastic perfection, while the other ends in the image which addresses itself, as its name indicates, primarily to the imagination, and for which only a modicum of skill is required. These two postulates of painting alternate according to different schools and could serve to define their ambitions.

Both means are equally opposed to the *free beauty* about which Kant speaks in the *Critique of Judgement* and which defines works of nature, crystals or flowers or the human body. It goes without saying that this anterior beauty is destined neither to satisfy the taste nor move man's heart or memory. Yet men recognise it in the fact that each of the models it proposes contains no element which could not simultaneously be the cause and effect of its own form as well as the totality of which it is a part and which today's science would doubtless call teleonomic.

I will now return to the illustrated mannequin that has been the source of my reflections. I allowed it through its specular games to reveal to me that, if we are formed from the fragile material of our daydreams, the converse is still more certain, even if its obviousness sometimes causes it to be forgotten. Dreams are deformed reflections of ourselves – less stable and more ungraspable than we are, upon which we in our turn assume the right to reflect upon and to determine. And in this way we are led to the dream through the limbo of a light with no source to a cafe in a state of dereliction, that no one looks at and that perhaps no one can see. At the same time I experience pleasure in the phantom landscape, in the doubly deserted effigy, that confirms my idea that the art of painting, that of representing (without considering a third and more ancient approach), a source of forms which seduce and astonish, partakes in the universe of appearances (without coinciding with it and in incompatible ways) and is liable to resound in a sensibility vaster than the pure harmony of colours and proportions, and it is precisely here that dreams stir, obsessions take wing and analogies are connected, so that finally this mythical element surges forth. This is never absent from assured works. Those that sow the seeds of the imagination.

*****

published in *La Lumière des songes* Paris: Fata Morgana

translated by Paul Hammond and Michael Richardson

*****

ROGER CAILLOIS (see volume one p 219)

GHERASIM LUCA

I Love You

A few lovingly assorted objects such as the button from a bodice or a doorbell, a spider's web between the teeth of a comb, a bar of soap next to something unknown or to a ring, and the mythology of the orgy continues towards the sensually modern meaning of fetishes, of things which excite and kill each other for other things, and since it is known how water loves drowning itself in flames, or the voice converses with its own echo and that living as an effigy as steel knows how to or swooning like plants is really just a way of living, I enter a mist of frozen gestures, breathe in the scented fog that two entwined objects give off, listen to the passionate cries of the atoms and for no other reason than to see the spurt of their blood I sink my teeth into a piece of wood, stone or cloth, just a handkerchief myself amongst these fleshy objects whose bosom seems ample enough for me to risk hiding my face in it, to stifle a sob that is more allusion than reality, more impersonal and idealised, before continuing my dead-end path through these objects in a state of full erection, of full certainty, and while my ever more uncertain blood runs drop by drop along the length of an unbearable knife their own gushes out but flows back in again with the rhythm of the spasms, of the laughter and the sensual pleasure, blood upon blood just as after violation comes the violet, like the sacred in the massacred where the chair takes the carnation's tongue between its teeth, pulls it down with it as it falls and they tumble together on a living carpet from which rises a steam of ecstasy and insanity, where the comb strokes the cheeks of a mirror which reflects not man, the deceiver, but the object, the unhoped-for, objects tousled, stripped, delivered, carnivorous, magical, women with limitless sexes, secrets which their own veils unveil, cold glassy desires, thunderbolts, the mask of a virtual avalanche whose snow is none other than the void, automaton mask, automaton chair, automaton flower all in an automaton room giving off an automaton smell, Hero of Alexandria, Bacon, Van Helmont and all the makers of automata I think of when I look at an object and see it in a mirror that watches me, in seeking out a door, a wardrobe, a wax doll, I automatically make them automata, operated by sublime shadowy golems, desire, always ready, and pleasure, always surprising, are in them at the same time, touching a fork unleashes a tangle of possibilities, a factory of questions, impulses and spectres is set in motion at once, and if I fix it with my all-seeing metal eye it is entranced, fascinated, as for the fork it crosses the room, sleepwalking, pushing doorbells as it goes, and with its long rhinoceros fangs it kisses me passionately on the mouth into which, after a moment, it pushes itself, the fork, the moon, a glass of water and anything else are just the marbles which play with a child before choking it, objects meet, stare each other out, breathe each other in and, with a bayonet and a swallow in their heart, part again, turn the corner of the first street on the right and next left where, in the blackness, the glass from a lamp coaxes a wrinkle out of an antelope hide or throws itself naked into the foliage, and if instead of watering it like a garden I sit it on my lap next to the thunderbolts everything leaps up, and the automata cross in front of me, brush past me, pass through me, I rub against them with both sides of my skin, I hide behind the door so that the table has to search for me, and under the table so that the penknife forgets me, taking part in this gentle game between no and no are the forest, the elements, the four birds of prey the fiercest of which is solitude, my necklace of pearls is playing too, and my black gloves, my pallor and its echo, like a beacon or even an agony, the voluptuous clitoris of this echo lights my room and as if nothing was the matter, a plate slips from the sideboard onto the floor and from there straight to the nothingness from where it brings back to my memory the old sorceress who cured me of epilepsy when I was a child using two bristles from a broom and a few lead pellets, and if the ash from my cigarette was rising into the air instead of falling, it could have been the trembling tree in which the dust bird sings with an inflammable voice, the virus of this voice, its movements those of a tiny wild animal, its leaps beyond the real, wavering, panting, its return to the flame, the landslides in the sparking match, the stick no bills of compasses, the strictly no entry of dental surgery, the windows leaving by the emergency exit or the stones coming in by the service stairs, all just so many ways of overcoming taboos, so many corridors giving our progress the chill of a pack of wolves in pursuit of a sleigh and if, for my own personal use, a bit of dynamite grows tame like a little tiger while, on the other hand, my tie only waits for a moment's lapse of concentration on my part to leap at my throat, I would still have no qualms in offering this axiom: two mirrors placed to face each other reflect a third, a fourth, a fifth, and it is the mirror I bathe in, the mirror I fall asleep on, all the objects around me are mirrors infinitely reflecting their images, and sometimes mine whose bones are throbbing beneath their transparent skin, all my nerve-endings exposed, a flag unfurled at the window, and my ear glued to the wall so as to hear the mad gallop of the approaching bricks, and I ask myself: have I really left behind the place and the span of my childhood? am I not still racing around the world on a ridiculous wooden horse, drunk with the rattling of sabres, the battle cries of my fever and the apoplectic fit, rising inside me on my breath to my lips, and while in my bed all kinds of massacres rage on the comb and the hair copulate shamelessly like serpents?

★★★★★

published in *La Brèche: Action Surréaliste* no 7 December 1964 translated by Krzysztof Fijalkowski

★★★★★

GHERASIM LUCA (Bucharest, 1913 – Paris, 1994) A member of the Romanian Surrealist Group until exile in 1952, since which time he has lived in Paris. Author of a vast number of works exploring the phenomenology of material living, especially the strangeness of language. A major poet of surrealism, Luca looks to establish a non-Oedipal relation with the world in which nostalgia would become redundant.

PAUL NOUGÉ

Feldheim's Secret Notebook

Detached Pages

She was sitting opposite me in a public establishment. I hadn't noticed her. But she crossed her legs rather high, exposing her knees so I could discern the start of her thigh, in the shadow. She remained like that for some moments then uncrossed her legs. I don't know if I then really noticed a gleam of white flesh at the edge of a well-stretched stocking. The woman was distant or perhaps nervous. She crossed her legs again, but not so high as before and it was necessary to recreate the image I had detected with the aid of the little she presently allowed me to see.

In actual fact, I don't believe she was at all aware that she was the object of such extreme interest. My eyes now very slowly slipped over the surface of her dress, trying to follow the veiled curves of her legs, deepening the narrow space to be imagined between them, grazing her belly and haunches defined very clearly by the blackness of satin on the seat's red velvet, then reaching the calm hands, a very pure arm, the slow palpitations of a chest which did not surrender the secret of her breasts and finally a face without make-up which turned a little red under the persistence of my gaze. With an astonishingly discreet movement she set her charming foot beside the other which was just slightly swaying and restored the edge of her dress on the carefully joined knees with a very simple gesture.

How did I establish a conversation with this very reserved woman, what words did we use and how much time had passed in this way? It is hardly worth an effort to remember. When she rose, I had not touched the hand she had abandoned to my side.

Her step as she crossed the cafe was extremely discreet, and was without the shadow of provocation. I followed her and as she bent over slightly to move a chair out of her way I caught a glimpse of the delicious hollow made by her legs at the level of her knees.

She went into the telephone booth to make some inconsequential call. I followed and shut myself in the confined space with her.

A lamp very near her head flooded us with a violent light. Her hips could not avoid touching my body. She stretched her hand towards the receiver but the hand stopped, hesitated for a second, and then relaxed on the shelf, accepting the risk of the encounter.

I plunged my tongue between her lips and teeth which separated softly and I tasted the fresh humidity of her mouth and for a moment the movements of a tense tongue responded to my caress.

Her tongue suddenly seemed to die. She emitted a feeble cry although without flinging her head back. As it imprisoned her hips my hand hardly felt them quiver although my fingers and palm passed lightly into the barely desecrated secret of her dress, touching at the same time the border of silk stockings, which seemed rough to me, and the silky warmth of her flesh, that luminous thigh I had glimpsed. Meanwhile, as I took firmer control of her lips, holding her body more tightly against mine (with her hip heavy against my belly and leg, I was aware of her firm and round shoulder against my chest), my hand advanced with infinite care.

At times I was afraid of resistance. The warmth perceived by the back of my active hand, becoming hot and moist, was suddenly transformed into a pressure of trembling, burning flesh that soon died down and withdrew. The whole of her body moved and I thought she was going to defend herself but after having pressed my hand between her outstretched legs for a moment, she opened them to my caress rather more than before and suddenly, rubbing against delicate linen, my whole hand touched her most secret flesh. She was moist and burning, to such an extent that I could not doubt the strength of her desire.

Then for a long moment my motionless hand seemed only to be interested in clinging to the slightest fold of this agitated flesh and in discovering how far it extended.

I felt slightly rough hair crushed at the top of my wrist but my palm felt something similar to her mouth as I crushed it on my lips. But I existed in that moment only thanks to the incredible sensations which rose from my naked hand as it was squeezed motionless over her half open and disordered flesh.

It then seemed to me, in an almost imperceptible way, that she was trying to gain greater support and push the whole of her weight onto this attentive hand.

And suddenly, with a brief sigh, she moved, and with a slow and deep movement, an octopus movement, she shifted her wide-open flesh on to my roughly extended hand.

My fingers then wandered across her tender humid folds, encountered the firmness they sought and began to caress it, gently at first but then with increasing fury which became almost painful for my wrist. The woman shook like a tree in the storm.

Her mouth was now separated from mine. I saw this mouth remain half-open, still more abandoned, this lip fall open uncovering moist teeth, as the head – eyes closed and hat strangely shifted over her hair as it came undone – the head gave way, slipped, and fell against the kiosk partition.

My hand persisted with increasing, almost brutal violence.

Not a word was spoken. The narrow space in which we were shaken by this strange storm saw its silence overwhelmed by the creaking of the worn out shelves, of an oppressed breath which suddenly became quiet, a crumpling of material, a foot which slipped, banged against something but recovered, and then in the very heart of this silence, more urgently and strongly, and more clearly the rhythmic sound of kissing and water that came from the toil of my persistent hand.

My eyes then left this face in a state of dissipation that was approaching death, turning to stone, going through flashes of strange and brief shudders, becoming very pale, and in the midst of this pallor her closed eyes entered into a bewildered black circle which spread out and became ever darker.

My gaze ran down the length of her strangely distended and contorted body. The shoulder which was leaning against me was pushed into the corner of the kiosk. The arm which was not pinned to my waist tightened in a strange way so it was finally supported by the ends of separated fingers on the end of the shelf.

The folds of a dress were raised in disorder around her breasts (it had suddenly moved imperceptibly along her thighs and hips with a sort of silky crackling and crumpling). I then saw the slight surges of delicate and pale linen as it trembled. Her thighs were completely naked to the tops of her stockings; then her legs sheathed in black trembled, causing the delicate shoes of her clenched feet to crackle against the boards of the opposite partition. One of her thighs managed to lean between my legs and I started to move against her.

But my eyes now settled on my furiously active hand.

Huge, swollen and fearful, she seemed to persist for her part in some mysterious work whose true meaning escaped me. Its movement is the heart and the focus of the whole game now being played out. Everything around this furious movement is immobile or animated with imperceptible and brief tremors. Then her knees separate with a strange indolence to leave still greater liberty for the excited hand. I suddenly make out a brilliant thread as it slowly slides down her white flesh, seemingly having emerged from the dark hair as my palm crushes it. A lighter one makes a similarly winding path, completely round, standing out from the matt whiteness, I stare for a moment at a gleaming drop.

The vision then lost its clarity and became confused.

The movement now seemed to sweep away the whole

extent, the whole depth of our enjoined bodies. I moved more solidly against this taut naked thigh which came to life, which seemed to seek, persistently, over and over, to discover something within me.

Once again my eyes see this white face pitted with black, veined with pink and blue, recalling a land threatened with disaster, and in my ears the liquid and rhythmic humming mingled with some sweet raucous clamour rising from the depths and leaving her mouth motionless. I no longer know if my hand, which I have ceased to watch, still exerts itself. I sometimes feel in my wrist and arms, something resembling a fleeting pain. I now await the face – anxiously, delightfully – with an intense curiosity for the upheaval I now feel so close at hand.

Suddenly I know that my hand has increased its harshness and speed tenfold. My fingers suddenly felt a profound change, not of the folding and harshness with which they worked, but in the unctuosity of the flesh whose indefinable modification they suddenly discerned.

And then it happened, surpassing everything I could have expected. The whole head, the whole body capsized in a harsh tortured beast's yell, in the soft shock of our bodies against the partition, dominated for a moment by the shock of a heel against the shelves and the grating of a silk sleeve tearing up to the shoulder. Drenched hair issued from her armpit with an overwhelming fragrance. Finally we fell, barely feeling the pain of my hand crushed in the vice of her stiffened legs, crushed against her, ah! I exploded with my whole body, digging my teeth into her moist and white shoulder. I couldn't say what happened next, how we left the kiosk with tousled heads, tense, trying to allow nothing to be read in our gestures, as we went through the cafe that was filled with light, and how, with a whisper, I left her forever on the pavement skirting the night.

I have retained only a single image of these moments, while from the kiosk, still closed and saturated with smells, standing, her leg naked and with her dress in disorder, the point of a breast very visible under thin silk, her face mortally pale and run through with brief tremblings, and my bite which slowly darkened her shoulder, she stared, eyes shocked and moistened with tears, forgetful of the fact that she must repair the disorder of her body, motionless and as though absent, at that useless nail that had been hammered, for no logical reason, in between two shelves.

★★★★★

published in *La Brèche: Action Surréaliste* no 7 December 1964

★★★★★

PAUL NOUGÉ (see volume one p 82)

XAVIER DOMINGO

Borne On The Red

They wanted to be as red as a sunset sky as it plunges into a final fire. They no longer wanted to see the world except through the edge of the blade or through the never sealed gash the wind had to completely pass through as water passes through illusions or as illusions pass through the night while the strongest will and calm fervour in combat spreads over the skin with the sound of an engine, while skin softer than clay asks about solitude and sets out its stall as it would at a flea-market where birds find their fetid ration of fat and honour in its raw state as scrap-iron, skin visits the evening like a vast battleground which makes revolution of servitude, coldness of power and bacon of milk whenever sorrow is denied.

They wanted to be red with blood and the judges of blood in the white deed of their scrap-iron approach impalpable black blood and very slowly running through slender and harsh filaments of skin along the padlocks of the chains of mirrors hooked directly on to the skin offering in no time at all the whole mechanism from outside without taking account of the rust of time or the hail of insults pearled with laughter they walked in procession like madmen without saying a word to whoever would have finally stormed walls and doors and who would have provisionally been left in peace to bear witness outside to their bitterness from inside.

They wanted to be as red as the silence with which their skin shivered in the bites and convolutions of their nerves that hernias pulled about hither and thither by irons nailed like earwigs so they could walk straight and resolute without deviating an inch from this immaculate redness to which they had aspired since childhood and for which they grew stronger in needles and nails open like a chest of toys, or tools, or irons, as in the lumber room of the blacksmith, plating their skin with the remains of his castings in order to affront the transparent air with stubbornness and no more ardent than that.

They announced the redness of the future while for men it will be a matter of recuperating in the wastelands reddened by death the remains of what could have been if river-banks had been made of chains, memories of keys, balloons of lances, and if ants had been left with the responsibility of devouring altars in order that triumph would be something other than patronage and paradise something other than an institution closed to those who would not carry with them the credited receipt of their payment to travel by rail which would lead precisely where it was not necessary to go under pain of falling into this ship without a hold. They dyed themselves with the vibrant redness of the duel once released by women who invented the art of painting on the rocks of caves the redness of battles between men and animals while they fought to the death for issues of style and it is from there that the magic to cause suffering comes in order to be better able to possess the embers if the fire dies in a final spinning of redness or if one plunges white iron squarely into water.

They aspired to the moist redness of dying stars hung on high like punished people fragile orbs ready to burst beyond with purulent blood rotting flowers of celestial mud with eyes on the point of being put out by rockets with gothic arches on fire launched from the cape of the victim by men in rubber with soft teeth and heads close-shaven like cigarette-butts. It is the redness of the gland crossed through and through by the knitting needle of masturbations that they came alone or with several friends all attracted by the same desire for lava and eruptions. Oh yes! red as an assault on modesty of which the incandescent glowing would disturb the little girl having a wee-wee on a level with the sky while pink flamingos would throw out their powdery flame over a blueness as pure as Caribbean islands at first dawn.

Red at full speed like a Ferrari hurtling along for it is rather finer than being white or yellow or being green or grey-green or maroon it is more beautiful as well as more magnetic the red attracting the sound of bugles to the sheet, birds with horns which fly low at the sight of half-moon blood the weapons of their forehead darkening on Mars which spreads its wings and turns on itself majestically red and open like a wound on the sand rounded and encircled with grey discharged by robins and then kissing as does the whore's fingernail on the skin of the sex the river of minium red which turns round and plunges onto the cadmium mad with love with an equality of wounds exhibited by the bearers of gold.

But as shamefully reddened by the bites of an irritated leprosy expelling them immediately by the force of its vermilion of dejected or black things which hang around behind tombs no longer knowing what to make of their boredom and leaving them alone in their midst the contagious and nasty reds like impair and rouge social problems inflicted with a burning sulphur their skin swollen in a way similar to that of women punished with the perfume of vitriol and again seeking with iridescent and thirsty lips the kiss of the vampire-pimp.

Redder than a naked hennaed beauty in the Sahara of pimento birds the tears of her eyes droplets of strawberry on mulberry-flavoured milk but in the red taste of wine that is drawn from grapes tramped in the press of languages between the Red Sea and the river of the same name and boreal colour, a drink that favours great menstruations of rock faces and leads to precipitations of extinct volcanos.

For it is the dormant redness of the brain's magma that they want to draw out and set on fire lotuses and tulips with the coagulated light of a tranquil hatred for the rose which betrays the shadows of the night in a splendour less scarlet than it needs to be in this garden of violated tuberoses.

And it is hung up like skinned oxen that the lovers of red would end their torrential vigil bathed in all the pores of their body and strengthened with the smell of innards burned under the low flame of their irons crayons of unfeigned stigmata of everything that causes evil in the world and provokes the welcome of blood and gold so sought-after by transformers of the disposition of stones.

Finally red without concession those who would have wanted with all their passion to make their skin from this blood hauled up to the mast or nailed to the stakes liver salt on the streams piercing the muscle beaten by the skilful palms of the tomtom drummers who cause the drum with the skin of a gorged pig to speak and which throughout the night will ceaselessly tune their dance with that of hanged hearts throbbing emeralds distilling the alcohol of drunkenness of the lovers of red.

It is only the clairvoyance of red that these sorcerers will offer to the scoptophiles and that will be enough to cause their eyebrows to burn and their pupils to scorch and will mark their faces with an ineffaceable seal similar to that which iron leaves on the hide of a beast while its master wants everyone to know it belongs to him and one could never ever raise this imprint nor free himself from the slavery in chains of threads of blood nor break the alliance brought to an end by the sacrifice of those who walk on the blade between their orbits towards the roost of the red eagles.

At the smelt of uranium the arrows will leave towards the top of the house and soon they will be only a drop of blood on the mother's breast and the pleasure of those who are borne on the redness will begin with this convolvulus of snow.

★★★★★

published in *L'Archibras* no 2 (October 1967)

★★★★★

XAVIER DOMINGO a member of the French Surrealist

Group during the sixties, Xavier Domingo is a Spanish (not as incorrectly stated in the introduction to volume one, a Brazilian) surrealist.

JEAN FERRY

My Aquarium

For some time now I've nurtured thoughts of suicide. And I must say I've really come out of it very well.

During the day they say nothing and sleep in their little ebony box. But you need to realise that, when night falls and I raise the cover, everything swarms and fidgets fitfully.

They have little flat heads that are whitish and triangular, like certain record needles, needles of a model I think has been forgotten. These little creatures are extremely pleasant and so easy to feed. They eat everything I give them: sorrows, extracted teeth, wounded pride or not, worries, sexual inadequacies, heartaches, regrets, unshed tears, lack of sleep, they swallow it all in a mouthful, and still want more. But what they like best is my tiredness, and that's really useful since there's no risk that there won't be enough to go round. I stuff them, but they leave some of it and there's always more. I can never completely get rid of it.

You'll tell me I'm wrong to feed them and that things will end up badly, that they'll become too fat and escape from their box. But I keep the box in a drawer that is always locked with the key of the large chest of drawers that has a heavy marble top. Old Marie once cast toffee on this marble top.

I don't believe, even if they got out of the box and spilled into the drawer, that they would be able to raise the marble top. Clearly they never have. But what would I do with all this tiredness then?

*****

published in Jean Ferry, *Le Mécanicien et autres contes* Paris: Gallimard

*****

JEAN FERRY (see volume one p 40)

MARCEL LECOMTE

The Familiar Object

This long black glove, slightly swollen from a recent presence, feigns sleep on the side of the table bathed in shadow. Because there is perhaps a secret to hide in the sculpted fingers which would have animal or reptile forms bestowed with motionless life emanating from a very authentic pale and furtive female hand.

(And in fact there was just now an arduous setting in motion of this hand in the dark tunnel of the glove to undergo the disturbing and bewitching constraint of the troublesome lining.)

But there is no longer a secret: the woman has long since stopped contemplating the long black glove, she has noticed that in this way it revealed to her externally a kind of shape of her hand, interrupted, a material resonance of her person, plunged into the solitude of an autonomous existence at the side of a table bathed in shadow.

And in the too-familiar room, in front of the curtains of evening, meditating on that part of herself, in other words on her own hand whose particular existence, marked by signs appropriate to its existence, had been revealed to her by the image of the glove, she realises herself, obsessed with the idea that, when she is dead, her hands, and her face, will still be bearers of such acute signs.

*****

published in Marcel Lecomte *L'Accent du secret* Paris: Gallimard

*****

MARCEL LECOMTE (see volume one p 164)

NANOS VALAORITIS

The Hand

The hand is moving slowly without hesitation and is gaining ground, climbing up the wall, holding onto the periwinkle and the ivies – with such artfulness such an intelligence all of its own – as if it had a 'brain', as if it knew where it was going, a hand which is at least at the level of an animal, which moves blindfold, with a 'tropism' all of its own.

So it is moving as if someone is guiding it, and it was coming towards me. It is like a fatal and inevitable movement, like the flow of a river, like the falling of snow, of hail, of water. Slowly, methodically, it is gaining ground, grasping as if it was 'real' anything that crosses its path. Now that it has reached the soil – the parterre – with the flowers, it parts the flowers like a human being – and I am waiting for it steadily with the butterfly net hidden behind my back so that it won't see it. A stray hand, something still rare in these parts, now reaches a point nine feet from where I was standing and stops, skulking for a while, and waits to see what will happen. (Things are not going too well because what was happening in my mind was different from what was happening in reality – the world is double, triple, it is 'open' like a cut watermelon). It was just a matter of time, of seconds: either it would leap swiftly on my neck to grab it and throttle me or I would catch it first in the net, mentally aiming at its probable move. But at that moment the hand 'spoke' – with a faint nasal voice, as if from a small wireless set.

"Why are you hiding it behind your back? Have you perhaps mistaken me for a butterfly? I am not a butterfly, nor a snake either. I am a friend. . . I want to live with you but without restrictions, I want no more arms."

The voice was almost in my ear now, bitter, sarcastic.

The hand was speaking telepathically: "Whose are you?" I asked half to myself and half aloud.

"Nobody's," it answered immediately, "I'm yours – take me."

The spontaneous tone of the hand moved me:

"All right – I said – you can stay – but take care, I said, bear in mind that I can destroy you if I want – I have the means to shatter you."

"You won't do that, it said in a whining voice. I'm not bad. You'll see."

It came leaping like a puppy and sat on my knee:

"It squeezed my knee – and then started to stroke it, – and it was moving upwards, upwards. It reached my cheek, my hair, the nape of my neck – for a second I thought it was trying to squeeze my throat, but maybe it was just my imagination.

"I love you, I love you," whispered the voice in a nasal, whining tone in my ears.

I lived with the hand for some time. – It was better than the most stunning mistress. It even fed me, it went shopping on its own.

The nights were inconceivable. Nobody can imagine such an ecstatic torment. And it kept whispering in my ear – and speaking to me in soft-spoken words such as I had never heard before in my whole life from anyone. Once or twice I interrogated it to find out where it came from.

"From somewhere," it would say vaguely, and it gave me to understand that it came from an unimaginable, inconceivable place, beyond the grasp of anyone's mind.

I started imagining a stunning woman who was – the owner of – the hand. The caressing, slightly ironical and nasal deep voice spoke inside me mingled with memories. Sometimes I thought it belonged to an old love of mine from my adolescence, sometimes I believed it was one of those exotic creatures I had encountered during my travels in sleep, non-existent imaginary beings – princesses, priestesses, soothsayers, Tartar women, ghosts. Sometimes it seemed sent from the world of 'death'. The hand would guess my thought: like a voice on the telephone – it kept telling me – no I am not like this, I am not like that, – I am not what you think, I am something else, you will never find it, do not seek it. The hand went away twice. I started being jealous of it. "Where have you been, what have you been doing?" – Whenever I asked it, it would always react as if I was being indiscreet: "I have my private life too", it would tell me.

Finally, one night after a 'terrible' quarrel – the worst we ever had – it left – and never came back. When the initial sorrow had passed I felt a great 'relief'. I gradually got used to the disappearance of the hand and my former loneliness did not appear so terrible.

One day I received a phone call. An unknown female voice wanted to see me. She spoke with an accent – in a foreign language, which I didn't know very well. The bell rang: on the doorstep stood a Japanese woman.

I was stunned: her face was completely covered with white make-up as one sees in the theatre. I asked her in: she offered me her hand. I took it. She squeezed my hand gently and I immediately recognised something familiar in the 'touch'. I looked at the 'hand' but it wasn't the same one. Still the touch was the same. I made her sit on the sofa. I sat down beside her. I took her hand without a word. She started to caress me, but wouldn't let me touch her.

Her hand caressed exactly like the other hand, and amazingly it touched me erotically everywhere in a miraculous way. After she had completed her job – she rose – bowed – and left, without a word.

At that time I was studying various Buddhist theories – I had happened to read the life of Milarepa, the story of his 'struggles' against black magic, and magic in general. He was an athlete of the spirit who performed 'miracles' to teach the way. He subjected his disciples to incredible disheartening trials, he used to treat them with unthinkable cruelty.

"I did that," he would say, "to awaken them."

Those who could not take it left – they gave up.

The genuine ones, the strong, endured to the end and became in their turn great athletes of the spirit and succeeded the master and would one day perhaps reach absolute understanding and be enlightened, they would become one with the principles which govern the universe.

Those days I was also preoccupied with another world: the world of the people who walk 'stooping' as though they carried a horrible weight inside them – an invisible and wretched burden – the corpse of another self or of a dead love.

This world, or rather underworld, of sorrow – exercised an almost destructive attraction on me. Its shadows visited me day and night, they would not let me sleep, eat, rest.

I was the captive of their desires.

They dominated me as though I was subject to an unknown monarch.

Was it the stray hand – I wonder – that was acting from that other side of things, which we only dimly discern through the twilight of beings?

*****

first published in *Talking Ape or Paramythology* Athens: Aigókeros, 1986

translated by Sophia Voulgari

*****

NANOS VALAORITIS (Lausanne, 1921) poet, prose writer and critic. Of Greek origins, he has lived in London, Paris and San Francisco. Translator of Seferis, Elytis and other Greek poets into English and French. Participant in surrealism since 1939, he edited the Greek language journal, *Pali* (1963–7). Has published extensively in Greek, English and French and was curator for the 1991 exhibition on Greek surrealism at the Beaubourg.

BERNARD ROGER

'The High Tone'

The *cry* spreads across the window which has been closed for a long time: what had then become of the forest? A new sign had caused it to re-emerge among us. *The shadow of laughter* flitted about there between the leaves of precious metal. The last stroke of midnight was just sounding and everything settled down in the *act of gold*, but it seemed impossible to say at what fraction of a second the door would open. At the back the velvets of the twelve dancing princesses whispered: "The metallic chaos produced by the hands of Nature contains within itself all metals and yet is not metal. It contains gold, silver and mercury. Yet it is neither gold, nor silver, nor mercury."

The duel has not yet taken place, but it could not be long in so far as the veil is unlaced in a lascivious way. Some flashing names are pronounced in the high atmosphere, to which the very ancient echoes of caves of the earth respond, as along a golden thread extended from the Zenith to the Nadir.

In the close-by breeze the invisible blacksmith's anvil resounds: the dew burns old Saturn's skull to ashes at the moment when the moon rises and considers the crystal. It has not yet been understood, but the sound has completely penetrated the *yellow sky*. It is the premonition of deserts in which one navigates at one go, urged on by the mizzen-sail, scattered from the miniature volcanos in which red eyes gleam, to the enamelled slopes of the multicolored blossoms of lavas. On the horizon, the star hides the tree; it is, like its roots, shaped with fish scales. "The sun is formed from the purest part of prime matter in which earth and fire dominate."

In truth the traveller is already on his way: he is intimate with the large metamorphosing animals, and of lively words of tin forests. He hears the spring which flows three steps away in the forest, in the streaming words of the rays of dawn, in which memory is sketched out to the earliest years of things. Without haste he approaches the metallic cliffs with their gleaming cracks, but his approach has already led him in joy to the transparent crossroad where the encounter of the internal world and the world of the internal takes place.

*****

published in *Poètes singuliers, du surréalisme et autres lieux* (eds) A. V. Aelberts and J. J. Auquier Paris: Christian Bourgois, 1971

*****

BERNARD ROGER (see p 99 of this volume)

ANDRÉ PIEYRE DE MANDIARGUES

Moon Wardrobe

So white is the ground in the vicinity of Safara and so white are the houses in the small village devoid of any activity but coastal fishing, so dusty, from white dust, are the streets and lanes, and so rare are trees or shrubs with the exception of a few poorly flowering oleanders almost devoid of leaves, that one would say that in that place death had cruelly planted its essential colour and that life dwelt there only in a state of inferiority, beneath overpowering conditions of oppression. However, the macabre South has charm for many young travellers in the modern world, and a rather unusual hotel, the Minos Boarding House, welcomes them above the large stinking plastered square of the fish market that is brought to life only three times a week when the truck collecting sardines for provincial canning factories passes through. Terraced balconies go around each of the two floors of the Minos Boarding House and there is nothing to prevent anyone from going from one room to another, especially at night when the heat forces people to leave the French windows open. The young boarders remain excitable until dawn approaches. A few guitars keep their spirits up before sleep overcomes them and they rest for the greater part of the day.

Did Luc Laon take advantage of this opportunity to enter the monastic room in which Barbara Bara was lying naked with just a light sheet covering her as, by the electric light on the bedside table, she read a hefty tome of moral divagations published in the seventeenth century by a Neapolitan Jesuit? Did the book slip down to the white floor paving following the reader's motion of surprise upon seeing the young man's silhouette in front of her and did she sink deeper into the small bed to hide under the sheet even though it revealed her figure from head to foot and her bare shoulders and arms? Did she, in silence, but without raising her gaze from the intruder's lips, listen as Luc spoke with respectful ardour about how he had noticed her as she dined alone, at a late hour, in the boarding house's dining-hall, close to where he dined at a table in the shadows; how he had observed her throughout the meal and how he had been vanquished by the light blue gleam of her large eyes highlighted by her very brown tan and under a fringe of her hair that was less auburn than blonde, wavering above her dress, amply low cut at the back, when, in order to serve herself with a large shrimp or with fried red mullet, she turned to the plate at her left; how he had been delightfully enchanted by the intelligence of her choice of dish no less than by her sleek beauty and by a certain element of gleaming freshness which had much in common with a flower just blossoming in the undergrowth, or a fresh mushroom, as much as a rare fish glimpsed through the aperture of a diving-mask; how he had understood that this young woman was the very form of the desire he had absent-mindedly and lazily experienced in respect of all the young women who came within range of his arms, the absolute form of his perpetual desire, which could never be satisfied other than on the skin of she who was separated from him by no more than a yard or two, but with whom he had already had an intimacy comparable only to what he found in mirrors when confronted with his own image; how he had found out her name and the floor on which she was staying and the location of her room, and how he had entered through the window (anyway this was what most of the lodgers at the boarding-house did), to ask her to surrender to his passionate wish and allow him to clasp her in his arms before the clear nocturnal sky, to the sound of guitars plucked by the young men who had not yet found partners; how he hoped she would agree to his request without tiresome complications, something common among modern wanderers during the summer, in the southern regions, and which should not have caused her any surprise other than that of the revelation, that was, after all, flattering, he believed, of a desire as intense as the ones that, under the collective name of love, have inspired authors of the most beautiful poems of the past? Without moving underneath the sheet which made of her long body the most carnal effigy in any crypt, did Barbara Bara respond to him that she felt a sense of marvel rather than surprise at the way he had articulated his demand and that as she experienced it, she similarly recognised the longing she had within herself to meet her desire in the same way that lips meet their image in the mirror and cover it, but, as amazing as it might seem, she was a virgin, and that a room of the Minos Boarding House, a kind of pleasant brothel, as he had himself described it, was not really the ideal place to surrender herself to a sacrifice whose approaching execution she desired, yes, but to which she wanted to abandon her whole thought, in meditation and fancy, for at least twenty four hours? Did she add that the following night the moon would be full and that such an occasion would gain a certain maturity propitious to the harvest of blood and pleasure? As for the place, had the young girl elected the cemetery on a dominant chalky plateau high above Safara, and did she tell Luc Laon, initially disconcerted by such a choice, that it would be there and nowhere else, among the tombs of the ancient Safarites, that her body would be joined with his in any posture that pleased him, and that she would literally submit to him more exactly than an image could to the object sustaining it? And finally did Luc Laon hear Barbara Bara ask him to be dressed only in white on that night when they would meet so they could be in closer harmony, for she would be wearing a dress of white jersey whose front would be clasped around her neck, leaving her back and shoulders completely bare, a dress which would not therefore allow any brassiere and under which even a slip would have been unseemly, the sort of dress given to mad young girls who flag down motorists in the pine-woods close to resorts during the evenings of dog-days and are then taken away by three or four unknowns who would undo the knot during the journey and would touch all the pinnacles of her conquered nudity before stopping in a back lane and consummating, at times to the point of excess, what had perhaps only been a daydream of furious innocence? After Barbara Bara had become silent, did Luc Laon watch for a few more moments, without saying anything, and had he then returned the way he came, without holding out a hand towards the hoped-for body, which was still as motionless as that of a dead woman under the sheet?

The following day, after they each took dinner late but separately, did Luc Laon again meet Barbara Bara at the end of the white portico on the main street, and was she wearing, apart from the promised dress, only white leather sandals? For himself, in answer to the young girl's wish, was he wearing white espadrilles, trousers and a polo neck pullover, both of white cotton, an attire that would have gained him entry to the most elegant of summer galas? Did they smile, finding themselves as they had wished the previous evening and as they glimpsed each other in the dining hall? Did they take each other's hands? Did they leave the village via the chalky gravel path which rose abruptly toward the cemetery on high? Did a population of white cats which, on the outskirts of the village, fed on the remains of fishes and were eaten away with mange in consequence of such a diet, disperse to right and left as they walked by between blocks of that limestone called mountain milk thrown up on both sides of the path? Had their attention been drawn, a little further along, by the barking of two white harriers which the moonlight isolated over the sky and which were sinister like heraldic animals supporting the arms of a very ancient race of killers? Did a white owl take off from the chalky desert as they approached, with a cry that could have come from a woman's throat on the point of being strangled? Did they reach, after around half an hour's silent ascent, still holding hands despite the difficulties of the track, augmented by the satellite's illusory light, the end of their journey as demanded by the young girl?

Did Luc Laon and Barbara Bara, as they faced the Safara cemetery, which had neither an entrance nor a door, nor a wall nor perimeter fence, and seemed to project across the wide plain of soft chalk like a lake upon which the tombs appeared like ships in distress, did they, or did one of the two of them, not recoil for a moment and then did they not remain dumbfounded before the bizarre sight of funerary monuments, which are of only two types, one of which is masculine and comprises a small column shaft topped with a sort of Phrygian cap and the other feminine, offering the crescent of the new moon or the horns of some divine heifer over a block carved into a sugar-loaf, not as high as the virile shafts, and all of which are made from the limestone used to construct all the houses in the village? Having recovered from their amazement, did the young people, Barbara leading Luc, advance haphazardly, since there is no path traced in the Safara necropolis, among the gland-topped columns and horned sugar loaves? Then, after having walked a little here and there, did Luc suspect that his companion was not as lost as he was as she made him take detours between clusters of tombs that were reclining as if at the whim of tempestuous waves which, in reality, conducted him towards a still faraway monument that was also more elevated, wider than the others and distinguished from the neighbouring whiteness by the dark gleam of its bulk? Did the young girl not hasten her steps, upon approaching it, with a certain air of not being in unknown territory, while Luc stumbled once or twice on fragments of shafts or crescents, since he was looking at his guide rather than the ground? Was he more amazed than initially when he realised that this thing towards which Barbara Bara had led him was nothing but a colossal mirror-wardrobe, or rather a monument in the form of a mirror-wardrobe, whose two mirrors were real mirrors while the structure which would have been walnut or ebony had it been a piece of furniture, was of blocks of black granite which must have been brought from far distant lands to be erected in the burial field. Pulled up by his companion's hand, did he clamber up two steps which brought the two of them to the base of the large wardrobe, a rectangular platform on which a thick layer of very white, very fine, and very clean sand had gathered? Had not both of them reached the foot of the monument, above which the moon had become a little lower than it was when they left the village? Did they contemplate the image of them both in the double mirror bathed by the cold light spilled over it by the satellite, mirrored also on its sidereal path?

Was it written on the pediment of the monumental wardrobe in silver letters of roman capitals, HERE LIE (in the language of the vast land which comprises Safara), and did the engraved inscription, devoid of anyone's name, soar like a pale vulture over the two mirroring panels upon which the reflections of Luc Laon and Barbara Bara were framed like painted portraits? Did he look towards her reflection, towards her eyes that were now clearer, her hair that was blonder and more gleaming than ever, while her skin in contrast was browner and her body more beautiful as it was shaped by the clinging white gown? And, for her, did her gaze remain fixed on his refection as his face darkened above the white silhouette, on his imperious mouth and on his teeth as they sparkled in a half-smile, on his pale eyes under the double arch of his bushy eyebrows, on his forehead blended by his tan and his chestnut-brown hair that was cut almost in a crew-cut. "In Spanish, a mirror wardrobe is called a 'moon wardrobe'." Did this phrase break the silence for the first time that evening as it was pronounced by the young girl, perhaps intended for the night forces, if they existed, or for all those of Safara recently or since time immemorial entombed, as much as for the thickset ears giving an engagingly brutal appearance to her companion's reflection? Did she then make a movement, which put an end to the long immobility of the reflected couple as it did away with the illusion of a double portrait?

With an emotion which suddenly hastened the course of his blood, from heart to brain and belly, did Luc Laon see Barbara Bara's hand rise up as she stretched out her thumb and index finger towards the knot of ribbons that alone held up her long dress behind the nape of her neck and which, no sooner unfastened, fell at once, leaving the beautiful warm statue in complete nudity that, first in a vertical position and then, when he had rested her on the sand, horizontally, he was able to explore with fingers and lips, without reserve, before penetrating her with his stiffness and flow into the humid tautness of her torn-open intimacy? Did he wonder whether he would be able to control himself enough to place his body and the proffered body of the young girl in such positions that he could observe to the end the spectacle of profanation in the moon-wardrobe?

Did a violent wind suddenly gust – but where had it come from, on such a peaceful night – before the ribbons holding up the dress were untied? Did the double mirror turn like a revolving door on an axis which might have coincided with the fastening of the doors of black granite? Was it the reflection of the couple, or the original pair, the true characters of Luc Laon and Barbara Bara, that this weather vane movement conveyed inside the funeral edifice? Did the young couple find themselves – under its roof, which may have been of crystal as it allowed the moonlight to enter unhampered as though the large tomb was open to the elements, at the top of a double spiral staircase? And did they have any alternative but to descend the parallel spirals, separated by a balustrade with railings, above which they still held each other's hands, with, however, their arms raised because of the high bannisters which almost reached their shoulders? Did music (German or Italian from the eighteenth century), whose source was as doubtful as that of the unfortunate wind, accompany their descent? Did it control their footsteps by means of a counter-point whose extent could have been interminable, as could the steps along which there was no reason for them to cease moving?

How far will the double spiral engendered by the double mirror of the sepulchral wardrobe descend, and will there be an extremity to this sort of spiralling, or will it continue right through the earth? For, as the little iron bed of a room at the Minos Boarding House creaked in the light of the almost full moon, Luc Laon brutally thrusts his hard sex into the downy soft moistness of Barbara Bara's, from whose body he has forcibly pulled away the sheet, which he rolled up as tightly as he could around her head and arms to prevent her from crying out and struggling, while the bedstead swayed more or less in rhythm with that of the guitar outside, and disturbed the fragments of the electric light which had joined on the white floor tiling *The Useful with the Pleasurable*, which was opened up at the title page to reveal the name of Father Carlo Casalicchio of the Society of Jesus, the author of the weighty tome.

(Venice 20th August 1970)

*****

published in André Pieyre de Mandiargues *Mascarets* Paris: Gallimard

*****

ANDRÉ PIEYRE DE MANDIARGUES (see volume one p 226)

COLETTE THOMAS

The Fragrance Of Nature

The woman started. What had happened? She was still plunged right in the centre of suffering. In all probability nothing more real existed in this world. What power dared venture into such a place outside itself? What enormous burden could cause it to shake?

Suddenly her limbs stiffened. She closed her eyes. *Someone* was there. When she opened them again her unbearable anguish increased but she *knew*. Her body started to sweat at what she saw at the corners of the foot of her bed – two candles. Instead of a bedstead there was a mortuary sheet. She did not need to turn round to know that two other candles burned above her head. "So this is *my* death," she thought. "Not any old death, not that which everyone speaks about and which has never existed. Nor that which has existed specifically for a particular person and thus that we have not touched. Rather it is my death, uniquely mine and necessarily mine. Genuinely mine. My substance transformed into death. My substance in a catafalque, in candles, in anguish and in mortal dread. The glacial breath at the back of my head and this skeleton as thick as decay is myself. The scythe of time," she again thought. "So that's what it's like."

She then succumbed to weakness. She heard a voice pant out: "Your death will take you if you do not immediately leave this coffin, if you do not pass over this mortuary apparel in order to *pray* to the death that is *rightfully* yours. Kneel down at the side of the catafalque, go and find your nurse and pray, pray for the dead woman you must become and who will not exist thanks to your *faith*."

The unfortunate rose and sought out her nurse and they knelt down at the side of the bed to pray.

From that time on this woman lived but she bore the mark of shame.

Later she understood that it was not simply a matter of suffering but also of dying and *overcoming*, and that she was not dead but that she had been afraid.

One evening she went into a coffin,and her smile did not leave her face for one single moment, and with her hand she fingered the planks of her box. It did not amaze her to feel the planks sticking more tightly to her legs as the sap of the tree flowed in the wood and the bark crackled and the moss appeared.

This woman bears the fragrance of nature over her.

★★★★★

published in *Obliques no 14–15: La Femme Surréaliste* Paris: Obliques 1977

★★★★★

COLETTE THOMAS Although not connected directly with the surrealists, Colette Thomas was engaged in a parallel quest that was stimulated by her friendship with Antonin Artaud during the last year of his life. Her only book *Le Testament d'une fille morte* (1954) is a scintillating exploration of the nature of being.

NELLY KAPLAN

Solidary Pleasure

Who would have many Visits must not stand
Too great a freight of flowers on stone which my hand
Lifts with the strength of those past joy and sorrow

Stéphane Mallarmé

Now I'm dead I have all the time in the world for reflection. And I amuse myself by watching them, those who still fuss over me, tearfully receiving the condolences of all those imbeciles I never could stand. How agreeable it is to be able to watch them without being obliged to smile or ask them about their vulgar spouses and idiot brats! How I would like to stick my tongue out at them (you can imagine the panic that would cause!), but unfortunately my muscles no longer obey my desires. I am dead, after all.

My husband looks distraut. He loved me a lot, in his way. Me, no, not at all. I found him stupid, petty, *so* awkward. I was never happy with him. And if I did nothing to hold on to life during the operation, he is largely responsible. I regret it now. It would have been more sensible to have left him while I was still alive. But you always understand these things too late.

The people now assume an ultra-tragic air. My husband leans over to kiss me one last time and some of his tears fall on my nose. Normally that would tickle me, but I no longer feel anything. It's true he was never too worried about discovering them. . . Oh, if I could but hate him, him with his parsimonious impulses, the honest tax-paying chemist.

A lock of my hair is cut off as a keepsake. My mother-in-law furtively slips my emerald ring off and pockets it. I still don't know what my new powers will be but, no matter what, I must try to return one of these evenings just to frighten her a bit, the horrible creature.

They close my coffin, but I see as well as ever. They lift the whole thing (a little more care, please!) and set off. Soon I won't be obliged to listen to them any longer. A worthy recompense, despite everything. Alone at last. . .

The final ceremony. I hear them proclaim my exemplary virtues. Fools, if only they knew what I thought of them! Earth tumbles down in a singsong of hail. I'm curious to know what comes next.

I need to get used to another dimension. Or rather to a lack of dimension. Time, for example, can no longer have any meaning. And boredom? Will it still exist for me, now? I feel my neighbours swarming around me, intrigued. But I know no contact will be established unless it is desired. And I want to be alone, as before. I have much to think about.

Life seems so far away. I don't regret it.

Nevertheless, I know that there is something I do regret: love, which I have never known. Goodness knows, I would have so liked to thrill to, with, under, in, against a man. . .

I feel that something marvellous has been stolen from me, that I was made for love and that being dead and buried today at the age of twenty-five without having been transported on tides of vertigo represents a sort of crime against everything most sacred.

But since everything is finished, what's the point of grumbling? If only I could have seen this clearly three days ago. Now it's too late.

I would like to sleep, but it is useless. Perhaps the dead don't sleep. I remember a fable that was told in a film: apparently women who die without knowing love do not find rest and return to earth to haunt the living. We shall see.

For the moment I look at myself: no sign of deliquescence. I am just very pale, beautiful even. I can see myself without the need of a mirror, as easily as I observe the landscape above ground. Night has fallen. Already. It seems that time no longer counts for me.

All is calm outside. No, not all. Someone is approaching. He stops. The moon illuminates a newspaper he has in his hand. He compares my name with that in the obituary column. He is young, extremely handsome, and his manic eyes would frighten me if I was not already one of those who should rather provoke fear in others. He looks around, and appears satisfied that he is alone. He comes to a decision and starts removing earth from above my new home. Poor idiot, he does not know that my mother-in-law has already stolen my emeralds. But how can I let him know that he is working for nothing! Even today they won't leave me alone.

His excitement seems to increase. What a strange individual! Yet I don't find him unsympathetic. In the last analysis digging up corpses is a profession like any other, full of the unexpected, risky and sometimes thrilling.

Amused, I await his moment of disappointment. I have nothing of value on me but my mortuary shirt, a woeful booty.

He approaches, he is here. With just the right tools (he's a real professional) he raises the coffin lid. His breathing is heavy. Is he afraid? Now he looks at me; more than this he devours me with his burning eyes. He seems more and more excited. He passes his hand under my shirt, raises me like a feather – how strong he is! – and clambers out of the grave with me.

What does he want? He is not looking for jewels. He gently removes my shirt and sets me down on it. And he speaks to me passionately in a low voice. He touches me. He leans over me and kisses me on the eyes and on the mouth, which he tries vainly to open. He runs his hand over my body.

Ah, if only I was not dead and had the power to respond to him, so handsome, so amiable, does he seem to me. He kisses me all over. I am ashamed of remaining cold and inanimate when he loves me as though I were alive, with the same regard, the same tenderness, the same madness.

I now know what I previously only felt in an obscure way: that love can exist, even for me; or rather, that it could have existed. But even so I am happy to know that this man, whom I love now with all the horror of my inanimate body, all the ardour of a spirit which can no longer communicate, will himself be happy because of me.

He opens my body with his hands, with his lips, with himself. And he clasps me to him, our bodies as one. His cries of passion scandalise the dead, who I hear murmuring. Myself, I am happy, or almost so. I only regret not being able to add my joy to his. He covers me with caresses, he buries his head in my hair, and he loves me, a dead woman, a thousand times more than he could love a living woman on earth. This seems to be an old habit with him. But this evening he says it in his ecstasy without knowing that I hear him, and that's different. He does not grow tired, does not have the disgust of that first weariness, almost wishes – supreme proof of love – that I was alive, that I could be happy with him, help him to love me, to satisfy my whims, those whims that I wonder how much they were always within me.

A strange, fleeting feeling passes through me. It is perhaps the sensation of desire that I *could* feel, a desire *so* powerful in my mind, more lucid now than it ever was during the whole of my idiotic life. . .

If only I could begin again, now that I know that this God-Devil business is a swindle, that I know a little of the earth's secrets, that I feel that love is possible for me, a love that is here, gripping me with a despair that renders ignoble the tears shed by my husband, sobbing into my deaf ears that I am the woman he has been looking for, in every town and every cemetery, possessing me, tirelessly, for hours, without realising that the moon was waning and that soon we would have to part forever, even before getting to know each other.

No, *I do not want*, inert mass that I am, to separate myself from him, my love, my one and only love. He is inside me again, and I start to imagine I can feel his weight, and to believe that my body responds to his caresses, that I secrete the balms to help him straddle our prodigious sabbaths, that his delirium is only one with mine, that he stops biting my lips because I open them to tear at his lips, *like so*. . .

I suddenly sense that I possess my lips, that it's true I bite him, and that I open my eyes to encounter his, and that I stiffen with the whole of my being beneath his violence, and that the most exquisite joy spills out inside me for the first time, warming my body with countless flames, and that I become a living vine, adhering to my lover, to complete together the most marvellous of voyages amidst fury and delight.

We look at one another. He is not surprised. Nor am I. Alive once more? Why not? It was something I sought with all my willpower the moment the man I love, who loved me, who possessed me, wanted to lead me back to life. Love's co-ordinates seek nothing less.

The dead, with whom I can now communicate at will, tell me that this happens at times, though extremely rarely. They wish me the best of luck until next time, and they promise to watch over us.

My lover looks at me, kisses me, covers me with his cloak, is worried I might catch cold. It is cold, it's true. To warm ourselves, we carefully cover over my grave. You would never be able to tell that anything had changed since the mourners had left.

I look, amused, at my epitaph. And then at my love, who I find handsome, marvellous; who finds me beautiful, marvellous. Day is breaking. We leave the cemetery arm in arm. No one sees us depart. We walk slowly towards the town, stopping every few steps to kiss, overwhelmed.

And myself, who now possesses all the memory of the world, *I know* that we will live happily ever after and that we will not have children.

*****

published in *Le Réservoir des sens* 1962 & 1988 Paris: Jean-Jacques Pauvert

translated by Paul Hammond and Michael Richardson

*****

NELLY KAPLAN (see volume one p 194)

CLAUDE TARNAUD

Orpalée

Death, macaronic as always, was dressed as a gigolo from the age of tangos. The Young Drowned Woman, sitting modestly on the humid sand in an organdie-pink cloud, sipped a King's Ransom while delicately chewing a branch of red ceranium. A sea-gull cawed out as it perched on her shoulders. The pallid clown chased it away with a flourish of his ebony cane and a fuzzy flight bore it off, transformed into a noctule, to the high cliff of noble stone where it vanished into a crevice – we followed it there for some moments, carried along by sharp rapids of granite, feeling the wind of the schists blow in our hair, on the way through caressing the humid face of the amethyst deposits, to the small bed-rock clearing where we awaited, under a sardonynx sun, all the iridescence of a needle-sharp and crystalline fauna.

"My favourite snacks are the last looks of lost sailors: this seaweed that I nibble contains the unspoken and anguished cry of a young narcissist. As for this laminaria, beautiful as a wasp, it hastens the whole life of a master-harpooner in chaotic images." Then, pointing to the out-of-date dandy with clean-shaven face, the young woman added: "This one considers I'm too frivolous. He is, you know, the keeper of the now disused lighthouse which warned of the entrance of the neighbouring ria and whose tower shelters a colony of large crabs which, from one ebb-tide to the next, exchange melancholy aphorisms with this slight sound of moist kisses which serves as their language. . . Out of love for me, he has transformed the fixed fire into a gigantic magic lantern which he uses to project onto the cliff's luminous forms which, playing among the fissures, the overhangs and the high-reliefs – sometimes sharp, sometimes minutely polished by the waves – form images which cause ships to stray towards the deadly breakers – enchanted visions of cities, high corniches bordered with mansions, forests of enlightened cranes – and it is thus that I collect the seaweed with its mortified colours."

Ever since then we have known these cities, these phantasmagoric harbours. Deserted, ghost ships drifting over the bare steppes, set in the Dolomites of ostentation or run aground in basaltic shallows, they offer to us an unspoken consent contradicted by the light stiffening of the muscles which announces the great ebbings of passion. Overcoming our anguish, we pretended to stray there, into the canyons of cement and asphalt where incomprehensible machines lay scattered and jammed with rust, over the immense alleys, of which the mass of sea comes alone to shake the torpor, and along the piers of seaside resorts where, lured by the mixture of spray and rare fur, elegant predators once lurked. But whatever town was described to us, our steps led us always to the alley where we dared not venture and that due to its imprecise orientation we had called 'The Passage of the Sea Eagle'.

This was a narrow street, a hundred years long and cut in a straight line between the glum and cracked facades of residences that had once been well-to-do. Before rejoining the avenue, we noticed that it crossed at the other end a small sunny market place, circular and bordered with arcades, whose centre was occupied by a low fountain, in the form of a flat boat which strangely recalled Bernini's hopper. Its basin had been polished to excess, to the extent of gaining this transparency, this opaline immateriality, which turns a Roman fountain into a fountain in every accepted sense of the term, at once boat and calyx, sumptuous barge and debauchee's bath for some capricious and cruel queen of antiquity. If we hesitated each time to break the charm which held us prisoner for hours at the entrance to the Passage of the Sea Eagle, we never spoke about the strange attraction it exercised over us, nor of the tacit interdiction of which we were the object.

The autumn equinox came. One evening, before chancing the sinuosity of a new unknown city where the twilight had already caused all the windows to blaze with a blossoming of maniacal fireflies and coralligenes, we climbed into the tower to welcome our two engineer hosts. Leaning against the glazing of the hall of fires, Clélie (that was her name) said in a muffled tone to her companion whose gaze we never met: "The rose that Matilda offers to Ofterdingen, like an unexpected challenge to Klingsor's didactic euphoria, is, in a single tegumented and sumptuous spiral, the whole city over which the old poet misrules in their name. But the initiator owes it to his character to accept the supreme humiliation of ignorance and immolation. You have ruled over the void for too long: a merchant of deadly images, rather poorly stocked, you have been nothing to me, neither begetter nor lover, and you now come to grief on the sacrificial altar. It is not the sterile vat sanctified by none of your victims. Know that it is the rose that Matilda offers and that it is also the Boletus of Satan."

It thus seemed that our visit was ill-timed and we prepared to descend the shaky path of spiralling stairs where the frightened crabs fled before our steps with an astringent grating that still chilled us. We did not see the gesture that Clélie was to make, but we noticed that the lights cast above the cliff allowed us a bird's eye view of the proteiric city for the first time. Under our alarmed eyes, the image started to turn on itself more and more quickly, in a terrible fermentation of lights whose acceleration turned for a few moments into an insupportable whiteness. We understood that the axis of this demented gyration, the hub of the shadow pierced with light towards which we were each time mysteriously beckoned without ever risking ourselves in its centre, finally managing to take our bearings. . . And we were again alone, our souls broken down, in the face of an immense surface of dark rock which suddenly seemed to our battered gaze to be of jet. A large block, sticking out like a toothing stone, blazed forth for one final time and then came away, bouncing from relief to relief, and rolled on as far as our feet.

Of all the great treats granted to us, I do not know of any more bewildering than those far-off long walks along the cliffs of Orpalée.

★★★★★

published in Claude Tarnaud, *Orpalée* (1965) Paris: M. Cassé

★★★★★

CLAUDE TARNAUD (Maisons-Laffitte (Yvelines), 1922 – Ap, 1991) Poet, storyteller and object-maker, Claude Tarnaud co-founded the group *La Revolution la nuit* and participated in surrealist activities after the Second World War.

RIKKI DUCORNET

The Volatilized Ceiling Of Baron Munodi

For my friends at the *Equator*.

The museums of Europe keep curious portraits illustrating the assumption that the body gives the soul its shape. Da Vinci imagined a woman with a monkey's face, Rubens human lions, Della Porta a man with the profile of a ram. I myself am albino; I look like an angel and so inspire acute passions. Longing for a purifying fire, men would defile me, or, taking pleasure, be absolved of sin. If I have never shared their fevers, it is because a woman has stolen my heart. Black and clairvoyant she claims that one day the world will shrivel in the sun like a plum. However, this is not the story of our love affair, but of an obsession justified by my friend's bleak vision. As my love for her, it has withstood the teeth of time.

*

One evening in the early seventeen-hundreds and shortly before the tragedy which was to deny the promise of Eden, the Baron Munodi described for his little son those metal mirrors made of four isosceles triangles once cherished by the Greeks. At the point where the triangles converged reigned a sacred and a potent (and potentially dangerous) conjunction: here air was transformed to fire.

Later, in lieu of a bedtime story, the Baron took his son to see the temporary workshops installed in the arcades and galleries of a new palace near Naples. Little Gustavo had heard of the workshops, everybody had, and his curiosity could be contained no longer. Over ten thousand pieces destined to be incorporated into the geodesic marquetry of the ceilings were in the process of being conceived, cut, painted, and dusted with gold. The child perceived the workshops through a refractive fog; the air was saturated with particulated gold and he was dazzled.

Baron Munodi told Gustavo that because of their beauty and the knowledge they conveyed, the paintings were deemed evil by a repugnant authority he did not choose to name, but which wielded a tragic power.

"Some believe that these images can make beasts talk", the Baron told his son, "in the manner of the serpent which tempted Eve; and that I have the power to excite tempests". If it is true that the Baron was powerful, his power, as the ceiling which blossomed in the torchlight, oscillated on the verge of an abyss.

With eager eyes, Gustavo devoured green lions and gravid elephants, a submerged city of mermen shining beneath the moon, a laughing cupid, a man with the face of a camel, a girl as naked as a lily. From out of a blue oval the size and colour of a puffin's egg, a one-eyed sun gazed at him with such urgency that he blushed before he looked away. Then, peering around a smocked and spattered elbow, the boy saw an image which vibrated so mysteriously that he was not content to touch it, but must lick it with his tongue and, putting it to his quivering nostrils, deeply inhale.

This potent picture imprinted itself not only on the child's brain, but upon the imaginations of future generations. I have awakened from startling dreams which reveal to me just what was now being revealed to Gustavo:

A mature albino ape, its heart pierced by an arrow, falls from a tropical tree. As he falls he attempts to catch the bloody ropes spouting from his breast. In truth his wound is fathomless, a mortal fracture in the body of the world. Gustavo sees that the ape's hands are very like his own.

As in the swelter of torchlight Gustavo gazed enamoured of the ape, the image was gently taken from him and the cipher 666 painted on the back. Then it was set down among many hundreds of others which lay scattered in the manner of the zodiacs which animate the vaults of Heaven.

Soon the features of the room and the painter's faces dissolved in a vortex as red as the wings of angels: a swarm of apprentices had descended upon a freshly varnished set of pictures to dust them with gold.

That night a conflagration raged throughout the Baron's workshops. By morning all that remained of the palace was char, and of the painters a fistful of calcinated teeth. The ten thousand images were reduced to smoke; the secret of Baron Munodi's ceiling had volatilized.

Proof of the catastrophe's perfidious nature, the Baron was found assassinated, his heart pierced by a long nail with such force that his body was secured to the boards of his bed. Awakening drenched in her beloved's blood, the Baroness – whose lucidity was legendary – was bound and carried off as one possessed to a madhouse. There she gave birth to my ancestor who, I know from one famous portrait in the Prado, I do not resemble. Gustavo died before reaching maturity; I, sole heir to the Munodi line and memory, am childless. A friend who knows such things has told me that this explains my compulsion to capture what I can in black ink on white paper.

⋆

Baron Munodi's properties and his little son Gustavo were seized by the executive officers of the Inquisition. After an exhaustive search, a pentagon was found freshly painted in an attic, and among the Baron's things a ball of feathers and a shoe studded with pins. A globe was found also, and a map of the heavens that showed the planets in orbit.

Gustavo was stripped of his silk shirt and dressed in a penitent's shift of sacking. The vivid curls of his infancy were shorn from his head, and he was forced to spend the lion's part of his days among God-fearing arsonists in prayer.

As he had neither pastimes nor companions to ease the morbid placidity of monastic life, Gustavo courted vertigo in the shape of a memory. From incessant practice he could within an instant conjure the ape and carry it perpetually before him. Image 666 was his own elementary secret, the exact centre of his mind's incarnate mirror. Try as they did to discover the exact nature of the umbilicus that joined Gustavo to his past, his father's assassins had to admit to failure.

The monks explained to the Grand Inquisitor that they did not know the object of the child's worship and so could not subvert it. They knew only that it was an alien practice. The heresiarch's son was prey to an incomprehensible exultation which had nothing to do with Jesus Christ; his fervent prayers were all his own. No one knew that as the others fixed the cross, Gustavo gazed inward upon that image of the ape which was Baron Munodi's metaphor for loss, dolorous spiritual mishap and detour, and a primary element in a vast, coded message of incendiary significance. Just as the Baron's enemies feared, the ceiling was no idle inventory, but the revelation of an itinerary. Now as I write this, as the very atmosphere escapes into sidereal space and the world's balloon deflates, I fear its vanished alphabets spelled out *the only itinerary*. Gustavo had seen the unassembled pages of the Book of Salvation. Envy, greed and groundless fear had destroyed it.

*

One rare afternoon of peace in the monastery gardens, Gustavo chanced to witness a bitter argument about the nature of the creature evoked in chapter thirteen of John's *Apocalypse* which reads: *May he who is intelligent calculate the number of the beast. The number is that of a man, and his number is six-hundred and sixty-six*.

Delirious with joy, Gustavo ran to the circle of contentious monks and cried out:

"I know! For I have seen it! And see him even now! He is an ape! Oh! A beautiful ape!"

Lifted into the air by an ear, Gustavo received such a slap that the ear was nearly torn from his head. Then he was kicked down corridors of stone and thrust into a cell, windowless but for a vertical aperture just wide enough to send an arrow into the heart of the forest.

From that time on, Gustavo, in concordance with the *Instrucio*, was struck each night to hammer the cruel nail of piety deep into his skull, and again at daybreak to banish whatever fancy might have slipped down his festering ear as he slept. It was said that the Baron's son could not be saved, not even by an extraordinary act of grace, that his words had divulged an unforgivable heresy:

"The child", the monks informed the Grand Inquisitor, "implies that the son of God is an ape."

What the assessors, councillors and judges of the Inquisition reviled as a crime of *lèse-majesté divine*, is today, except within the most reactionary enclaves of the Middle-East, North Africa and North America, common knowledge. The exemplary science of genetics has corroborated the marvel: the ape's number – give or take a chromosome or two – is the mirror of man's.

Once vigorous, a boy who delighted in pictures of the rope-dancing elephants of Rome and Pompeian acrobats, Gustavo was now but bone and nerve, subject to visions of subterranean demons. His ravaged face refused to mend and a mortal fever gnawed at his mind. He did not notice the crusted iron cross which hung suspended from a nail, threatening, at any instant, to shatter his skull. As a moon the ape had risen, and it orbited his thoughts. I who have shadowed gorillas with the hope that the quintessential nature of my ancestry be revealed to me, understand that infant's *idée fixe*: it is my own. You see, I have inherited my purpose from a child dead over two hundred years. Some spontaneous influence, perhaps electric, has caused all the Munodis to share Gustavo's obsession: my great-grandfather spent a lifetime investigating the footprints of the *Yeti*; my father's father lived among the *Macaca speciosa* of Thailand; my great aunt Dolorosa, when she was not tracking baboons, wrote an excellent book on Rosalie-Zaccharie Ferriol – the ravishing French albino (and according to a precious engraving, my Doppelgänger), whose celebrated eyes burned so brightly they pierced the hearts of everyone who saw her; and an essay on *Moby Dick* in which she notes that, unlike white apes, white whales are common (or, rather, *were* common); whales of any colour are no longer common.

★

It is now time to return to Gustavo who is dying, and who dreams he is once again in the Baron's workshops. In the light of resinous torches, apprentices run up and down the mazed avenues of the painter's tables, seeding the puissant images with gold. The air is so charged with gold that when Gustavo opens his eyes for the last time he sees that his dreams's luminescence has flooded his cell, that he is held in the tender embrace of the beloved ape. An angel exiled from Heaven, it has fallen onto his verminous pallet of straw.

When the monks find Gustavo's body, they burn it. It is written in their erroneous books that a toad hopped from the flames and that a viper circled the pyre. These are fables. The truth is that a morbid agitation disrupted the questionable peace of that wicked place thereafter and led to its decline.

My own researches into albinism and, inevitably, melanism, have taken me to the far reaches of this our own shrinking planet and evolved into a study of the coded alphabets which are visible on the backs and faces of all the beasts of the animal kingdom. Above the 40th North Parallel I have, in months of incessant night, tracked white wolves and blue foxes. In the smoky depths of forests on fire I have seen hermaphrodite snakes of ink and milk, their eyes the colour of the caviar of scallops and so rare they can be counted on the fingers of one hand.

Recovering from malarial fever in France I have recorded the white spots on the backs of piebald crows (*turdus merula*), which, having beaked the tainted waters, plummet from the pollarded trees. I have spent an entire decade mapping the markings of capricorn beetles and even the ears of tigers; their seed is crippled irretrievably. Just as the whales, the apes, and Baron Munodi's miraculous ceiling, they too shall vanish.

★

Recently, as I lay beside my mistress, I dreamed a disturbing dream: I had bought several pounds of fresh squid to prepare for many illustrious friends, all who had, miraculously, survived the gas chambers. The squid were slippery and wet, and, as any inspired intuition, hard to hold. They were also perfectly white. I took each up one by one and with a very sharp knife slit them open, revealing a perfect little figure of a man, white as ivory and dressed like the princes of ancient Persia – studded turbans on their heads and scimitars in their belts. They wore neatly buttoned vests, and one had caviar – tiny white pearls of it – clinging to his loins and inner thighs.

With care I slipped each perfect man from his casing of flesh and severed the head. Then I cut the arms from the torso, and after that the legs. I feared they would waken and scream, but all slept and if one bled, his blood was pale, hardly blood at all; the blood of a fish. When I had finished I realised with a shudder that there had been one hundred and eleven manikins, and that I had sliced each one into six.

I have described this dream to a psychoanalysist, a philosopher, and to my mistress.

The psychoanalysist insists that the squid is the symbol of the penis, the sleeping man I would kill rather than arouse. The philosopher suggests that these mermen are the metaphor for the soul's longing for gnosis which the mind assassinates from fear – grace more terrible to the uninformed heart than eternal darkness. I believe that my mistress's answer is by far the most satisfactory, although I know that all answers are fragments in the puzzle of the True:

"The dismembering of the body symbolises its dissolution, the first step towards regeneration, and without which resurrection is impossible. The water that spills from the squid's body, as the blood from the heart of the wounded ape, symbolises the amniotic fluid, and above all the primal waters from which all things descend: green algae, blue foxes, men and women both white and black."

*

The years pass too swiftly. Like a fantastic doctrine become ashes before it can be read, my lover and I will be reduced to dust. In one brief lifetime, I cannot undo the tragic loss of a child's life, nor begin to reconstruct an alchemical lexicon; nor can I, with exactitude, chart a family tree. Even the finite combinations on the backs of common beetles elude me. Yet I am certain that should the world survive, others will be haunted in much the same way and dream similar dreams. This is my greatest hope, if Eden is to be one day reconstituted.

*****

The Volatilized Ceiling of Baron Munodi first published in
1991 Angers: Éditions Deleatur
reprinted in *The Complete Butcher's Tales* 1994, Normal, Illinois: Dalkey Archive Press

*****

RIKKI DUCORNET (see volume one p 208) In the past year, Rikki Ducornet has received an award from The Lannan Foundation; her novel *The Jade Cabinet* was nominated for a National Book Critics' Circle award.

ALAIN JOUBERT

Art, Pleasure And Gardening

He was sick of living within four walls grey with dust in the tiny two-roomed flat with kitchen washbasin and toilet on the landing in the tenth district which a lucky (?) chance (and a little help from his sister) had provided him with the opportunity to invest in a couple of years earlier. While lying on a more or less collapsed spring mattress which was set out on a level with the floor, he let his gaze linger on those miserable grey walls with torn wallpaper on which it was still possible to discern, here and there, a few bunches of grapes trying vainly to serve as decoration but which had been definitively devoured. In this way the minutes were drawn out and by degrees were turned into hours without the slightest desire having passed through his mind. But suddenly, when twilight had ceased eating away what little light appeared to him through the dirty windows that opened onto another wall without windows (it was six in the evening and February had never been the most cheerful month) he decided that what he would do would be to buy a plant. That was the first day.

*

On the second day, he went to the flower market on the Ile de la Cité. After some dreadful hesitations and a titanic internal struggle, he finally chose a *Monstera deliciosa* of the *Araceae* family, whose leaves, twelve inches long and ten inches across, stretched out in the form of a heart and deeply cut between the secondary veins, threw many strange shadows on his walls when he installed lateral lighting.

Passion then overcame him. An *Aechmea fascianta,* some

Bromeliaceae, a *Cissus antartica,* some *Vitaceae*, a *Diffenbachia*, a *Fatshedera*, a *Peperomia* together made their appearance in the flat and something tropical began to rise up from between their foliage. That was the third day.

★

On the fourth day, as he scrutinised the hothouse at the Botanical Gardens seeking new species, he had an encounter. In front of a *Scindapsus Aursus*, which originally came from the Solomon Islands and whose heart-shaped leaves very much intrigued him, his gaze met that of a charming young woman, whose long hair lightly flowed and who appeared to be – like him – fascinated by the plant world. Later, as they lay on the spring mattress, which as discreetly as possible had accompanied their amorous journey, they decided to turn the two-room apartment into an enchanted place in which the plants would occupy pride of place in the room as they already did in their lives.

★

No sooner said than done. They bought a quantity of peat and wood hummus and spread it far and wide over the floor and took the plants they had already bought out of their pots and, after unpotting them, planted them in open ground, together with a good dozen newcomers they had spent the day collecting in more or less the usual way. In the evening, exhausted but happy, they slept together, naked, on a bed of palm leaves after having refreshed themselves with fruits. That was the fifth day.

★

On the sixth day, they were surprised to see that the plants had sprung up in a way that had nothing natural about it. From morning, a tangle of branches, leaves and liana prevented them from moving about the flat easily and by noon they had to become resigned to tracing out a path with a machete if they wanted to get from one room to the other. They found this extremely poetic and were pleased with the astonishing humid heat which reigned in the rooms, something which encouraged them to dispense with the slightest clothing on their radiant bodies. Water streamed down the walls, serving to complete the illusion but completely ruining the wallpaper! Dozens of birds came in through the windows and mingled their songs with the sighs of our two young savages, who were more in love than ever!

★

The next day passed as if in a dream. Strange and succulent fruits had appeared on some of the plants – which soon turned into trees – and they even saw an iguana, which sprang up from who knows where and took a trip around the room before vanishing into the undergrowth. They spent their time savouring its flow, caressing one another and re-discovering the pleasures of forgotten senses – or the meaning of forgotten pleasures. In short, they weren't bored! That was the seventh day.

★

At dawn on the eighth day there was a knock on the door. An old man with a long white beard, flanked by a tipstaff and a policeman, read out a declaration printed on official paper that announced that they were being evicted forthwith, failing which they would suffer a severe penalty. And this is how they were ignominiously thrown out of Paradise Road for having tried to create it there again! Since then he has worked for the Social Security, while she became a teacher. As for the flat, they say no one has ever been able to get inside, so intensely has the vegetation grown. But then they say so many things.

★★★★★

published in *Homnesies* no 1 (April 1984)

★★★★★

ALAIN JOUBERT (see volume one p 268)

ZUCA SARDAN

The Sun And His Rose-Pink Buick

Cruising very slowly down the Milky Way, the Sun finally arrived at the hospital in his rose-pink Buick. . .

On Earth, the cold had long ago frozen even the Eskimos. . . All human life had died. Only a few lichen had managed to survive, invading abandoned palaces, churches, libraries, covering a book by Swedenborg left on the table. . .

Concerned, Dr Star ordered the Sun to have himself admitted to hospital. (There was no point in pretending. . . There might still be a few purple rays, for a while, perhaps. . . Then. . .)

The rose-pink Buick remained where he had left it, near the park. And years and years went rolling by, along the precipitous rim of the Great Zodiacal Ring.

The Sun no longer left his bed. Out of an ingenuous vanity, however, he continued to wear his Raybans and an Indian silk scarf in blues and violets.

On the bedside table stood his small white retro-chic radio, resembling nothing so much as one of Buck Rodgers' rockets. And from it, amidst the crackles, on the shortest of short waves, emerged the unmistakable voice. . .of Elvis Presley.

The Sun glanced at his photo of the Moon, looking lovely, the low neck of her dress artfully awry to reveal her large breasts, very round and white, the breasts he loved so much.

Smiling sadly, he bent over, got his fountain pen and a pad of orange-coloured writing paper out of the drawer and began:

"Dear Moon, my little cutiepie. . . It appears that I am dying. . ."

*****

Translated from the Portuguese by Margaret Jull Costa

*****

ZUCA SARDAN: (see volume one p 250–1)

MARCEL MARIËN

The Ghost Of A Shadow

In spite of a modest education, Hubert Stassar had been in turn a surveyor, a freelance journalist, a broker, a guide and an insurance agent. He also had a favourite hobby, which was to worry about history. Or more exactly the minor aspects of history, for he was one of those odd characters who are exclusively interested in secondary figures, those obscure types whose names have appropriately but almost by accident survived the material disappearance to which most people are subject.

Thus it was that Stassar in the course of his reading came by chance across the Chevalier Thomas de Bonnepierre who had played a forgotten role at the court of Louis-Philippe. Chateaubriand mentions him somewhere in his correspondence, praising the sincerity of his views and his great vivacity of mind. What exactly had he done in the shadow of the sad monarch of July? This was not by any means clear and, prompted by someone who stood out only slightly in the madding crowd, it was at first with curiosity then with passion that Stassar threw himself on the track of his potential hero, burying himself deeply in the impenetrable dust of forgotten memory.

After long and laborious research he established that the chevalier had been tutor to the royal children, a post he retained after the abdication, and that Guizot esteemed him as a young man with a fine future ahead of him. This added up to something but not very much. Hubert might well have had to abandon his investigation had he not discovered a little later, in a second-hand shop in Rouen, a mass of old religious-books among which a slim pamphlet (whose cover bore no details) attacking Napoleon III and the imperial court had impudently been slipped. In it Eugenie de Montijo was insulted in crude terms and the Emperor described as a 'phantom knave' and a 'bloated vermin'. The name of the author could be read at the end of the text in fine Elzevir capitals. Hubert was astonished to see the name of Thomas de Bonnepierre clearly printed there.

He bought the booklet for a few francs and resolved to continue his quest in Paris. He found nothing at the Bibliothèque Nationale, but at the Arsenal discovered a further copy of the ancient booklet as well as another work, whose content was more innocuous and, doubtless for this reason, was, unlike the other one, not completely without publishing details. It had been printed at Alençon, at 11 rue des Marcheries to be precise.

His job as an insurance agent allowed him to organise his roaming through France more or less as he liked. A week later he arrived in Alençon and was fortunate enough to find that the printing house was still at the same address, proudly displaying on its nameplate the legend: 'Business founded in 1850'. In the studio was an old bookbinder named Eugène Grindel, who no longer did much work but who was kept around because he was well respected. Stassar was able to talk to him and encouraged him to go over his oldest memories in the hope of discovering new clues.

Obviously the old man could know nothing about the chevalier, but Stassar did learn from him that a vast archive of material had been deposited in an adjoining warehouse when the main buildings were given a general facelift. That had been forty years earlier but it was not impossible that he might find some information going back to the earliest days of the firm.

Hubert Stassar had no difficulty in gaining authorisation to go through the confused mass providing he did not disturb anyone and replaced everything when he had finished. He set to work at once. Luckily he soon realised that the bundles had been arranged in a particular order that more or less respected chronology. Consequently he was able to save a lot of time and the very look of the yellowed and crumbling paper permitted him to quickly go back to the time of the chevalier. After three days of minute excavation, Stassar, on the stroke of eleven, stifled a triumphant cry. Right in the middle of a mass of accounts' papers, in faded ink, he laid hands on a copy of a note dated 21st April 1855 addressed to Thomas de Bonnepierre at no 12 rue de Bois-Sabbat at Dreux. The imprecise and fixed outline, which contained only a name and a few sentences, caused a stir to pass through him.

The object of the note, for a sum of twelve francs 10 sols, was not specified, but Stassar thought it most probably concerned the printing costs of the booklets. As he went to the door, he noticed an abandoned bath tub in which a solitary spider sauntered. 'Spider of the bath, hope', he mechanically murmured since it was still morning. He left the print shop, not without thanking M. Grindel for his friendly help and, as he still had time, took the road to Dreux straightaway. He arrived early in the evening, found a hotel, and next morning took up the hunt once again.

At Dreux Town Hall he needed to negotiate with a grumpy clerk to gain access to the archives. A few lies accompanied with a tip were sufficient to arrange matters. The registers were well-ordered and it took him little time to discover that the chevalier de Bonnepierre had lived in Dreux (his native town) for nearly a quarter of a century, that he had married a certain lady named Blanche Capel, who had given him two daughters: Sanguine, born immediately after the marriage, and Sabine, who was born two years later. The latter's birth seemed to have cost the life of the mother judging from the coincidence of dates.

Stassar also learned that Sanguine had vanished when she was fourteen, no one knew why or how, and it appeared that she had still not been found after a search that took place two years later. Soon afterwards, the chevalier moved from Dreux with his second daughter to Cambai.

Stassar had time: his work could wait. He left straightaway for the old archbishopric of Fénélon, land of the swan and mint toffee. Fresh research brought more facts: Thomas de Bonnepierre had lived for two years in a family *pension* in rue des Clefs, the Pension Pilate. It was there that Sabine married a gentleman named Henry Cube, a horse-butcher from Grasse, where the couple would live. The young bride was only fifteen and so special dispensation was necessary. This was granted, doubtless in order to repair an ill-timed pregnancy since, just four months later, on 15th January 1878 to be precise, little Hector was born.

Without waiting for the happy event the chevalier, who had remained in Cambai after the marriage, left the boarding house just two months later and departed for Germany. That was all the public records revealed, the vaguest of paths.

Not in the least discouraged, his appetite whetted, rather, Stassar again took up the trail and disembarked at Grasse railway station the following evening. He took a room at the Hotel de la Poste and, before going to bed, had an initial look around the perfume capital. The butcher's shop in rue Droite no longer existed, its place having been taken by a dairy. Still, as he carefully examined the facade, Hubert was almost sure he could perceive the trace of a horse's head which must once have served as the shop's sign. Even under electric light, the difference in tone in the face of the panelling was clear enough to be discerned.

Next day he confidently made his way to the Town Hall, but was soon disabused. A fire had since destroyed part of the public record archive, precisely for the period which interested him. Stassar came out of the Town Hall mortified and wandered aimlessly around the town, again going purposelessly past the dairy. This time he could clearly make out the discoloured trace of the sign, which only served to add to his disappointment. He had made such good progress and now the chain linking the past with the present had been broken thanks to the fire. He ruminated on his misfortune when chance led his steps to an avenue planted with palm-trees. At the end there was a small square with benches in a circle around a sort of obelisk. He sat down on an unoccupied bench and found himself facing a monument to those who had died in the Great War. The air was fragrant and the weather radiant. A few dun-coloured sparrows skipped around, chirping.

Hubert had been sitting there idly for a quarter of an hour when his eyes fixed on a large bluebottle which had just landed on the column and proceeded to flitter, head-down, across the names engraved in the stone. Mechanically, he started to read the names of the dead one by one in alphabetical order when suddenly his heart skipped a beat. Between a Roger Bodart and a Louis Dubrau, the name Hubert Cube leapt out. This could only be the grandson of the chevalier.

He rose and went in search of a telephone box. Thumbing feverishly through the directory he came across the address of a war veteran's association, which he noted down there and then. It was not very far away, in an old private mansion situated in the centre of garden grounds behind an iron barred gate. He rang and waited for a while before a little old man with a blotchy face under snow-white hair came to open it. His lapel was festooned with military ribbons and he limped with the aid of a rubber-tipped cane. He was nonetheless very friendly and it was with a broad smile that he invited his visitor to follow him inside.

The old man's name was Alcide Bava and he seemed heartset on providing as much information as he was able, as though he hoped thereby to atone for the shame of not having been massacred alongside those whose memory he kept alive. The archivist consulted his card-index and found Cube's dossier. Immediately the link which Stassar had feared broken was renewed in an unhoped-for way. Everything was again enmeshed and wonderfully so. Hector Cube had fallen at Douaumont on 3rd June 1916. His body had been taken to Grasse and buried there. His widow, Anne-Marie, died soon after the Armistice, leaving a son, Hilaire Cube, and a daughter named Marie-Anne.

Although it was outside his province, the conserver of the past had augmented his documentation with much ancillary or subsequent detail relating to the families of the deceased. By passion or pastime (in the event rather like Hubert Stassar), old Alcide could not help recording everything that turned up in connexion with his brothers-in-arms. This was how Hubert learned that the male descendant had turned out badly. A press cutting gave details about a knife brawl which led to his spending a few days in prison, and it recounted that, aside from his bellicose temper that, as a child he sometimes stood at the first-floor window and spat on the heads of people in the street. Later, the butcher's shop having been taken over by his father, he stirred up a mob of customers against him, not without vilifying them too "in the name of all our murdered brother horses!" Reaching manhood, his trace was lost among the Africa Corps and, although his remains were never recovered, it was assumed that he had died during a skirmish near Wadi Djefar.

As for Marie-Anne, she had been charmed by a customs officer from Lorraine whose name was Grein. She followed him to Colmar, where he lived, which is as much of a displacement as that experienced by the poet meeting the Andalusian woman in Barcelona, but such is life. Afterwards, although they were never officially married, a daughter was born who Marie-Anne, still attached to her mother's memory, had baptised Anne-Marie. The latter, who retained the maternal surname, was born on 11th July 1937. Today she must therefore be – as Bava remarked – forty years old. She appeared not to have left her town of birth and had remained single, though in between times her mother and natural father had died.

Stassar noted all this down, including the address of the last descendant of the chevalier de Bonnepierre. More impatient than ever, he took leave of the amiable archivist and immediately made his way to the station.

The following evening he disembarked at Colmar and, since he had slept through the journey, felt an urge to take a stroll awhile in the night. A taxi took him to the frontier. He made the driver wait as he meditatively strolled along the roadside. He gazed at Germany, amorphous and immense, covered in deep shadow like an ocean at rest. Somewhere over there, a hundred years before, his hero, the chevalier Thomas de Bonnepierre, had vanished.

He took the road back to town and got out at the centre. He went on foot in search of 25 Grand'Rue. As he passed rue des Clefs, he recalled that of Cambai where the chevalier had lived. Was he finally going to find the key to the door?

At the appointed address, he found a small hairdressing salon of an elegant if modest kind whose sign, 'Anne-Marie Hairdresser', seemed to confirm old Alcide's information. He restrained his great desire to ring the bell as it was past midnight and there was no point in disturbing his hero's great-granddaughter now that he was on the point of meeting this distant reincarnation in the flesh. How things went would obviously depend on how he approached her and the reception she would give him.

In spite of the late hour, he was able to find a small hotel, a little sleazy it's true, and he spent the rest of the night tossing and turning in his bed, annoyed by the noisy love-making filtering through the flimsy walls.

Finally daybreak came. He got ready and had breakfast in a hurry, paid, and left, and wandered, slowly and with a little anxiety, to Grand'Rue. The little shop was still closed. He had around half an hour to kill. A female silhouette appeared, alert and graceful, and unbolted the door before she went about her business inside the shop amidst the chairs and hair-dryers. Stassar crossed the road and pushed open the glass door.

Anne-Marie welcomed him kindly and when he told her that he was preparing a study of her ancestor and the role he had played in the history of France, she was at first taken aback, but then offered to help him with the little she knew. But the bell over the door that marked all the comings and goings had just tinkled to announce a client. Anne-Marie apologised and said she would be free at seven in the evening. Without ceremony, Hubert invited her to dinner and they arranged that he would collect her after work. Already, through their words, they had entered into a kind of intimacy.

Truth to tell, barely a word about the chevalier great-great-grandfather was uttered during the whole meal. Stassar was won over by Anne-Marie's openness and by the captivating charm this lively brunette, on the threshold of maturity, had retained. The fine dinner, rather too well accompanied with drink, no doubt, did the rest. Since both of them were free, they continued the evening longer than is usual on a first date. So much so that, two months later, they were married.

In the meantime, Stassar had sold off some of his possessions and had obtained a fixed position which allowed him to live in Colmar. He hoped to be able to develop the hairdressing salon and to employ more staff in order to free Anne-Marie. One day he acquired a small villa, very close to the German border. The couple went there every weekend with a kind of common satisfaction which, without going so far as intoxication, no less bore a semblance of love.

One fine summer's night, as they embraced, Hubert observed Germany, distant beneath a starry sky, through the open window. He imagined the millions of couples experiencing the same feelings as they did at that moment, as they held each other, bodies entwined and souls melted together. And, in a flash, the past century, that century whose stray thread he had picked up again, triumphing through tenacity over neglect and oblivion, appeared to him summarised in one second. By means of this obscure journey – from name to name and town to town and culminating in this body trembling with life – it was as if he had availed himself of superhuman longevity, carried beyond ordinary horizons by dint of this mysterious and inexhaustible transmigration of flesh through flesh.

While his wife slept, Hubert remained thinking for sometime. His fate seemed to him like a continuous enchantment. He sought to comprehend the circuitous routes that had brought him to this bed, to the side of this sweet woman, from the faraway and faceless chevalier to the real and agreeable body of his daughter's great granddaughter. He imagined the blood circulating impetuously from heart to heart, from Sabine to his sleeping wife, through the intertwinings of the Annes and Maries, from birth to death, like an irresistible river mocking the closed lock gates of the skin. He also asked himself if destiny had a meaning and if he should conceive of a link between the Alençon weaver and the archivist of Grasse, between dead Sanguine and joyful Hilaire, between the butcher's shop and the customs-post, the spider in the bath and the alphabetical fly, not to speak of all the wars and that strange profession which consists in dressing other people's hair. In short, to have entered body and soul into his hero's family was no mean feat. How many historians could claim as much? On this thought he departed imperceptibly from the world, double-locked in a deep dreamless sleep.

One month later, Anne-Marie told him that she was pregnant. With a girl most probably, Hubert immediately thought, and added, in his heart, that they would call her Marie-Anne so as not to disturb any of the links of the strong chain of time.

A few weeks passed before something occurred that was to plunge Stassar back into his original quest. Anticipating the appearance of the child with whom Anne-Marie was now heavy, the couple had decided to rent out the hairdressing salon and definitively settle down in their villa on the border. They bustled about emptying the flat in Grand'Rue where the new manageress would set up home.

In the course of this activity Hubert, as he cleared the attic, came across a chest containing a mass of old and varied objects amongst which, right at the bottom, he was amazed to find a large oak box. It was oblong and had been hermetically sealed, bearing the name of the chevalier Thomas de Bonnepierre, followed by his German address, the Gasthof Kreutzer at Mayence. A label and multiple seals revealed that it had been sent first to Cambai and then to Grasse, addressed to Mme Henri Cube. The reason for its being returned was given, concisely and simply in a single word: *Gestorben*. The chevalier had therefore died in the meantime, around the month of April 1878, if one could believe the stamps from across the Rhine. This made it barely three months after the birth of his grandson. It was hardly surprising, then, that the young orphan and mother had no inclination to open up the chest which had lain forgotten at the bottom of the trunk, a neglect that had been contagious since his descendants had taken no more notice of it.

Hubert carefully set about unnailing the cover. It was a slow and arduous task since it seemed that, to ensure that the contents would be properly protected, the chest had been varnished all over to seal up the joins. He called Anne-Marie and she sat at his side, moved mimetically by her husband's feverish impatience. A tear even came to her eyes, which she was unable to explain.

However, the package contained only a few carefully folded clothes, apparently those of the chevalier. There were several complete suits and cloaks, hats and shoes, all dyed black and everything in a perfect state of preservation, although they had been excessively pressed down for a whole century.

Stassar emptied the box in an almost religious way, placing each item delicately at his side. There was also some immaculately white underwear and some as-new black silk stockings. Anne-Marie eyed this display of obsolescence without saying a word.

Finally, at the bottom of the empty box, there remained only an unsealed envelope from which Hubert took an old sepia-toned photo. It was a daguerreotype taken by one Halleux, an 'artistic portraitist' in Cambai, which had obviously been taken the day of Sabine's marriage. With heart beating fit to burst, Stassar recognised beyond any doubt, alongside the pregnant wife, in a white dress despite her condition, Henri Cube on one side (a fine figure of a man sporting a superb black curled-up moustache above a joyful smile), while on the other stood – in the flesh – serious and reserved, stiff and gaunt, the chevalier Thomas de Bonnepierre.

"Ecce homo!" Stassar could not prevent himself from exclaiming, overwhelmed with emotion and happiness. "There's my man! And he looks exactly as I've always imagined him."

And all of a sudden he had the realisation of finally understanding why he had been obscurely attached to the chevalier as others are to those gods or heroes who illumine millions upon millions of ardent looks. It was because, above all else, and in a way that was unparalleled, Thomas de Bonnepierre more than anyone else had *the correct bearing*.

Anne-Marie acquiesced in her husband's enthusiasm yet without sharing it. She had difficulty in conceiving how someone could entertain anything but indifference towards such a far distant ancestor. This did not prevent her from having an inspiration and exclaiming: "But Hubert, now that you possess all his clothes, you could dress like him!"

Without his wife's remark it is not certain the idea would have so readily come to Stassar. As far as size was concerned, while the clothes fitted in length, they were a little small around the chest. Where the chevalier's profile had been elegant and slender, that of his admirer was palpably corpulent. Well, that being the case, he thought, if the clothes cannot come to me, then I will go to the clothes. And so, without hesitation, he imposed a diet on himself to quickly lose the necessary weight. It was only a matter of a few pounds and it would only do him good.

If faith can move mountains, then admiration, if it be sincere and deep, can equally well cause fat to melt away. Hubert's sincerity was hardly in doubt. Having proscribed himself all fats and glucose, he infallibly lost weight with remarkable speed. Two months later, having limited himself, as they say, to ship's rations, he was able to don, in a state of considerable emotion, the chevalier's clothes. They now fitted as though they had been made to measure. He immediately vowed never to wear anything else. He had already, upon seeing the photo, had his hair set by Anne-Marie in the same way as her ancestor.

Naturally, fashions having changed since the founding of the Third Republic, Stassar's romantic appearance, unwaisted frock coat and tight trousers, was rather odd. While he was not completely at ease in the picturesque and spectacular clothes of long ago, his attire smacked a bit too much of disguise to pass unnoticed. However, the strict severity of the costume preserved him from laughter and ridicule. Besides, Hubert did not go out very much during the day and, when he did, a sombre greatcoat effected, between the vestimentary dress of two centuries, a compromise acceptable enough not to scandalise the locals. In any case, the times favoured anarchy. The thing was that Stassar had passed the age to subscribe to it.

The only real problem was the opera hat, which was far too visible and even gaudy. He considered half flattening the crown and adapting it into a felt hat with a wide brim. In this way he would be wearing the ancestor's hat as its owner had without it being obvious.

Time passed and Stassar's character, by nature expansive and sociable, became oddly sullen. Each day saw him more depressed and his teeth were continuously clenched. Anne-Marie did not dare draw attention to this due to the fact that his dress from another age had alienated her to such an extent that she felt at a handicap in his presence. Even when he undressed, his stiff and old-fashioned underwear kept her at a distance. She felt powerless in the face of the sadness that increasingly dominated his soul held captive by a hundred-year-old dead man who had no significance for her. It was a question, it seemed, of a close identification which was getting worse, a sort of deep empathy, perhaps irreversible, in which, with revulsion, she caught a whiff of unpleasant taints of incest or necrophilia. What was more, he no longer worked or even helped around the house.

She would have ended up completely benumbed were it not for a gnawing concern with her pregnancy and impending confinement. When the baby came into the world (a girl, as Hubert had expected and who was of course called Marie-Anne), there were difficulties and complications which kept her in the clinic for longer than usual. Once back at home she observed that her husband had employed his solitude by withdrawing even further into himself. Stassar barely recognised her, responded with hardly more than a yes or a no, and these were sometimes back to front. She went about her everyday tasks without saying a word, but with anxious brow and heavy heart.

One day he journeyed to Mayence and returned a week later, more taciturn and gloomy than ever. Then, every evening, as the Earth turned on its axis, Hubert went out into the countryside wrapped up in his greatcoat, his double hat braced to his skull. He would return late at night. By then Anne-Marie was in bed, henceforth resigned to neither wait up nor try to understand him. Her generous zeal a thing of the past, she devoted herself entirely to her daughter, who grew up apparently unaffected, a perpetual smile on her lips. Soon the couple took separate rooms without, it seems, Stassar feeling either pleasure or regret. He continued to go out at dusk, prowled around the frontier, and came back exhausted. More sombre than the night itself, he aged visibly.

Anne-Marie, taken up with her mother's role, ceased to worry about it. She told herself that it was because he dressed permanently in the chevalier's belongings that Stassar had assumed such incurable melancholy, which was perhaps part of the profound nature of his ancestral model. But something she could not in the least have suspected, and which perhaps, consumed in his anachronistic dream, Stassar himself refused to admit, was that while the chevalier Thomas de Bonnepierre (Dreux 1810 – Mayence 1878) had taken a shoe size of only six, Stassar himself needed size eight shoes.

★★★★★

originally published in *Les Fantômes du château de cartes*
Paris: Julliard

★★★★★

MARCEL MARIËN (see volume one p 115) Marcel Mariën died in Brussels in September 1983.

ANNE MARBRUN

The Man With The Hundred Knives

In the station
the gothic novel
the cast-aside novel
lies
at the end of the bench

A little girl could open it, slip her hair between the pages and learn the chapter headings by heart. She will not do it. Little girls do not like soiled books covered with suspect stains and soiled with the weariness of sleeping travellers. They prefer large dolls with blue and stupid stares, or else the jostling of loud-mouthed boys who laugh spitefully as they shake their fists. But that's not the case for mothers, mothers love cast-aside novels that tell the tale of the man with the hundred knives. They devour the words without reading them, they shiver as they seek out the traveller who has passed by, the one who is never seen. The pulse of the waiting room beats with a deep sense of unease. The emptiness is peopled with various lightfingered fugitives whose feverish hands rummage in the pockets of tramps to seize the key to the mere moment.

By the gleam of a lighter, the station master came by to inspect the platform where boredom lay in wait in the shape of a novel.

"You'll have to leave, madam. The trains are no longer running. All journeys have been cancelled. The camshaft which, when you were a little girl, carried away your insignificant joys, has been lost."

The mother, the thief of the cast-aside novel, crumpled

her ticket. "I just want to sleep for a while. To sleep on this platform where the fresh wind of history blows. That of the man with a hundred knives."

The departure boards announcing the trains have been turned off. A sweeper spits on the passing of days and mingles his fag-ends with the flakes which hum *The Javanaise* on the tiled floor.

"We are closing, madam, we are closing."

Beneath the glass dome, the rails interlaced each other for the night. In secrecy, the ballast and the fragile wild poppies prepared to open their black hearts to the light breath of smoky dawns.

The thief of history made up her eyebrows. She thought of all the men who have placed chrome on her memory. To each of them his bed. Finally everything fissures. It is like make-up, to want too much, to lose everything, everything peels away.

While the sweeper turns his back, she holds out her hand towards the abandoned book and fondles the dirty cover. Under her fingers the hundred knives rise up and irritate her skin with mischievous pricks. The thief opens her bag and slips the gothic novel of stations into it.

The neon lights in the roof crackle in a sign of impatience. It's time to have done with these lights. It's the end of the line, madam. To have done with all these stories of secrets to confide, of over-red hearts and knives bared. Certainly the fugitives with ardent hands have fled.

The station master crosses the hall following the division lines of the floor tiles, a foot on each slab. He was careful not to cross the lines. He took off his cap and every six steps donned it in oblation to the station clock.

"It's just a matter of politeness," he murmured to himself.

Then, returning all of a sudden towards the thief: "As for you, stop doing dirty things with that book! I can see what you are up to, you know. From today, novels are banned."

He went back to his hopscotch on the tiled floor, without sun and without moon. An orphaned hopscotch.

"The trains are no longer running and novels are banned."

He took a false beard from his pocket and affixed it to his chin with the elastic over his ears. The cap, by the way, winked at the departure board which would very much like to lie down somewhere underground.

In the darkness
dull distress
underneath the station

The mother, a woman and a thief, the thief of cast-aside novels, the cheat of early evenings, the woman was lying down on the bench. She placed her bag under her head. The novel was in the bag. She knew the station was empty and that everyone had left for home. They always leave, men with vague hearts and flexible shadows. As soon as she tightens her mouth in a tarantula smile, they slip away. Pale hares seeking the footpaths of sleep. She fondled them, with her too slender arms, she sometimes grasped hold of them. They slipped away, in a jog trot with deep sighs.

In the bag, the book moved around.

"Be good," said the thief. "Tomorrow you will love me."

In the roof a neon light went out and two others followed. Jog trot. A sleeping train took advantage of it to let out a prolonged sigh of pleasure. A sweet undulation passed through the whole train in a stifled clicking.

The station master has stopped, ears alert. Everything being in order, he resumes his hopscotch. Soon enough it bores him. He looks around. Nothing moves. Even the sweeper is asleep, leaning on his broom. The dust flakes had become quiet.

The station master makes a decision. He crosses the hall to the bench. The thief is not asleep, she is thinking. He sits at the end of the bench, near her feet.

"You think, madam. You think too much. That's the trouble with you."

With his hand on his heart he sought some lyrical words: "Your sadness weighs on my old heart."

The novel rebelled in the thief's bag.

"Instead you should travel."

"On which trains?" the woman enquired. "They've all stopped running."

"The trains have all stopped, yes, that's true, but. . ."

He did not find the word.

He found it. "But love is a stowaway."

The novel roared so much with laughter that it roused the woman's head. She punched the book to make it stop.

"Don't worry about it," said the manager indulgently. "It's just youth."

"Not at all," she objected. "It's not even young, this one."

"Well. . ."

It was the station master's turn to think. He thought so hard that the false beard stood on end, sketching out a complete transformation in the form of filched entrechats. A passing fly distracted the acrobatic beard and was absorbed by error into the station master's mouth. He sputtered as he spat out nylon hair. The thief became impatient.

"Stop doing that. You look ridiculous."

"I know, madam, I know, but what can one do when things are so disobedient?"

And echoing his lamentation, a great uproar shook the silence of the hall. The station master looked round.

"Well, the loudspeaker as well."

"That makes one liar less," said the woman with her eyes fixed on the ceiling.

"Falsehood is also something that has to be excused. It is like youth."

The woman bit her lip in a gesture of annoyance: "I have no interest in that."

"Fair enough," he said while thrusting his beard into his pocket.

They both turned their eyes away. The silence bounced against the walls in blue bubbles.

The silent leap
Of the void
Absorbs the night

The sweeper woke up. He pressed his broom silently on the tiled floor. The dust flakes succumbed to the touch. Without taking precautions against it, they found themselves gathered up in a heap in which each of them wound round each other. Still without a sound, the sweeper placed his broom on the ground and took an amulet from his neck in the form of a match. He struck it against the sole of his shoe and safeguarded the flame which arose between his palms. The small gleam dazzled his look of love. He leaned rather slowly towards the pile of dust flakes and discarded the burning pearl. The fire took very quickly. The dust flakes woke with a start from their blissful slumber. Caught unawares, they tried to gather together their memories and recall the steps of a graceful farandole. The dance began to take shape, but very soon crumbled away in ephemeral spirals. Like frightened butterflies, some of the dust flakes thought of flight. The flame grasped them by the sleeve, slipping words of love into their ears. They could resist no longer and slipped into the blaze with a sense of delight. They died smiling.

On the bench the guardians of silence did not want to see what was going on.

In her mind, the woman added a new chapter to the story of the man with a hundred knives, "Landrin," she murmured.

"What did you say?"

"His name."

"Well, well," approved the station master as his eyes wandered over the reflection of a languid dromedary in the glass door of the entrance.

"Landrin, that's a fine name for a criminal," the thief of novels affirmed.

The dromedary moved away slowly one step to the right, one to the left. He observed the swaying of the atmosphere.

The play of light on the glass intrigued the station master.
"What crime is he accused of?" he asked distractedly.
"Hundreds of crimes," the woman replied indignantly. "He's a monster!"
At these words, the novel fidgeted in a gesture of protest. It managed to free itself from under the head which fell heavily onto the bench. The woman righted herself and, angrily grasping hold of the bag, took out the book and flung it across the hall.
"Ah!" it said as it crashed down at the foot of the departure board.
"And what's more it complains about it," she sighed.
"Make less noise," ordered the station master. "You'll frighten the dromedary."
As if to prove the point for him, the dromedary fell to his knees and pulled in his hump which was in danger of disappearing altogether.
"I knew it," said the station master irritably. "It will end up with him vanishing."
"Goddammit," grumbled the thief. "Landrin's left me."
"That's what it is," thought the station master, "to discover love."
But he said nothing. Even so he knew something about it. At that very moment, the dromedary which he already loved, slipped away from his glance. Its outline of light faded from the glass and took the form of a sensitive ectoplasm. There was still a slight trembling, and then it completely vanished into the dark shadow of the great cemetery of oblivion.

Languid
Dromedary
Cemetery
Of oblivion

The station master held back his tears.
The thief, sitting on the edge of the bench, openly turned her back on the novel about the man with the hundred knives.

Forsaken on the tiled floor, the latter suddenly felt quite stupid. A shiver of regret passed through its weary pages. It was afraid of never knowing its own ending. This woman, with her brutal touch, her cutting lips, her burning thirst. . . This woman who turns her back.

A violent gust of wind came from the deserted platform and caused the doors to bang. A poster was torn with cries of abandoned kittens. It smelled of sulphur. A lace ventilator lit up beneath the departure board. It became aware of the drama of the station hall. The fetid smell of the drama hung about the museum of farewells forever, stealing its way into the pages of the cast-aside novel. The man with the hundred knives slipped his arms between the words, his hundred feeble arms as flaccid as worms. The knives fell one by one on the cold paving stones. Pinpricks on the mirror of regret. The ridiculous man whistled in the depths again raised his trousers with an august gesture and ran breathlessly up the stairs. When he reached the platform, he staggered over, a lamentable puddle of deja-vu.

On the bench the thief sought a new story. The one about the lost traveller (perhaps) who asked for the way (perhaps) and indeed in his eyes the lamp of proffered love glowed. Perhaps. It would be necessary for him to have some unhappiness and that truly it would be she who would burn the old yellowed page, stiffened with dried tears, for ever and ever.

The station master hummed. He has again put on the false beard and he rubs his feet together. Love is fin. . . Beneath his feet the floor tile moves imperceptibly. Who has never, ever. . . With a tap it rocked back. What if the two of us. . . In the fresh earth of light and dark fragrances, a wild poppy was impatient to blossom out.

*****

originally published as *L'Homme aux cent couteaux* Bédée: Wigwam (1992)

*****

ANNE MARBRUN (Clermont-Ferrand, 1947) Has published in the reviews *Toril*, *Camouflage*, *Le Château lyre* and currently edits *La Dame ovale*. She has alternately published stories (*Ratora, La Course au pré, Le Feu des anges*) and poetic prose (*La Petite, Casus belli*).

PAVEL ŘEZNÍČEK

VILMA

The domain of Overstolz spreads out so much it is sometimes necessary to empty some of it with a bucket. At times the baby gets thrown out with the bathwater – or rather, as once happened, someone gets thrown out with the contents of the bucket. Then, this someone fell into the cogs of an immense wristwatch which was lying about on a rock. The cogs ground the poor fellow up, transforming him into minutes and seconds which then floated over the land and formed time. "Time is born from unfortunates," sighed Vilma. "If everything was made from unfortunates I couldn't even manage to heave a sign. It would be the same as if time was made of soap bubbles."

A young man with a drummer's astonished face walked along the road into the rocks. Far in the distance a wooden cross loomed up, twelve or fifteen feet high. "Another quarter of an hour and I'll be there," murmured Heinz Lühne. He continued walking, scattering confetti as he passed. Suddenly the cross vanished as though a new slide had been placed in the projector. It was replaced by an immense samovar made of meat sporting, what's more, a white and hairy lid. Vilma froze at the castle window. Heinz Lühne went pale. He sensed that the coins in his purse had started to squabble. The big hand on his wristwatch put out its head and belched. Lühne automatically put the watch into his inside pocket and attached the purse to his wrist.

All around – I am not afraid to say it – nature was glorious. The pines swayed proudly in the noon breeze, calm spread across the rocks they dominated. Noon. A sweet song reached the village beneath the rocks, the grass being greener than ever. A young girl slept, curled up beside a half-extinguished fire.

Heinz Lühne knelt to pray. The flowers in the meadow, swaying under the caresses of the breeze, prayed with him.

On the horizon, the samovar was once more replaced by the large wooden cross. Heinz Lühne gave out a sigh of obvious relief.

From the window of the castle, Vilma dropped her handkerchief. Heinz Lühne untied the purse from his wrist and put it in his jacket. He took out his watch and tied it to his wrist. The road into the rocks had become steeper and steeper. Near the fire, the young girl woke and watched Heinz Lühne in amazement. In the village, the sweet song was silence and immediately replaced by the beating of flails. Calm deserted this corner forgotten by God, to settle in the oasis of the local cemetery. From the tombstones the oval photos of bakers (one still hastening to finish his croissant), cobblers, blacksmiths, wheelwrights and coopers, as well as that of Imperial Councillor Prügelsack, a native of the land, watched with lifeless eyes. Beside the stream the young girl who, a moment before still slept near the fire, now drank fresh water from the palms of her hands. Heinz Lühne watched her in amazement. The clouds in the sky had dispersed, the pine trees on the rocks assumed an even greater pride as they swayed back and forth.

Suddenly the cross vanished from the horizon. A six foot long pipe appeared in its place, stuffed with tobacco. Was it expecting a smoker, or was it expecting a butcher? Heinz Lühne thrust his fingers into his jacket pocket and uttered silent threats against the cemetery baker. In the cemetery the crunching of the croissant became more and more insistent. At her window, Vilma lit a cigarette. Heinz Lühne, breathing heavily, continued to climb to the top of the mountain. He had once again affixed his purse to his wrist and put his watch into his pocket.

The pipe left the horizon. In the village, the flail let up for a moment. Even the baker, on the cemetery photo, stopped eating his croissant. The young girl who had drunk spring water once again slept by the fire.

The large wooden cross again dominated the horizon. Near the fire, Heinz Lühne woke the young girl and told her to drink the spring water from the palms of her hands. The cross on the horizon lengthened by three feet and widened by as much. At the window of the castle, Vilma lit a second cigarette. The cross lengthened by another three feet, as its arms retracted by as much. Beside the stream, the young girl refused to drink more water from her palms. Heinz Lühne shrugged his shoulders wearily. The young girl put out the fire and, with slow steps, went back to the village. On the horizon, the cross again lengthened as its arms retracted – to the extent that a straight line rose up on the horizon bearing no relation to a cross. At the window of the castle, Vilma successively went pale and turned red. The straight line vanished from the horizon and was replaced with a bloodstained cotton tampon. It was twelve feet high and twelve feet across and twelve feet long. It was bleeding and assumed an air of self-importance.

Heinz Lühne took the purse from his wrist, took his watch out of his pocket and then, throwing them both away, ran off.

The young girl, who had first been sleeping near the fire and than drinking spring water from her palms, was frozen with amazement. The sight of Heinz Lühne in flight was more than disturbing. As he ran along he lost first one arm, then the other, then both legs came apart from his body, followed by his trunk. . . until all that was left was a head floating in mid-air. The young girl, whose name was Xena, sobbed gently.

The massive bloodstained cotton tampon left the horizon. Heinz Lühne's head also vanished. The horizon was again dominated by a wooden cross, between twelve and fifteen feet high. On the cross Heinz Lühne's re-constituted body struggled.

In the window of the castle, Vilma lit another cigarette, then went to set the table.

*****

*****

PAVEL ŘEZNÍČEK (Blanski, Moravia, 1942) Situating himself on the margins of Czechoslovak surrealism, Pavel Řezníček is a prolific poet and storyteller passionately fond of jazz. His novel, *The Ceiling* had been translated into French.

RAÚL HENAO

Billiards

In the afternoons I hung out with the fat man in the corner of one of the local cafes. As we downed a few bottles of beer, we watched a tie salesman approach displaying his merchandise that consisted of half a dozen silk ropes, acquired at the various scaffolds erected around the city. The fat man asked to be shown certain ones of a particular size and quality, and while he executed that delicate operation, we heard the harping of the main speaker at a political rally outside, who exhorted for the initiation of an implacable crusade against the vice and anarchy that were about to seize the reins of power. A mounted guard entered the cafe on horseback and, making his way to the counter, ordered an enormous hamburger whose mustard ran out of the corner of his very thick lips which persisted in devouring everything in sight. Considering the grave situation of civil unrest, which we heard about continuously in a news bulletin on the radio, we left the place. Visibly satisfied, the fat man dragged me into the street by the arm. As I looked at him again – alarmed by the persistent smell of embalming fluid emanating from his clothes – he rolled like a billiard ball across the green cloth of the pool table, disappearing into one of its pockets.

*****

translated from the Spanish by Cindy Schuster

*****

RAÚL HENAO (Cali, Colombia, 1944) has collaborated with the journals *Dunganon* (Sweden), *Ojo de Aguijon* (Paris) and *Arsenal: Surrealist Subversion* (Chicago). Poet and essayist, he has published several books and edited an *Antologia de la poesia para-surrealista* with Stefan Baciu (1981).

ANDREAS EMBIRIKOS

The Road

Misty at dawn, the road is shadowless; as bright as the yellow tones of wind instruments at noonday in the sun. Objects, shining buildings, all creation seems *en fête*, rejoicing in the light, like a cock crowing on a fence.

Without a care the road unfurls, like one who whistling (spring wind among the reeds) goes by without a care, and as the light grows stronger, the traffic on the road (of passers-by, pedestrians and riders) increases and becomes more numerous.

The travellers are too many to count. Among unsung poets and nameless saints, among long-haul lorries, everyone, middle-class and proletarian alike, goes by, all of them obedient to something, to something often very well disguised (which is to say, obedient to Fate) some on foot and some mounted on wheeled vehicles, on conveyances of every sort, a motley transport, passing amid the tumult and the uproar, in Citroëns, in Cadillacs, on Vespas and on carts.

The road, gravel-surfaced or dressed in asphalt, passes through everywhere always – Athens, Moscow, Yaroslav, London and Peking, by Santa Fé de Bogotá and Guadalajara, the Sierra Madre Oriental and the Cordilleras, through sacred sites like Delphi and Dodona, through famous sites like Salona, the Alamana bridge, as well as many other places of renown, such as that city of the world that voluptuously stands on the banks of the grey Seine.

But the road, although it passes through everywhere, is not always one for an idle hour or habitual reflection. Sometimes cries can be heard in the night, the cries of a woman raped in a ditch by many men, or at other times, other cries – *Halt!* that ominous demand that once instilled such terror in the hearts of wayfarers, when daggers flashed, and muskets or blunderbusses, appeared before the breasts of travellers, when on this selfsame road an evil fortune cast them into the hands of brigands, who, in their grubby kilts, the way they sprang from the mouth of a cave, resembled the braves of Odysseus Androutsos, as though the place had been the Gravia Inn and these travellers the soldiers of Kioshe Mehmet or Omer Vryoni – just like that, as starting out from Pikermi, passing through Dau Penteli, by this selfsame road, the brigands drove their lordly captives (fair-haired sons of England who came to Greece and left their sainted bones) towards impenetrable pathways, prodding them with knives (oh Edward Herbert! oh Vyner, de Boyl and Lloyd![1]) until they should reach the fastness of the lair, hard by the landing-places of Oropos, in the wilds of Dilessi, to earn a royal ransom or be put to the sword (*lambs to the slaughter at Salona, at Chrysos rams*) to earn a royal ransom or die like lambs (*'tis in an evil hour that Death has come to take me*) just when winter was ending and Easter approaching, and all around was the strong scent of pine, of thyme, to earn a royal ransom or die like lambs, (oh Takos Arvanitakis! oh Christos Arvanitakis! oh Yeroyannis and you, wretched Katarrahias!) to earn a royal ransom or die like lambs, hard by the landing-place for Oropos, in the wilds of Dilessi.

And so the road unfurls, passing with comparable details through everywhere always (the Grand Canyon, Makrotantalon, Akrokeraunia, the Andes), by the banks of the Guadalquivir that waters all Córdoba, by the banks of the Amur and the banks of the Zambesi, the road passes through everywhere, and everywhere the road is hard, so very hard, as always to endure the tread of all those passing feet and the wear of the heavier vehicles, through towns

[1] English travellers kidnapped by brigands outside Athens and murdered in April 1870 near the village of Dilessi, in the most notorious incident of its kind in 19th-century Greece.

and villages, mountains, plateaux and plains, past the lakes of Finland, Tierra del Fuego and Extramadura, until suddenly, every now and then, a road sign, visible only to those who are called, always appears to each, wherever they may be, whether indigenous or travellers, a road sign with lettering broad and simple: 'Terminus. Make ready. River Acheron.'

At the same moment, whatever the country, whatever the landscape, it becomes a final Venice with a Grand Canal – a vision always divine and for the senses a last farewell – a final Venice by whose jetties black gondolas are waiting (I almost said, like hearses) and an itinerant gondolier, pale and spindling but powerful in the arms, each time calls out to those who are coming to the end: "This way, gentlemen, come this way. This is your boat. Embark." And those who are called, with the gaze you see in the eyes of the condemned, in the final moments of their lives, before the levelled barrels of the firing-squad, at the matins hour appointed for executions, in the split second before the volley rings out and their bodies turn to writhing heaps upon the ground, all come this way and enter gondolas, without luggage always, and depart.

And the road continues to unfurl, and the road is hard, harder than ever, gravel-surfaced or dressed in asphalt, and it softens only, whatever the country, whatever the landscape, beneath the radiant gleam of immortality, and only to the tread of those among the poets who are matchless and immaculate, and of their kin the Holy Saints.

Athens 23 January 1964.

*****

published in *Oktana* (1980)

translated by Roderick Beaton

*****

ANDREAS EMBIRIKOS (see volume one p 107–8)

JEAN MALRIEU

Pergamum

First there is an armchair, barely lit by a sparse light from the street; it must be Winter, a Sunday, even, redolent of rain, as we might sense the mud, the drizzle and the odour of raincoats. In this light it rains on the disaffected tax-office in the suburbs, the leafless trees, on this row of stakes, this moist clarity that chills the blood, it has been raining for centuries, a rage of rain, a rage of centuries, and this armchair witness near the sitting room window, this gilded armchair in the corner with unpolished grooving, alone, lost, is an orphan saved from torment. And why *that* particular one? No one comes into this room, it no longer exists. It had been sold when Tatiti died. Now it is a cafe. There is a juke-box, a billiard table, a nickel bar, an aquarium, and people come and go, striding over the armchair, passing through, sitting in the corner where the piano of black wood could be found and over which there is, in the half-light, a large painting. It is difficult to discern clearly, it is always closed. The pier of a port and a ship which starts to rattle. The port traffic is intense and from the other side of the bed, over the bed where she died, there are the 2 Orphans. It is a painting which lives on. I no longer remember the colour of the tapestry. Otherwise my memory is blurred. The 2 Orphans over the bed in a heavy golden frame, crowned with the crown of Napoleon III stamps with, in the middle of the room, a table with a marble top and legs of a lion which beast appeared to be a prisoner in the wood and was starting to metamorphose; not to forget that old musty smell of dust when the rain starts to make the roofs tremble. Someone walks over the slates. Someone breaks into a room which does not exist.

This ray of light which falls from the attic, this ray of an electric battery in a cave of dust which is warm since it must be cold outside. No one passes by in the street, the light in the cafe that laid its foundations on this vanished city has gone out. It would be possible to find some of the fossils of music if one sought closely and why this strange armchair which appears very clearly and fully haloed. A proof, a historian's illumination! in the same way that Troy or Pergamum was reconstituted. Dust floats into the light, a tiny star, a note which escaped from the phonograph into its red coffin with the enormous horn and records (where are the records?) marked 'Pathé'. The music started in the middle and because of the contours of the table and the wear and tear, the same groove was replayed over and over, with the singer announcing the title of the piece: Griselda, song of Alain, Griselda, song of Alain, and so on and so forth because time has caught a cold.

She had a limp and wore long red boots buttoned up by means of a hook. The sound of her steps was also that of the rain. She pulled a hood over her head, before going into the courtyard, but now it was so dark that it was through habit that one found one's way into the labyrinth. A garden which opened onto the street, with the savour of wisteria, magnolia, pigeons and rabbit hutches. Very far away in the distance the rusty sound of the creaking gate, and the summer encumbered by those cornucopia which are the Trumpets of Jericho. She had 2 passions: the pigeons, whose eggs she coveted, and the rabbits she hid in the flower pots. It was odd. The writing-desk was opened and out fell a cat and a hen. And in the left-hand drawer, in a bowl, the expansive evenings when she took out her nephew's appendix who had died in an operation, she cried. It was a sort of red tube in a brown liquid. The operation on the child had taken place right here, white sheets had been extended all along the walls for the prophylaxis. And then the passion for her mother – she was 80 years old – an old fossil, the widow of an industrialist of the Empire. She had had 2 children and lost her milk when the mobilisation of 1870 was announced and her husband – his portrait with waxed moustache was hung beside the spotlight – had been sent to Perpignan. As for her, she had lost her head and no longer recognised herself in mirrors and said hello to herself, especially in front of the wardrobe which reflected part of the garden in which a cock's cry had remained musty with a smell of moss. She spoke to the lady opposite: "You appear to be rather charming, Madam. But why don't you open the door?" Then she opened the door and out fell a rabbit that Tatiti had shut up. "You have been playing tricks on me, Madam, you are a rabbit." Finally she lost patience. And the other one called her, "Little Mama! Little Mama!" and spent the whole day looking for lost keys to open the cupboard, the chest, the store-room where all the coats hung, true Bluebeard's wives as far as this chauffeur's cloak in colt's hair, for in 1914 she had had a car, a chauffeur was necessary and a pair of dark glasses and then the car had been sold and there remained only the 2 headlamps, like 2 veritable storm-lanterns that were sometimes placed on the table to evoke vanished outings.

They said one went to these 'ladies'. Lentils were brought for sifting. Near the wood fire, and then she gave a piano lesson and she passed her hands from right to left, went through the octave, and I glanced into the light and the movement of shadows, the travellers who crowded the pier and especially this pirate in a corner with a monkey on his shoulder who made signs like a conjurer. He said "Hurry up! They're about to raise anchor" and music heightened the waves and hands smelling of rabbit passed all over the place, I fainted, I heard no more than the dissonance of G-sharps with something indefinable about them, the felt-covered doors which open up, the avenues of discovery and the flight over the nerves. "Little mama", said the other and the one started to recite without anyone knowing why, thanks to the failure of the G-sharp, that set a clock in motion, everything being so fragile:

Hardly had we left the gates of Trezene
He was in his cart, ranged around him
His sad guardians copied his silence
Lord, I have seen your unhappy boy
Dragged along by the horses reared by his hand
He falls and soon his body is merely a wound
Hardly had we left the doors of Trezene
He was in his cart. . .

Griselda, song of Alain, Griselda, song of Alain. A small pebble in the memory and that cut short, the same routes leading to this immobilised time, the 2 Orphans, the marble table with a fat book that had a red cover, 'Journey on the back of a Whale' in the Hetzel collection with illustrations to make one dream and the shadow of muslin of the curtains which opened on to the street. It is fine out now. It must be just before spring and the shadow of the acacias plays over the window panes. Trinkets chime in the window as old as the Tanagras or the amulets of museums. Some morocco-leather slippers that no one has put on and which climb the wall with passe-partout mounting portraying – they were childs' drawings of a man playing the flute and a little girl in a light dress on a swing 'That was me'-. A mirror in a mirror and so on to infinity and this poor nephew who died in the operation, quite chubby cheeked, obliquely watching the door in a strange way for objects finally correspond, long use unites them and they get on well together, an arrangement, in short, and the housework is done and slippers are wiped without even shedding one tear. It is an atmosphere in a bell-jar, under pressure, an underwater wreck and the visitor in the rarefied air revives the colours, calls out a word, its complement, and reconstitutes the submerged galley. It is enough simply to skim the surface of the slime and sand and straightaway everything in the whirlpool turns upside down and settles again. From the armchair as strange as a meteorite to the bunch of flowers that no one dares any longer to throw away. It has been put into the dustbin a hundred times, but has returned.

It is there, still new, on a marriage table. There is a large oval mirror on which a swan moves about on the frozen lake. Catherine Almayrac had taken away all the caterer's covers in the evening, and that had caused a lot of problems. A rather long time afterwards they were found in the wardrobe with a rabbit that had died of hunger. The doors of the glass-fronted wardrobe had been opened and the sheets were imitating the layers of the earth and on occasion a gold watch and silver covers had been found between the folds of the pliocene. Another had settled over some champagne bottles, 4 or 5 under its bottom and its feet were raised up in the air like a gymnastics instructor. And then the ball. . . I now know who had made this hole in the armchair's groove. It was the headmistress of the school, for she had clambered all over it in high heels and had nearly tumbled as she felt her foot being held captive.

She died. She no longer had any age. In the same room, there was a Bed of State. 'Securities' were found in the piano. This was why it played so badly as the keys were muffled with certificates. The heirs had done some excavations. They were infatuated with it and its scent. Some Egyptologists. There was a large dish and lots were taken, then pieces of paper were drawn out: The Louis XV rosewood chest of drawers, some old cloaks and two dozen solid silver spoons, not to mention the emerald ring. Later the gestapo had stolen everything. The emerald ring whitened a little on the east coast. They say that these stones mature. Presently it is completely white at the bottom of an Austrian lake. As for her, she no longer moved and a woman fell at the foot of the coffin in a single heap and I was naive, I believed that she had fainted and tried to raise her up by the sleeve and she kicked out. How unseemly!

He had a dental swelling and the other told the person who led the mourning "Above all, don't look at me as you would cause me to burst out laughing", while to those who came to offer their condolences, he clasped their hands and said "How are things?" in a convivial way. The pirate with the monkey on his shoulder had left. As is customary, the mirrors were covered with large white sheets so that the soul would not become the prisoner of its reflection and a window had been left open. . . Once again a light illuminated the assembly. Like the telephone, objects still answered one another. A variable geometry, an electrical current which was going to be cut off. The glance of the 2 Orphans of the industrialist, the trinkets – with one's eyes closed, one would have been able to completely reconstitute everything and that smell of moth-balls which fell from the fur coats like dead landscapes from the top of wardrobes.

The last time she was going to take the plane. All the formalities had been completed and she had actually crossed the barrier into the narrow passage that led to the runway. She looked round, completely burdened down with luggage – in my turn I crossed the barrier and told her I was sorry I had not written to her more often and that in any event I thought about her so much – "Since you are here," she said, "Why don't you come with me?" "Oh," I said, "I'm too awkward. At my age – to go to America!" "But you could bring your father back!" My father had been dead a long time. I didn't know it then. "Kiss your husband," I said and as I moved away the memory came back to me. But her husband was dead, I thought. What a gaff! Some old people awaited me at the exit with widow's veils. But she was also dead. Then I woke up completely covered in tears.

*****

published in *L'Archibras* no 3 (March 1968)
translated by Michael Richardson and Peter Wood

*****

JEAN MALRIEU (Marseilles, 1915 – Penne-du-Terne, 1976) A poet who participated in surrealist activities from the fifties. His most characteristic volume is *Préface à l'amour* (1953)

Editorial Note

The two volumes of *The Dedalus Book of Surrealism*, which comprises *The Identity of things* (published in 1993) and the present work, offers the most comprehensive selection to date of surrealist stories in English (and perhaps in any other language). The richness of surrealist storytelling has been emphasised and the aim has been to present as representative selection as possible from around the world. Unfortunately it is inevitably not as comprehensive as one might like. The enormous difficulties involved in gaining access to stories in some languages has mitigated against this, as has some copyright difficulties. It is particularly regretted that it was not possible to include more material from Eastern Europe (Czecho-Slovakia, Romania and Yugoslavia in particular) and from Spain and Latin America, and that it was not possible to obtain any material from the Japanese surrealists. Also regrettable is the omission of anything by fascinating storytellers like Jacques Baron, Yves Ellëouet and Maurice Fourré who do not appear to have written any short tales that could be included, and that it was not possible to include anything from Mario Cesariny's *Titania História Hermética*... One hopes that the current work may encourage readers to explore some of these byways of surrealism for themselves.

Afterword

People have always told each other stories. The stories they tell illustrate the way they perceive the world and serve to embellish what would otherwise be a mundane existence. Stories are generated through intimacy and through a need to share common experiences and there is an indelible connexion between storytelling and the hearthside which provides the focus for community gatherings. Before the blazing log fire in dark houses at dead of winter or in front of the camp fire on a bright summer's eve, our habitual defences are lowered and we become more trusting and generous. The fireside joins people in friendship and receptiveness and the crackle of its flames is the germ that provides not only heat and light but also fosters the urge to recount tales. Like the fireside, stories draw people together and warm them with a sense of common destiny.

The stories that survive within us are those that partake of this profusion. They resound within our minds, illuminating our perceptions and suggesting connexions that had not previously occurred to us. They provide the links that help to establish our sense of identity and destiny. As dreams illuminate our unconscious life it is stories that do the same for our waking life. Like dreams, too, they respond to an elemental part of our being. Such stories are our myth of the world.

The surrealist Benjamin Péret spent much time during his life gathering together American Indian myths and legends for an anthology which was only published after his death. In his introduction he wrote: "The bird flies, the fish swims and man invents since he alone in nature is equipped with an ever alert imagination, and is always stimulated by a ceaselessly renewed necessity. . . If it is undeniable that the development of spoken language, an automatic product of people's need for mutual communication, tends to satisfy a social requirement, it is no less true that men assume the expression of a completely poetical form as soon as they are able, in a purely unconscious way, to organise their language, adapting it to their most pressing needs and sensing the possibilities it harbours."[1] This perception lies at the heart of the surrealist understanding of language and the necessity for stories that, for the surrealists, always take the form of myth.

As Péret asserts, the value of such stories resides in the fact that they respond to direct social necessity, but in a way that is not obvious in a society dominated by what is utilitarian and functional. Rather they represent a natural surplus of imaginative abundance that may confound or reinforce the way we perceive the world, but which never does so in a simple way. Even though they may have no direct social use, they nonetheless embody the actual state of real relations between people.

In our modern world this elemental quality of storytelling is denied. We live today in a world in which everything has its place and function and nothing must be left out of place. Storytelling is thus at a discount and like everything else in a world ruled by the laws of exchange value, literature is forced to submit itself to the requirements of the market and must learn, like any other commodity, to adapt and serve needs that lie outside of itself and its concrete value. It is forced to stand not for itself but for an ideological cause of one sort or another, whether it be political, social or literary. It cannot exist for itself: like everything else it has to be *justified*. And for this very reason the power of storytelling is automatically devalued. Literature is reduced to the status of complementary utilitarian functions: as a pastime to provide distraction and

[1] Benjamin Péret, *Anthologie des mythes, legendes et contes populaires d'Amérique* (1960) Paris: Albin Michel, p 9–11.

entertainment, or as a heightened activity that would claim to explore 'great truths' about the human condition.

Since surrealism was first articulated in the nineteen twenties it has fought tenaciously and uncompromisingly – if doubtless *uselessly* – against such reductionism. Denying that literature should serve anything outside of itself, it has asserted that stories have an elemental use-value that has no relation to the exchange-value placed upon it by the dynamic of capitalist society. A stubborn refusal of the conditions of twentieth century 'reality', surrealism has denied intransigently and consistently that modern man can live without a sense of the wonder of the world that was once embodied in myth. In approaching literature, it has aimed at restoring to the word its magical qualities, and at giving back to language the elemental power it once had within society. This determination lies at the heart of the surrealist attitude and distinguishes it radically from the modernism which took shape contemporaneously with it.

Surrealism and the contemporary novel

Given their attitude it is hardly surprising that the surrealists have evinced a distrust for the novel, something which dates back to the *Manifesto* of 1924 in which Breton offers advice on how to write false novels. From the beginning surrealism had a distaste for general fabulation and it would be vain to look in surrealist writing for any of the qualities usually regarded as pre-requisites for judgement of a novel. Realistic portrayal of the milieu, accurate mise en scene, character development and psychological verisimilitude are not at issue in surrealist narrative writing but nor, for that matter, is it a question of arbitrary invention. In *Nadja,* (1927/8), Breton details his objections against "all the empiricists of the novel who claim to put on stage characters distinct from themselves and present them, physically, morally, with their own habits, in the service of a cause we prefer not to know"[2]. This developed the com-

[2] Breton, *Nadja* (1928) in *Oeuvres complètes* Vol 1 Paris: Gallimard p 650–1.

ments made in the *Manifesto* which pour scorn on the author who "attacks character and, this being settled upon, parades his character to and fro across the world. No matter what happens, this hero, whose actions and reactions are admirably predictable, is compelled not to thwart or upset – even though he looks as if he is – the calculations of which he is the object. The currents of life can appear to lift him up, roll him over, cast him down, he will still belong to this *ready made* human being. . "[3] Nevertheless, what was involved in this surrealist distrust is frequently misunderstood.

Breton's diatribe against the form of the realist novel has widely been viewed as a disapproval of narrative writings as a whole. It is therefore curious to note that narrative writing was a central concern in early surrealism. In the journal *La Révolution Surréaliste*, for instance, extracts from novels by Péret, Soupault, Aragon, Desnos and Crevel feature prominently. True, Philippe Soupault was expelled from the Surrealist Group for his literary ambitions and a legend has been nurtured by Louis Aragon that hostility to the novel within surrealism caused him to destroy the manuscript of a novel he had been working on for five years, *La Défense de l'infini*. It is Aragon who has largely been responsible for the misunderstandings concerning the surrealists' attitude to the novel and it is therefore worthwhile to examine his evidence in a little detail.

Aragon, who was careful to wait until after Breton's death before advancing his contentions, suggested that he was a victim of an incomprehensible campaign by the surrealists against the whole notion of the novel. He even claims that his classic *Paris Peasant* was received with hostility, recounting how Breton goaded him into reading extracts so they could have a good laugh at Aragon's expense. Yet a more reliable witness, Jacques Baron, indicates that far from having to be encouraged, Aragon was always

[3] Breton *Manifestes du Surréalisme* (1962) Paris: Gallimard.

eager to read passages from the book and implies that this was a part of the ambience of surrealism at the time that everyone looked forward to.[4] This certainly seems to ring more true and in his introduction to the fragments that remain of *La Défense de l'infini*, published after Aragon's death, Edouard Ruiz has cast considerable doubt on Aragon's assertion that the novel was destroyed because of disapproval by the surrealists. Certainly a perusal of the fragments that remain (amounting to some 300 pages[5]) it is difficult to see how it could ever have been brought together into a coherent narrative and leads one to believe that in all likelihood the main reason for Aragon to have destroyed it was that it had become too much of a burden.[6]

Whatever the case, the recent publication of surrealist archival material has allowed some precision in the matter. In this series of interrogations, it can be seen that Aragon's novelistic activity does indeed come under scrutiny, but certainly not in the terms Aragon claims.[7] It is neither the content nor the form of the book that is fundamentally at issue but the detrimental effect it was having on Aragon's life: the concern was that Aragon was becoming obsessed with something that was of no importance.

In fact, in the same discussions, Robert Desnos, far from having to justify himself for the novel he was writing, put it forward as proof of his good faith as a surrealist. This

[4] Jacques Baron, *L'An 1 du surréalisme* (1969) Paris: Denoël, p 70.

[5] 'Enter the Succubi', included in *The Identity of Things* being part of it.

[6] In any event he waited for over a year from the time of the supposed interdiction before destroying it. If the novel really had the importance Aragon later attached to it ("all the novels I wrote before, or after, that one, have been merely child's play in comparison") then he surely could have resurrected the project: the destruction of a manuscript never means that an author loses the essence of what he has written – in fact it can serve as a spur to re-constitute it in a more effective way.

[7] see *Archives du Surréalisme Tome 3: Adhérer au Parti Communiste* (1991) Paris: Actual/Gallimard pp 26–27.

novel, *La Liberté ou l'amour* has always been regarded as one of the cornerstones of surrealist narrative.[8] And while the fact that Philippe Soupault wrote novels was held against him, it was his attitude that was found objectionable – indeed Soupault makes no attempt to justify his novels as such, saying that they are merely a way to make a living and have no other importance than that. Soupault was condemned because his attitude was considered complacent and opportunist, not because he was a novelist.

In fact from the first novels played an important part in the development of surrealist consciousness. *The Castle of Otranto,* (Walpole); *The Mysteries of Udolpho* (Radcliffe), *The Monk* (Lewis), *Melmoth the Wanderer* (Maturin), *Justine* and *Juliette* (Sade); *Wuthering Heights* (Brontë); *Peter Ibbetson* (Du Maurier); *Alice in Wonderland*(Carroll); *Le Surmale* (Jarry), *Impressions d'Afrique* and *Locus Solus* (Roussel), *Fantômas* (Alain & Souvestre), to name but a few novels, all had an enormous influence on surrealism, as did the work of storytellers like Achim von Arnim, Kleist, Nerval, Barbey d'Aurevilly, Poe, Villiers d'Isle Adam and O. Henry. This being the case it would seem somewhat hypocritical if the surrealists had dismissed the novel as a legitimate form of interest.

What was at issue was otherwise. Aragon and Soupault were criticised not for the fact of writing novels: it was their literary ambitions that were suspect. In the eyes of the surrealists such ambitions could only have the effect of leading them away from the essential concerns of their writing into the realm of literary conceit. What was at issue for the surrealists was, as Breton pointed out: "no longer essentially one of producing works of art but of lighting up the unrevealed and yet revealable part of our being in which all the beauty, all the love and all the virtue with which we scarcely credit ourselves are shining intensely – these immediate aims are not the only ones. Notably, it seems that now there is much to be expected of

[8] Recently published in English for the first time by Atlas Press.

certain methods of pure deception, the application of which to life would have the effect of fixing attention neither on the real nor on the imaginary, but on, so to speak, the *other side of the real*. It is easy to imagine novels which cannot end, as there are problems which remain unresolved. When, however, will we have the novel in which the characters, having been abundantly defined with a minimum of particularities, will act in an altogether foreseeable way in view of an unforeseen result?" The point is that it is not a matter of advancing the evolution of the novel but of returning to sources. As Breton had stated in the *Manifesto*, "There are fairy stories to be written for adults, stories that are still in a green state".

Unlike most other contemporary figures whose dissatisfaction with the nineteenth century novel lay in the fact that it seemed incapable of conveying the dynamism of the age of the movie and the motor car, the surrealists were largely uninterested in such a practical application of art. The novel mattered to them no more than painting or film-making as such. Where the critique of nineteenth-century realism by modernism was to lead to the re-creation of the novel by fragmenting it and establishing richer textures that served to advance its evolution, the surrealist critique did not have such a progressive function, either in theory or in practice. On the contrary, in this respect surrealism could be said to be 'reactionary', seeking to recover a magical and lost world. An injunction to 'return to childhood' was taken seriously by the surrealists and marks a clear breach between them and the modern movement that sought in the novel a closer identification with the alienation and fragmentation of contemporary life.

Towards a Theory of Surrealist Narrative

The breach between surrealism on the one hand and modernism and the avant-garde on the other has always confounded critics. The fact that the surrealists always denied that surrealism was an avant-garde has not prevented critics, always discomforted when unable to give something its proper place, from considering it as such. In art history, the fact that surrealist art embraces both abstract and figurative forms seems anomalous and unassimilable to the forward trend of modern development. The same anomaly is apparent in its literature, which can range from works that treat complex philosophical issues in a form that, too, is complex, to texts that are formally extremely simple and take a joy in their own exuberance. This very diversity disconcerts, especially when no immediate separation is made between different formal approaches. As in painting the surrealists regard formally original artists like André Masson or Max Ernst to be as important, but no more so, than artists like Clovis Trouille, whose technique is, from an art historical point of view, academic and pedestrian, so in literature the formal complexity or originality of a surrealist work is considered to be of no importance.

If we wish to understand the basis of this attitude, it is helpful to consider how surrealism fits in with the contemporary movement away from realist representation.

The reaction against realism began in the late eighteenth century with the rise of romanticism and the emergence of the gothic novel as a popular literary form. The surrealists were among the first to recognise the importance of the gothic novel and perceived that its form gave it a means to reinvent storytelling in a way that was both immediate and allowed the possibility of examining complex phenomena that realism was unable to engage with (the form of the gothic novel also implicitly contested the claims of realism to reflect the world directly by showing how artificial its structure was).

A despised genre for so long, recent studies have revealed clearly the multifarious implications of the gothic form and that it has had a pervasive influence upon Western art and literature through the past two hundred years and provided the base for an often neglected tradition within European literature that has challenged realism by focusing on uncomfortable social and psychological aspects of modern life which escape the frame of conventions established by realism.

In an influential book, *Fantasy: The Literature of Subversion*, Rosemary Jackson[9] has shown how this fantastic element had been a pervasive literary practice in Europe and yet has been barely recognised by conventional criticism that asserts the primacy of realism.

The frame of the fantastic is subversive, she asserts. It undermines those notions of time, space and character that have so laboriously been established by realism to provide the stability of its model. Instead it embraces all that is disordered and fragmentary. Like the Big Bad Wolf who is always on hand to blow down the most convincing sanctuary that realism can provide, the fantastic dissolves all the relations of stability upon which realism depends. This extends to the very texture of the world and even to the very discourse which expresses the language. Everything becomes uncertain and disturbing. This world is a world of dread and emptiness: rules and conventions are subverted and what is real and what is unreal is confused. Where realism upholds a conception of life determined by presence, certainty and fixity, the fantastic shows a world based upon absence, doubt and loss.

Rosemary Jackson rightly recognises that surrealism does not fit easily within this mournful model. Rejecting realism as the fantastic does, surrealism nevertheless refuses to embrace this sense of fragmentation and loss. Instead, she asserts, surrealism lies within what she calls the 'marvellous', which does not subvert realism, but heightens it. It is, she writes: "super-real – and its etymology implies that it is presenting a world *above* this one rather than fracturing it from inside or below."[10] However, this suggestion seems to play upon a misunderstanding, something that is highlighted if we consider that Jackson regards the 'marvellous'

[9] Rosemary Jackson, *Fantasy: the Literature of Subversion* (1981) London: Methuen.
[10] Jackson, p 36

as being characterised by writers like Tolkien, C.S. Lewis or Charles Kingsley, who created harmonious invented worlds in which the harsh reality of contemporary life is never confronted and realism is neither fractured nor questioned, but transcended. Writers within the 'marvellous' create a sort of parallel universe in which fantasy is allowed free play.

Superficially this may appear to connect with surrealism, especially in so far as the surrealists did indeed invoke the 'marvellous' to define their own aims. Nevertheless, that surrealism is to be understood as 'super-real' has always been unequivocally dismissed by the surrealists who have considered that such an understanding serves to travesty their activity. Specifically denying that surrealism ought to try to transcend realism, Breton called for an 'open-realism' that would disclose the possibilities of reality and in the process question the basis upon which realism's claim to be able to represent reality was based.

The gulf between surrealism and a 'super-realism' can be seen in a difference of narrative structure. In general, the 'super-realist', from Tolkien to more sophisticated contemporary figures like García Marquez, Isabel Allende or Sylvie Germain, uses essentially allegorical means to heighten a realist effect. In this world a homogeneous 'unreality' is created and this establishes the verisimilitude and authenticity the narrative requires. The contentions of realism are respected but are taken in a direction which realism in general does not recognise. In surrealism, on the contrary, it is this homogeneity that is brought into question, by a refusal to recognise an artificial divide between 'real' and 'unreal'. Again it is this that connects surrealism with the traditional fairy tale.

In fact the world of the fairy tale is not at all 'super-real' for an obvious historical reason: realism did not then exist. In the 'super-real' it is the structure of the world that is unreal: the events and characters are for the most part defined by the conventions of realism. What is 'unreal' in the traditional fairy tale on the other hand is not the setting but the events and characters, since it responds to different descriptive criteria from those prescribed later by realism. Where the 'super-realist' accepts the conventions of realism and strives to transcend them, the surrealist is looking to return to an immediate means of storytelling that is free from those conventions.

Surrealism, then, neither aims to subvert realism as does the fantastic, nor does it try to transcend it. It looks for different means by which to explore reality itself.

This helps us to understand the great attraction of the gothic novel, for what the surrealists admired in it was not the sense of fragmentation that was the crucial factor for the fantastic, but its quality of immediacy. The ability of gothic novelists to quicken the blood and offer a shiver of recognition of the most intense moments of human existence was a particular appeal. As Breton wrote (speaking of the novels of Ann Radcliffe), "A work of art worthy of the name is one which gives us back the freshness of the emotions of childhood." The power of the best gothic novels arises from their intensity, something that is established so forcibly because they are located on a borderline where distinctions between what has tangible reality and what is imaginary and unformed are blurred. Above all, the gothic castle is the perfect setting for this meeting of two worlds where contradictions tend to melt away and reality and imaginary merge into one another. "What is admirable about the fantastic," wrote Breton, "is that there is no longer anything fantastic: there is only the real."

The gothic novel was also crucial for the surrealists for its conception of character. Here the 'rounded personality' is treated with contempt and characters are evoked not in accordance with superficial appearances of verisimilitude, but to embody forces of desire in human form. For Breton, Matthew Lewis's Matilda (in *The Monk*) is the perfect surrealist character, being "less a personage than a continual temptation."

For the surrealists the marvellous "is at once in being and outside of it" (Pierre Mabille). It establishes its own domain beyond the frame of the model constructed by realism. As we have also seen, unlike the modern fantastic, surrealist narrative does not attempt to subvert realism – it simply ignores it, not to escape the exigences reality imposes but on the contrary to plunge ever deeper into the nature of reality itself. The fantastic is in complicity with the realist model in the claims that realism makes to represent the true face of reality. It points to the gaps and inadequacies of realism, but does not question the legitimacy of its claims to represent reality. The concept of 'suspension of disbelief' that beloved criterion of positivist criticism supposedly serving to establish the legitimacy of the fantastic, confirms this hegemony. As Rosemary Jackson says, "The fantastic cannot exist independently of that 'real' world which it seems to find frustratingly finite."[11] This sense of frustration is absent in surrealist narrative which, as it assumes its rights, renders the notion of 'suspension of disbelief' redundant. Even so, surrealism rejects the arbitrary and establishes its own logical structure.

The differences between surrealism and the general trend of modernism can be brought into focus by considering the surrealist aspects of Kafka's work. A modernist understanding of Kafka asserts that his importance lies in the representation of the bureaucratic anomie of modern life and reflects its absurdity. For surrealism, on the other hand, Kafka's importance lies elsewhere. Georges Bataille, for instance, praises Kafka's "totally childish attitude" and points out that his work "only becomes clear to us when we find our way out of it."[12] Kafka's work, Bataille contends, is not fundamentally a critique of a bureaucratic and inhuman world, but a celebration of the sovereign moment which denies utilitarian behaviour. Kafka, indeed, takes a positive joy in the very disorientation to which he is condemned. This connects his world with that of the

[11] Jackson, p 20.
[12] Georges Bataille, *Literature and Evil* (translated by Alastair Hamilton) (1973) London: Calder & Boyars.

traditional fairy tale and thus for surrealism Kafka's importance lies not as a negative portrayal of an inexorable destiny but rather as presenting fugitive moments of hope that point the way to the overcoming of such anonymity. This interpretation of Kafka's work is shared by the philosopher Theodor Adorno who rejects most of the conventional criticism of this author: "Of that which has been written on him," he writes, "little counts; most is existentialism." Rather, he states, "his texts are designed not to sustain a constant distance between themselves and their victim but rather to agitate his feelings to a point where he feels that the narrative will shoot towards him like a locomotive in a three-dimensional film. Such aggressive proximity undermines the reader's habit of identifying himself with the figures in the novel. It is by reason of this principle that surrealism can rightfully claim him. . . fate serves not to deter but to entice."[13] As we have seen in relation to the gothic novel, the quality of immediacy remains central. To understand surrealism we need therefore to be aware of the nature of this immediacy which was given concrete form as automatism.

The nature of automatism

Beyond surrealism, automatism has several meanings, but all refer to activity – whether it be mental or physical – that evades consciousness. Above all, the basis of automatism lies within divinatory practices, all of which assume that the sum of separate individual consciousnesses of the world does not exhaust the problem of knowledge. Its practice implies that the world contains elements that must remain beyond man's consciousness – and control – and towards which he can only strive in an intuitive way. It also denies agency and serves to undermine the way causality is understood in Western thought.

Automatism was put forward in the *Manifesto of Surreal-*

[13] Theodor Adorno, *Prisms* Cambridge, Mass: MIT p 246.

ism as inseparable from the very definition of surrealism: "Psychic automatism in its pure state, by which it is proposed to express – verbally, in writing or by any other means – the actual functioning of thought. The dictation of thought in the absence of all control exercised by reason, and outside all aesthetic or moral considerations."[14] This definition was soon perceived as inadequate and Breton modified it: "I deceived myself (. . .) in advocating the use of automatic thought not only removed from all control exercised by reason but also disengaged from all 'aesthetic or moral considerations'. It should at least have said *conscious* aesthetic or moral considerations." But if it is unsatisfactory in placing surrealism beyond conscious 'moral or aesthetic' considerations, it is equally so in surrealist practice, which generally seems hostile to the possibility of expressing the 'actual functioning of thought', an essentialist concept alien to the unfolding of surrealism in practice.

Automatism had been discovered for surrealism almost by accident. It had been in 1919 that André Breton and Philippe Soupault first explored its possibilities through writing their collective text, *Les Champs magnétiques*.[15] Breton's experiences as a psychiatric nurse during the First World War alerted him to the poetic possibilities of induced language (indeed the surrealists were soon to celebrate hysteria as an involuntary form of automatism), but to apply it to poetry was both to negate and yet, in another way, to take to its logical conclusion the poetics of symbolism in which both Breton and Soupault served their apprenticeships.

Writing with no pre-determined thought as quickly as

[14] Breton in *Manifestes du surréalisme* (1962) Paris: Gallimard.

[15] It has been translated by David Gascoyne as *The Magnetic Fields* (1986) London: The Atlas Press. The collective aspect is crucial to surrealism and was the basis of much of their most important experimental work, most significantly, perhaps, Breton's and Éluard's *L'Imaculée conception* (translated into English by Jon Graham [1990] London: The Atlas Press).

one could on a blank sheet of paper was a revelation, revealing that a great power opens up to us when we surrender to the impulse of chance. Nevertheless, pure, unmediated automatism had its dangers, as Breton was well aware. The second notable surrealist experiments in its use, the legendary period of hypnotic sleeps, had to be abandoned when not only the mental health but the actual physical well-being of the participants seemed at risk.

With automatic writing the risks were no less great, but tended towards a more immediate and banal difficulty, which was that the great surge of liberation that follows an initiation into automatism, that 'holocaust of words' as Georges Bataille described it, soon loses vitality and similar patterns tend to emerge with monotonous regularity. It became legitimate to ask what value the automatic texts had beyond offering evidence of immediacy.

That evidence was not negligible and many early automatic texts are still exciting if read today, especially Breton's own texts. However, too often we feel excluded from an internal dialogue between the writer and himself, with no concessions being made to the reader. The images may be suggestive, but it is generally difficult to take anything from the text beyond its immediate context. It can seem hermetically sealed from us. We can project something on to the text, since the rich images suggest a hidden wealth, but the effort is rarely worth it, and would tend to involve looking for symbols, the legitimacy of which surrealism always denied. For the reader such texts rarely if ever lie 'ajar, like a door' as Breton claimed was the surrealist intent. The problem of the reader's relation to the text is something immediately revealed by unmediated automatism. In fact, contrary to what is often believed, the surrealists were well aware of this and very few unmediated automatic texts were published; after 1930 hardly any at all. The main forum for such texts was the 'surrealist texts' section which appeared in each issue of *La Révolution Surréaliste*, where they are presented as objects of research rather than as texts to be read independently.

The other main form of direct automatism in early surrealism was the dream account, a wealth of which were recounted in *La Révolution Surréaliste.* Often these dreams attain a narrative strength of their own and, as with automatism proper, what is interesting is how collective concerns become manifest, rather more so than in directly automatic texts.

Nevertheless, it was soon recognised that the passive duplication of internal states, be they dream narratives or products of automatic writing, was only the first step on the way towards the illumination of the depths of human consciousness that surrealism sought to plumb.

This was not necessarily because the unconscious was unable to structure material in a coherent way. For Benjamin Péret, the storyteller par excellence of early surrealism, tales of indubitable charm would effortlessly slip from the tongue always charged with their own particular atmosphere. Péret's texts are entirely different in tone from other automatic texts from the period, especially in their structuring, which is always coherent, no matter how outlandish the events described, even though Péret wrote quite as spontaneously as any other surrealist. But Péret had a facility of being able to capture thought processes as they were on the point of becoming realised. Between 1922 and 1927 he wrote down a vast array of these tales. From 1927 to the end of his life (he died in 1959), Péret wrote hardly any further stories, probably because he could no longer be bothered to write them down. If the internal logic is spontaneously generated great richness can be the result, but one cannot live on oysters alone, and in the long run their very richness militates against them. Péret's stories are unique. No one could emulate his example, which is rather the exception that proves the rule that surrealism needed to use automatism as a springboard.

The real importance of automatism lay in the fact that it led to a different relation between the artist and the creative act. Where the artist has traditionally been seen as someone who invents a personal world, bringing into being something unique to his own 'genius', the surrealists conceived themselves as explorers and researchers rather than 'artists' in the traditional sense and it was discovery rather than invention that became crucial for them. As such automatism was a means by which 'poetry could be made by all'. It was above all a plunge into an unknown realm, and all one needed to explore it was the ability to swim.

Surrealist practice soon developed its own ways of mediating its material. The writer who most profoundly explored the implications of automatism was Roger Caillois and it was something that pre-occupied him throughout his life. What he saw as being crucial in automatism was not the fact of producing something – be it a text or an art work (indeed if this was the case it would be to surrender to just the sort of literary indulgence that surrealism wanted to make redundant) – than the receptivity of mind induced by the process itself. From this perspective, automatism was a form of contemplation and communication that sought to reveal the real relations between the phenomena of the world.

A particular application of this are the three books that Caillois devoted to stones. He considered that each stone was a microcosm within which the whole world could be read if one established the right form of receptivity. This required that one should locate oneself directly in the world and respond harmoniously with it instead of treating it, as we are habitually encouraged to do, as something to be dominated. We see here again the strong connexions between surrealism and divination, which seeks to understand the world by means that are external to man's direct control, assuming an affective rather than causative relation between things.

In automatism the intent was to capture the immediacy of thought, a thought that would be pristine and unsullied. It was necessary to engage with one's material in a way that disregarded possible consequences. No intermediary is necessary to pass from perception to representation since, in this sense, they are one and the same.

What was above all involved in automatism was the search for an activity into which one must throw oneself wholeheartedly, with the recognition that illumination does not come before but after the creation of the work. This could involve no literary aspirations, but called for a decisive purification.

The first step towards this purification was a negation of what passes for 'reality' in contemporary society, but surrealism also sought a path out of this negation. It looked for a means whereby literature could reclaim its rights and once more 'lead somewhere'.

Denying the utilitarian use of literature, the surrealists made a distinction between 'literature' and 'poetry', something clarified most lucidly by Tristan Tzara. In this distinction, 'literature' was understood as a 'means of expression'; that is it expressed utilitarian needs. 'Poetry', on the other hand, was understood to be an 'activity of the spirit', which would rather provide a way of exploring the nature of living in the world. It would respond to a necessity within us, something essential for our being and not to a need created by the needs of the market. It was thereby immediate: where 'literature' mediated the world through symbols with rhetorical and allegorical constructions, 'poetry' conveyed a direct experience of the world.

Thus the usual distinction made between form and content was obliterated: form became content and vice versa. In turn this gave to 'poetry' a natural and temporal quality implying no separation from the natural world. Meaning thus becomes transfigured and loses its textual referent. Rather than being inherent to the text, meaning extends from it and becomes dynamic. We can sum up the surrealist distinction between 'literature' and 'poetry' by saying that where the former is artificial, fictive and elusive, the latter is natural, real, direct and spontaneous.

Automatism thus had the effect of a purification revealing to the surrealists "a power they did not realise they had" (Aragon). The immediacy it offered and the fact that it collapsed form and content allowed insight into the nature of language, now viewed not as a system of signs and symbols through which people communicate but as a material entity actively precipitating the meaning created. As Paul Nougé said: ". . .if words allow themselves to be handled, it is with the help of infinite carefulness. One has to welcome them, listen to them, before asking any service of them. Words are living things closely involved with human life. . ."[16] This exploration of the reciprocity between man and language is central to surrealist concerns: one of the books by Michel Leiris, indeed, is subtitled 'what words tell me'.

Language and immediacy

By listening to words themselves, surrealism bestows upon language its own identity and it ceases to be merely a means to facilitate human communication. Surrealist writing therefore always endeavours to respect the integrity of language itself, which should never be conceived only as a vehicle for the expression of one's own thoughts. In so doing, surrealism rejects the arbitrariness of the sign, established by Saussure as a fundamental principle of structural linguistics, something which assumes a passivity of language which, as we have seen, surrealism refuses.

In the first place, different languages are not commensurate. The codes by which the relation between subject and object is established are not defined simply by the particular sign used, but also by the whole structure of the language. Saussure recognised this by making a distinction between parole (word) and langue (language) but this still assumes that language is an object that can be studied independently of its referents. Equally the subject that perceives and the object that is perceived cannot be separated from each other, nor can the connecting line of language be detached from the relation between them since the three elements

[16] quoted in J.H. Matthews, *Towards A Poetics of Surrealism* (1976) New York: Syracuse University Press p 108.

(subject, object and mode of communication) must form an inextricable unity. There is thereby a sense in which the process of naming confers both meaning and identity, rather than, as if often thought, a name being capriciously given to something that has a pre-established meaning. This notion is frequently encountered in popular superstitions when it is said that something does not genuinely exist until it has a name, and that a true name is a precious *object* that is disclosed at one's own peril.

The *material* relation to language was something the surrealists drew particularly from the work of Raymond Roussel, whose technique of word association served to interrogate words and allow them to establish their own meaning. On the face of it nothing could be further from the spontaneity of automatic writing than Roussel's laborious and artificial method, which involved taking words at random and expanding on their associations until they revealed up a meaning. And had such a system been directed to some pre-determined end, it would doubtless not have interested the surrealists, but Roussel used the method as a means by which to listen to words and allow them to speak without being imposed upon. It was therefore a method that helped to highlight the fact that automatism was a *discipline* that allowed *complete freedom* as surrealism conceived it.

The element of naming is an important aspect of surrealism. André Breton wrote, "Deliver the true names to me, prove that you have done nothing to molest your heroes."[17] Similarly, in *Nadja* he insists "on knowing the names, in being interested only in books left half-open like doors and for which one does not have to go looking for keys."[18] The surrealist does not write with the certainty in the stability of language assumed by most writers. One often has the sense that surrealists are writing on shifting

[17] 'Introduction au discours sur le peu de réalité' in *Point du jour* (*Oeuvres complètes* Vol 2, p 266.

[18] *Nadja, Oeuvres complètes* Vol 1 p 651.

sands, that they are trying to bring into being something that eludes their grasp. As will have been seen in many of the stories in this collection, non-sequiturs and gaps are common. Sometimes we even feel that the words are spiralling away from the writer who appears unable or unwilling to bring them back under control. Words are given an enormous latitude to say what they, rather than the writer, wants them to say. The most extreme example in our collection is perhaps Marianne Van Hirtum's 'Proteus Volens'. Here words are not used exclusively to communicate, but the writer seeks to become one with the words, to harmonise the relation so that her own message and that of the words become one. The literal effect may appear a tangled mess, but beneath the surface absurdity serious issues are being addressed. By giving words the latitude she does, Van Hirtum emphasises their contagious qualities: they become almost like viruses, with which it is necessary to put oneself in harmony by sympathetic magic if one is not to be overwhelmed. Thus the operation described in the story does not effect a cure through medical surgery but by transmutation. What is essential is to become one with the sickness, that is, in the context of language as a whole, to enter into contact with words.

Equally, the surrealists consider words as witnesses of life acting in a direct way in human affairs. To use words properly it was necessary to treat them with respect, for they were the intermediaries between oneself and the rest of creation. To abuse them was immediately to set oneself adrift from true being. Words need to be coaxed to reveal a little of their true nature, so as to close the breach that exists between the writer and the universe. The world is not something alien against which man is in conflict. Rather man and cosmos exist in reciprocal motion. We are not cast adrift in an alien or meaningless environment. The universe is intimate with us and, as Breton insisted, it is a cryptogram to be deciphered.

Thus, for surrealism engagement with the materiality of language is a first requirement. Inspiration is always familiar and is not reliant on internal individual subjectivity. Surrealism seeks a sort of science of lived experience in which generally accepted relations between subject and object are upset and the central issue becomes the relation of internal stimuli to external motivation and vice versa. Surrealism makes no invocation to the release of hidden forces. No question here of any innate creative gift. Poetry was available to all.

Intimacy and Recognition

This attitude towards language points to wider elements in the aim surrealism set itself: to combine the invocation to 'transform the world'(Marx) and 'change life' (Rimbaud).

We have already noted that Breton spoke of words 'making love' and the sexual metaphor in relation to writing is prevalent in surrealism. Breton also said, 'poetry is made in bed like love", and he called for a poetry that would be reduced to its simplest form, which is that of love. But the love invoked here does not refer exclusively to sexual relations, but to the whole of man's relation with the cosmos.

All surrealist activity is founded in intimacy and secrecy. A direct relation with the reader is sought, a one-to-one relation in which communication is experienced in its immediacy. Against the alienation of everyday life, surrealism sought to use literature to establish bonds between people. Its writing invites the reader into its world and challenges him to accept it on its own terms. As Paul Nougé insisted, the relation between writer and reader is analogous to that between players in a game of chess, in which each seeks to outwit the other. But what remains at issue is always communication. Georges Bataille put it in this way: "Though the immediate impression of rebellion may obscure the fact, the task of authentic literature is nevertheless only conceivable in terms of a desire for a fundamental communication with the reader."[19]

[19] Georges Bataille, *Literature and Evil* p 12.

The Revenge of the Object

"A man, a stone, or a tree is going to begin the fourth song", announced Lautréamont in his *Les Chants de Maldoror*, asserting an equality of relations that became crucial for surrealism. A 'fundamental communication with the reader' necessitated a confrontation of the relationship between subject and object, a relationship whose complexity the surrealists, with their basis in Hegelian philosophy, were well aware of. But there was also within surrealism an awareness that the unleashing of language that automatism opened up had implications for the symbiosis by which subject and object respond to each other. Neither of them had meaning without the other, which could reside only in the relation between them.

With this realisation, the object gains its own integrity and ceases to be at the mercy of the acting subject. Thus the writer becomes unable to impose a vision of the world: the world itself is given the opportunity to assert itself through the writer. The world, and our relation within it, is upset. In the process, *things* are given an *identity*, which in effect destroys their nature as things. Now "nothing that surrounds us is object," as Breton wrote: "all is subject."

A re-interpretation of Reality

Although surrealism – a praxis rather than a theory – never sought to establish a consistent philosophy, the parameters of surrealist activity are nevertheless fairly constant and can be seen to respond to what is – even if only intuitively perceived as such – a consistent philosophical position. This is grounded in an amalgam of Hegelian philosophy and Freudian psychology – although the mechanistic elements of Hegelian evolutionism were rejected, as were the clinical applications of Freudian psychology – and upon the analogical theory of correspondences taken from hermetic science.

These elements were utilised by surrealism in its own

way against the Cartesian notion of reality based on an identity of sensation and image. This is conveyed by the saying 'seeing is believing' and gives a privileged status to the sense data of one organ: the eye. What we hear is relegated to an abstraction of which music provides the highest form, while the sensations of touch, taste and smell are considered purely functional; what we see alone establishes reality. This in turn encourages us to respond to all sense phenomena in a passive way, causing an intellectual barrier to arise between ourselves and our experience of the world. We cease to respond to the world in its immediacy and try to dominate nature rather than harmonise with it. There is also a tendency, emphasised through literacy, to view the world as pure spectacle passively offered to the gaze.

Against this passivity, surrealism seeks to re-invigorate a sensibility made insipid through the one-dimensionality of realism. To lead the image away from its purely visual components was always the aim of surrealism. Rimbaud had spoken of hearing colours and seeing sounds and this energising of sensual resources is central to the surrealist attitude.

In this respect it was André Breton who defined the surrealist sensibility, saying, "the eye exists in a savage state". This quality of immediate sensation the surrealists sought to capture not only in painting but in all their activities. Reality was not equated with what was visually perceptible, but became established through a relation with what was imaginary. This relation is dynamic: "The imaginary is what tends to become real," Breton said.

Contrary to what rationalism might have us believe, the image is not formed purely from visual sensations. The findings of gestalt psychology and quantum physics have above all shown how what we see is mediated through a whole series of operations that involve all the senses : our image of a thing is not established only by its visual qualities.

In these terms the imaginary can be said to be a fluid

chaos of possibilities. The real is solid; in it the possibilities of the imaginary are brought to realisation. The motive force, providing the connecting line that transforms one into the other, is desire. Against the Cartesian model, which privileges a limited sphere it defines as 'real', in surrealism real and imaginary enjoy equal rights.

This leads us to recognise that surrealism has no quarrel with realism as such: it objects simply to the claims it makes to represent reality as a whole when it is no more than a particular perspective on it. Indeed, the surrealists admired naturalist novels – especially those of Huysmans – as well as the gritty proletarian realism of a writer like Nelson Algren, which were seen as escaping the ideological stranglehold of realism, while certain surrealist works utilise the realist model with great effect for their own purposes.

Yet surrealism also refuses the representation of reality: reality can only be; its existence proves its reality. Fiction thereby becomes impossible or is, by definition, false. This denies the Platonic distinction between appearance and essence and maintains (a fundamental of Hegelian philosophy) that essence and appearance are not qualitatively different things but elements of the same thing.

Thus the world created by a narrative has its own integral reality as an imaginary universe; it is not a reflection of a pre-existing defined reality, but brings into being a reality that belongs to itself. Sign and signifier here become one and representation is contained within itself. The difficulty for the surrealist narrator is not with representing a reality but with establishing it. Surrealist narrative tends, therefore, to be unstable.

In surrealist narrative to establish a fictional verisimilitude to a pre-established everyday world does not arise nor, conversely, is it a matter of playing with concepts of fiction and reality, representation and perception as it often is in the modernist novel. The surrealist has confidence in the nature of reality, for whatever exists is, by definition, real. Characters in surrealist stories are therefore not fictional: their reality is to be imaginary characters and they need to respond to their own motivations as such. In this spirit Raymond Queneau was not simply making a joke when he prefaced one of his novels (doubtless bearing witness to his own surrealist past) with the comment that "The characters in this novel are real. Any resemblance to fictional characters is purely coincidental." It is important to realise that it is as imaginary characters that they are real, however. This point can be illustrated by considering the example of the mirage, which is not an illusion, but becomes so only to the extent that it is mistakenly taken for something else. Its reality is that it is a mirage.

This conception of reality takes surrealism back to pre-Socratic philosophers such as Heraclitus and Parmenides whose ontology was not subject to the philosophical straightjacket of Platonism. We can in fact, through surrealism, perceive that these two philosophers, who appear to be saying the exact opposite, are really discussing different aspects of the same thing. Heraclitus believed that everything was change, a constant flow: one could never bathe twice in the same stream. Parmenides, on the other hand, asserted that nothing ever changed, in fact nothing could ever change; one was, perhaps, to extend the simile, consigned always to bathing in the same pool. This apparent contradiction is central to surrealism: change is immobile, there is a stillness that moves, fixity is always momentary.

This is the meaning of the surrealist notion of 'convulsive beauty', defined by Breton as being 'exotic-veiled, exploding-fixed, magic-circumstantial'. In this stillness that is at the same time movement, in this darkness that is at the same time light, change is founded not in the realm of ideas but in the energising desire that is realised through precipitation. Desire tends towards its own realisation and change takes place when the desire for it shatters the bounds of the possible, breaking the dialectical equilibrium holding together the framework of what is existent. It is at such moments that the imaginary flows into the real and overwhelms it, inundating it until it has been absorbed.

The energising force in surrealism is revolt, which is given a moral value in itself, as transmuted through desire. 'We are specialists in revolt," proclaimed one of the earliest surrealist declarations, and this sense of revolt has remained central to all surrealist activity.

For surrealism as we have seen there is a continuity between the will of the world and man's desire, a continuity that realism rends asunder. The points of convergence that break open the realist straitjacket and make us aware of this continuity was called by the surrealists 'objective chance', a notion taken from Hegel to express the way that necessity manifests itself as chance and vice versa.

In surrealism objective chance takes the place of causality and leads to a determination to follow the whims of chance wherever they might lead.

The shifting sands of the world, apparent in many of the stories in this collection, shows how much the surrealists were drawn towards an interrogation of what reality actually is. Unlike fabulists of whatever hue, there is a materiality in surrealist writing that resolutely keeps it, one might say, 'down to earth'.

Towards A Re-enchantment of the Universe

In surrealism the mystery of the everyday world is affirmed and the presumptions of Western rationalism and scientific progress are undermined in complex and multifarious ways. In surrealist narrative the structure of the everyday world is rarely fractured, but reality is redefined in ways that seem to connect up with the traditional fairy story, even if subject matter and thematic concerns are generally markedly different.

From this perspective, the surrealists would agree with the philosopher Ernst Bloch when he asserts that "not only does the fairy story remain as fresh as longing and love, but the demonically evil, which is abundant in the fairy tale, is still seen at work here in the present and the happiness of 'once upon a time' which is even more abundant, still affects our visions of the future."[20] And again he could be describing the impulse behind the surrealist narrative when he says, "missing meanings are fresh everywhere, and those that are not missing are waiting, as in the fairy tale. The happy ending is fought for and won." In surrealism too the happy ending is fought for, although perhaps not as often won.

[20] Ernst Bloch, *The Utopian Function of Art & Literature* translated by Jack Zipes and Frank Mecklenburg (1983) Cambridge, Mass: MIT p 163.